SPYING

A SEA STORY

MARK DAVID ALBERTSON

Irish Viking
publishing

OTHER BOOKS BY MARK DAVID ALBERTSON

Steaming: A Sea Story (2020)

Irish Viking
publishing

ACKNOWLEDGMENTS

There are always many hands involved in the process of creating a book. Being the author is just one of those hands. Many thanks to my fellow writer and wife, KE Meuir, who offered many suggestions, spent hours reviewing my manuscripts, and helped make the plot and characters workable as we sat on the back porch of Los Perros Locos Ranch over wine each evening.

I want to express my sincere gratefulness to ITCS (Retired), Ray Tuttle, for his work assisting in editing this book and providing his input on the accuracy of my descriptions of radio shacks and all things navy. Senior Chief Tuttle was generous of his time and talents. Not only did he have a great career, serving on the USS *Nimitz*, USS *Camden*, USS *Carl Vincent*, USS *California,* and many shore stations, but he is also a gifted and talented editor.

I also want to express my thanks to RMCS (Retired) Theodore (Ted) Denning, who graciously read my manuscript with an eye on the accuracy of my descriptions of the life of a radioman onboard the USS *Oklahoma City*. Senior Chief Denning served both on the staffs of the Commander of the Seventh Fleet and the Commander of the First Fleet and was onboard not only the *Okie*, but all the cruisers that served as flagships for those fleet commanders.

Many thanks to my publisher, Irish Viking Publishing, who believed in my writing enough to take this project on.

Finally, I want to express my gratefulness to the Naval Criminal Investigative Service Association History Project and their information-packed online resources. They were a great help in giving me an understanding of the organization and mission of the NIS during the 1970s.

Poker is a game of deception. I know, everybody understands a bluff in poker, but they don't realize that you can play the whole game using deception.

-RMCS Morris Lester

1

THE MUDAKS

Pyotr Ivanovich Makarov, dressed in a perfectly tailored grey Russian wool suit and sporting a brand-new pair of Tony Lama inlaid bicentennial cowboy boots, sat at the dark oak conference table, arms folded, with a scowl on his face. Makarov sat across the table from two young American men, who looked as out of place in the embassy as clowns at a funeral.

A couple of mudaks, thought Makarov, Russian for "shithead." Makarov sat, stone-faced, for several minutes, giving the room's tension ample opportunity to reach excruciating levels.

The two Americans looked everywhere except into Makarov's eyes. It was apparent they were entirely out of their element. Both looked with some awe at the lavishly appointed conference room, the polished Russian oak table, small gold sculptures on the side tables, and portraits of people of whom the two had never heard. Gradually, both men were becoming more and more nervous.

In his best, thickly accented, and rudimentary English, Makarov finally began. "Gentlemen, welcome to Embassy of the Union of Soviet Socialist Republics. My name Mr. Makarov. I am diplomatic officer here at the Tokyo Embassy." Although, in reality, Makarov was a Major in the First Chief Directorate of the Soviet Union's

Committee for State Security, better known to most as the KGB. His official title at the Soviet Embassy in Tokyo, Japan, was "Diplomatic Officer." Makarov had served in the KGB since just after World War II. He had a Master's degree in International Relations from the University of Moscow State Institute of International Relations and spoke six languages fluently. Now, at 56 years old, he was one of the top leaders in the Soviet Union's First Directorate, a sub-organization in the KGB dedicated to external spying. Their most successful program to date had been recruiting foreigners to conduct espionage against their own country. Amazingly, most of the successes came from scenarios just like the one unfolding in the conference room. People would simply walk into the embassy and offer to provide information, in exchange, of course, for money and other perks. Usually, such meetings were non-starters. To Makarov's trained eye, he had a couple of 'scamps' at the table who would offer nothing of importance. Makarov did enjoy talking with Americans, mainly because America's old west enthralled him. He had read every Louis L'Amour book written, could not get enough of Zane Grey, and the stars of western movies were of great fascination for him. Unfortunately, he could tell immediately that these two mudaks were, in the words of the cowboys, *plumb weak north of their ears.* He would warmly listen, then send them on their way. An hour of his day he would never get back.

"May I ask you, young men, to introduce yourselves and to please let me know what I might do for you?" said Makarov, attempting not to show his disdain for the two mudaks and to sound friendly.

Andy Anderson, Radioman Third Class, and James Bond Hilbreath, Radioman Second Class, looked at one another, imploring with their eyes for the other to start. Anderson, a tall and overly skinny twenty-one-year-old with a nose resembling an old potato, sat wiggling his right leg like he was running a marathon. Hilbreath, in his late 20's was a contrast to Anderson. Overweight, ruddy features, and three chins, Hilbreath had been in the navy for eleven years. He had barely achieved a rank that most sailors accomplish in the first three years in the US Navy. He had few prospects of gaining any further stripes for the remainder of his career.

Finally, because he had a slightly higher rank, Hilbreath spoke up. "Mr. Makarov, this is my friend, Andy Anderson, and my name is James Bond Hilbreath." Squinting his eyes and giving Makarov a wink and a smile, he attempted some levity by saying, "Yes, James Bond." Receiving not even a hint of recognition from Makarov, Hilbreath continued. "We are both radiomen, stationed aboard the USS *Oklahoma City*, a guided-missile cruiser, out of Yokosuka, Japan. Being a diplomat and all, you might not know it, but we are the Seventh Fleet Commander's flagship. Radio teletype messages come through our hands all day long that are super top secret, and we both have top-secret clearances, so we see a lot of interesting shi-- um, information."

Once again, no recognition from Makarov.

"Sir, we are tired of the crap the navy puts us through. There's no war going on, and we make shit for pay. We have access to a whole shitload, uh, sorry, a whole lot of stuff that we believe you Ruskies would be interested in. We've been thinking about this for a long time, and we took the bullet train all the way from Yokosuka today just to see you. Wow, I'm not sure how we made it because we couldn't understand where the stops were. You know, nobody seems to speak English around here? Um, anyway, we figured the embassy would be the best place to find somebody who might have an interest in what we have to sell."

Once again, Makarov took an uncomfortably long time to respond. "I understand, gentlemen, that you might have information useful to the Union of Soviet Socialist Republics. But you know that we are mostly interested in keeping peace with the United States. I, as a diplomat, of course, have no understanding of what my country might have an interest in. Still, I would warn you that you may have taken a dangerous course today with your own country. Your Clint Eastwood said it best: "Dying ain't much of a living, boy." The two looked at one another with blank stares.

Makarov performed another pause, this time even longer. Finally, unable to restrain himself, Anderson broke in. "We understand all of that, but, truth be known, what harm can it do? We aren't at war or anything, and we could help you a lot. Just to show you we've thought this through and are serious, let me show you what we brought. With that, Anderson picked up a bag and emptied the contents on the table. "Do you know what these are, sir?" asked Anderson.

Makarov looked at the envelope-sized cards on the table, each marked, "TOP SECRET." Each had small rectangular holes cut out at various places on the cards. "These are crypto cards from the KWR-37 crypto machine, sir! With these, you can decrypt the fleet broadcast and read every message sent to every ship in the seventh fleet! You would know where everyone is, what they were doing, and what they know. That's got to be worth some big bucks, eh, Mr. Makarov?"

Makarov immediately knew what he was seeing. Each day, a designated radioman placed a new card in a crypto machine at a specific time. Then the crypto was synched with the radio teletype equipment from the US Navy's fleet broadcast. Makarov looked down at them, then looked up at the sailors. "I have no idea if this is valuable or not, my friends. But might I ask, won't the custodians on your ship know they are missing?"

"Of course they will. We just brought these as examples, and we'll put them back when we get back to the ship. But we can copy the cards and get them to you, and nobody will ever know we messed with them," said Hilbreath.

"That's very interesting, my friends," said Makarov, feigning interest. If you don't mind, I'll take a picture of one of these, and pass it along, just to see if there is any interest on our part. Please give me a call in a week, and I will let you know. By the way, just out of curiosity, how much money did you want for this?"

"We both want $5,000 for the cards, but we can get you even better stuff. We can get ship movements, intelligence that comes through our shack, and more. It'll be worth big bucks to you, I'm sure!"

Makarov gave them his official embassy card, asking them to call in a week, and sent them on their way, each with an official embassy ceremonial pen. Both Hilbreath and Anderson smiled big smiles as they left the embassy to find the train station back to Yokosuka. Hibreath slapped Anderson on the back, saying, "I think we owe ourselves a beer!"

After escorting the sailors out of the embassy, Makarov's assistant quickly returned, shutting the door behind him. "What do we do with them?" questioned the assistant.

"Just because a chicken has wings don't mean it can fly," said Makarov. His assistant stood looking at him, having no idea what that meant. Makarov waved the back of his hand at the assistant, thinking he should find someone to work with who had at least watched *Once Upon A Time in the West*. "You don't dig up more snakes than you can kill. Contact Blue. Tell him about the contact and the two *mudaks* who have the potential of screwing everything up. Tell him there's a couple of yellowjackets in the outhouse, and they need to go away." Makarov's assistant ignored the unintelligible idioms but understood enough to nod and leave the room.

Two weeks later, Lieutenant Commander Davis McNutt, a Senior Special Agent with the Naval Investigative Service, worked at his desk in his office in Pearl Harbor. He looked at his watch and decided it was just about time to knock off and head to the Officer's Club for a work-out. Just as he was getting up from his desk, the phone rang. "Dave, it's Randy," the voice on the other end said. We've got a situation, and I need your help." Randy Glasscock was among the new breed of civilians serving as Special Agents in the NIS and was stationed at the NIS Regional Agency in Yokosuka, Japan. One year prior, Glasscock had been selected to be only the second female

Special Agent in the entire organization and was one of three NIS agents in the Yokosuka NISRA.

"Randy, it's good to hear from you! How is Japan?" LCDR McNutt inquired.

"Up until yesterday, it was great. We have had something dire happen, and I'm not sure that we have all the resources or experience to handle it. I'm calling you for your advice, on behalf of our Special Agent in Charge, since the Honolulu NISO has more experience at this than we do."

"You're sounding a little grim, Randy. What's up?"

"Last night, some fishermen found two dead sailors in the bay just off the beach from the Naval Hospital at Yokosuka. It was a homicide. We did an autopsy this morning and found a few interesting things. First, they had high levels of ricin in their blood – toxic levels. Second, they were radiomen stationed on the USS *Oklahoma City*, the admiral's flagship. And third, we found the business card of a Russian diplomat in Tokyo in one of their pockets."

2

BACK ON THE BOB E. CHICKEN

The winter holidays of 1975 were quickly approaching. Seaman Matt Bertram, "Matt" to his shipmates, laid in his bunk, known lovingly as a "rack" to the sailors on his ship, reading *Hopscotch*, a spy thriller by Brian Garfield. John le Carré was Matt's favorite author, and spy novels were his absolute favorite genre, but Matt had read all of le Carré's books at least twice. He was enjoying Garfield's novel.

Absentmindedly, Matt looked up at the calendar he had taped to the bottom of the next rack up, and with a bit of sadness, remembered he would not be home for Christmas this year. The year had been life-changing for him. He had arrived at his ship, the USS *Robert E. Peckham*, lovingly dubbed by its crew as the *Bob E. Chicken* just after Christmas last year. His personality and sense of duty to his shipmates had landed him in big trouble when he dove into Subic Bay after calling in a contrived race riot on the mess decks to get the officer of the deck away from the fantail of the ship. The reason for the dive had been to rescue Signalman Chief B.S. Boggs' dentures, which Boggs had spontaneously thrown into Subic Bay. B.S. had a long history of chucking dentures, and his wife, Adelle, had wrested a promise from Matt to protect the dentures at all cost, which he had faithfully executed. This act of fidelity landed Matt at Captain's Mast, a disciplinary process that might very well have led to a court-martial.

Fortunately for Matt, the Captain of the *Peckham* had been ordered to recruit and train something called a "landing force deployment team." The team was composed of a group of trained sailors onboard the ship, who had the weapons and warcraft skills to undertake smaller missions when more highly trained sailors, namely Navy SEALS, were not available. This concept was the disparaged but still active brainchild of the Chief of Naval Operations, Admiral Ira Stephens. The team was all "volunteer" and was required to have a radioman participate, none of whom had the slightest interest in exposing themselves to such peril. Because of this opening, the ship's Captain gave Matt the "opportunity to volunteer" instead of being punished, which Matt reluctantly did. The team's training was abbreviated and included, among other schools, Marine Force Recon training and a highly shortened SEAL-*ish* training. Both were virtually laughable. The team attended jungle survival training, and because Matt was quite a good shot with a rifle, Marine Sniper Scout training. Because the Vietnam conflict, after fourteen years, was in the process of winding down, nobody on the team had the slightest concern about actually being called to apply their ineffectual skills. Yet to the surprise of all, less than a month after completing training, they ended up on a mission to assist a marine platoon under attack by the Khmer Rouge. Two of the sailors on the team and four marines died in the melee, and, to make things worse, during a curious CIA "debriefing," they were ordered <u>never</u> to reveal the mission to anyone and were given no recognition for their role in saving the marines. And then, just like that, the Indochina war came to a specious end. Through a massive disinformation campaign, the US government had now successfully focused Americans on the Cold War with the USSR.

The entire episode left Matt with an abysmal attitude toward the navy, not to mention nightmares, night sweats, and a taste for too much alcohol to self-medicate. In the navy of 1975, Matt's poor attitude went completely undetected among the remaining flock of sailors with similar mindsets. As such, Matt's supervisors considered him to be doing a great job in the radio shack. The episode did solidify Matt's desire to be done with his hitch and as far from oceans and ships as he could be. Looking at his calendar, he noted that he had 901 days and a wake-up, and he would back home in New Mexico.

The US Navy had a pattern of transferring sailors about every two years to a new duty station. Matt had been watching many of his closest friends and enemies either end their enlistments, move back to civilian life, or go to new duty stations. The icon of Matt's division had been his friend "Stevie" Wundar, who had anointed Matt with the nickname of "Bert" and who had left the Navy to return to Texas. Others: Shroom, Scooter, Pigman, and Chief Boggs all moved on. Along with saying goodbye to his good friends, Matt enthusiastically saw his arch-nemesis, Lieutenant (Junior Grade) "Rock" Hudson, discharged. Rock had his penis severed in a fee dispute with a hooker on Hotel Street in Honolulu, which led to brain damage from blood loss. When Matt imagined that calamity, he cringed and smiled simultaneously.

Although Matt enjoyed some of the new radio crew, he was saddened to see his shipmates leave one by one. Charles Trueman, whose nickname quickly became "Harry," and Matt had become fast friends. Several of the other radiomen in the shack were less enamored with Harry, primarily due to his short temper. Matt realized that Harry's angry outbursts were short-lived and mainly directed at some piece of malfunctioning radio equipment. Because Harry's rants contained a dazzling array of profanity, Matt enjoyed hearing them.

Matt did not enjoy Harry's irritating habit of getting himself into wild bets that he rarely won. There was the bet that he could eat an entire oyster shell without throwing up, which landed him in sick bay for a week. Harry had a longstanding bet with one of the operations specialists that he could steal an entire set of coffee mugs left on the wardroom table by the officers. The wardroom was off-limits to enlisted men unless they were on official business. Harry was one cup short of a complete set before getting caught. He was written-up and restricted to the ship for three weeks.

When Harry started making bets that involved Matt, Matt began worrying about Harry's inept betting habits. While on deployment a few months earlier, the ship made a port call in American Samoa. Matt, Harry, and a few other sailors from the radio shack were in a club one night. Matt and the others at the table were trading sea stories. Sea stories were an essential part of navy life, much like fishing stories are crucial to fishermen. Also, like fishing stories, sea stories started with an experience that had some basis in truth but grew with each re-telling. The implicit rule was that everyone agreed that the increasingly exaggerated story was absolutely true. B.S. Boggs, Matt's former CPO, used to say, "The difference between a sea story and a fairy tale is that fairy tales begin 'Once upon a time,' and sea stories begin, 'Now this is a no-shitter.'" One of the sailors at the table was in the middle of a fascinating story about a night he and a friend had tried to go home with a hooker so they could have a menage et trois. It turned out to be an ambush robbery, so they had to jump out of a second-story window to save themselves. The sailor telling the story was getting to the portion of the story Matt loved best. Harry approached Matt with a frantic look on his face. "Bert, man, I've done something terrible, and you have to help me!" Harry shrieked.

"What now, Harry?" Matt said, with a hint of irritation in his voice.

"I promise Bert, this is that last time I do this," Harry said contritely.

"This is about the eighth time you've said that, grumbled Matt."

"I bet one of the locals that you were the best beer drinker in the navy and that you could drink an entire bottle of beer faster than he could," Harry screeched. "And I bet him $100. I don't *have* $100, so you have to help and win that bet. Pllleeeaasse!"

Harry pointed to a man at a table by the window. Across the room, a local Samoan man was occupying two chairs and barely accomplishing that. From all appearances, he was not a man. He looked more like a freight truck with a head. Matt looked at the man, looked at Harry, and looked back at the man. "Harry, this is the last time you do this to me," pronounced Matt.

Matt got up from the table, took a deep breath, and walked over to the man along with Harry. In front of the man were two bottles of beer. Unfortunately, bottles of beer in Samoa were huge. Matt guessed they had to contain at least a quart of beer. Matt looked at the man, sat down, and, looking him in the eyes while pointing to Harry, said, "This is the *tenth* time I've had to do this in the last month. I'm making this guy more money with these bets than I'll wager you make in a month, but if you insist on going through with this, I guess we'll have to take your money." The enormous man furrowed his brow, looking from Matt to Harry and back again, and then smiled.

"You ain't gonna beat me, skinny man," said the Samoan. I'm not afraid of that. You better have your money ready." Matt's ruse had failed. Seemingly having no other choice, on the count of three, both started chugging. A highly nervous Harry watched intently with beads of sweat appearing on his forehead. Matt finished the bottle, put it on the table, and looked at the Samoan, who still had a quarter of the beer left. Amazingly, Matt had downed his beer first, an apparent result of the significant amount of practice he had in the last few months. A look of shock came on the Samoan man's face, then a smile, and he said, "Two out of three?"

Matt smiled and said, "How about you just buy the next round, and we'll call it even." Matt looked at Harry and, pointing in his face, said, "Never again, Harry." Two hours later, two drunken sailors and a man the size of a truck walked down the road toward the port, arm in arm, singing "Island Girl."

3

AN UNLIKELY DECISION

S pecial Agent Davis McNutt was on his third conference call regarding the deaths of the two sailors. Like any other bureaucratic organization, the Naval Investigative Service seemed to have far too many layers to be efficient. The number of acronyms was quite astonishing, even for the military. There was NISOHQ (Naval Investigative Service Office Headquarters), NISO (Naval Investigative Service Offices) in ten locations, NISRA (Naval Investigative Service Regional Offices, which were smaller offices in about 70 places, and NISRU (Naval Investigative Service Regional Units) consisting of one or two special agents, scattered throughout the world. Besides the complex organization of the NIS, there was a history that had helped to form it, which went back to just after the Civil War, when the US Navy created the Office of Naval Intelligence (ONI). ONI played a large part in the second world war, and it recruited special agents from active-duty sailors. It wasn't until the mid-1960's that the Naval Intelligence Service organization came into being. Vietnam allowed the NIS to expand its mission, playing a large part in protecting the navy. Before the escalation of the navy's involvement in the Vietnam war, the organization had primarily focused on doing background investigations of sailors who had applied for security clearances in the early 1960s.

Davis was part of a dying breed of commissioned naval officers who were also Special Agents. The NIS of the 1970s had reclaimed its role to conduct criminal investigations, acts of sabotage, and international espionage. While the navy officers kept the command positions, Special Agent positions had transitioned to Excepted Civil Service positions. The positive side of all of the changes was that NIS had far more responsibility in more areas than it had in the last twenty years, including seagoing billets on aircraft carriers and flagships. The not-so-great news was that commissioned naval officers like Davis McNutt were gradually being replaced by Excepted Civil Service employees, not commissioned naval officers. McNutt had recently received word that he could be transferred back into the fleet or retire and transition to a civilian Special Agent.

The transition was not on Davis McNutt's mind at the moment. For days he had been working with Special Agent Glasscock on a strategy to address the deaths of Anderson and Hilbreath. At that moment, he was on a conference call, listening intently to the Commanding Officer of the Naval Investigative Service Office (NISO) in Yokosuka, Captain Stanley Berrycloth. Berrycloth was updating the personnel on the call, which included Randy Glasscock and McNutt's boss, Deputy Regional Director Bernard Fossate. "So, it's pretty obvious to our investigators that the Soviets are somehow involved.

"But what is more worrisome is that we have been keeping an eye on what we consider to be possible leaks coming from the communications division on the *Oklahoma City* for the last several months. We are speculating that someone has already been working with the Soviets on the inside. The deaths of Anderson and Hilbreath were quite possibly executed to avoid the two sailors from exposing a more established plan. After some investigation, we believe that Anderson and Hilbreath were simply two fuck-ups with an amateurish plan to enrich themselves. We have intel that they made a trip to Tokyo two weeks before their deaths, and we now believe that their purpose was to make contact with the Soviets."

"What does our afloat Special Agent have to say about this?" Fossate queried.

"Unfortunately, the downside of having a Special Agent afloat is that he is well-known onboard the *Okie*. Anyone with anything to hide is well-aware of our Agent, and, consequently, he's pretty ineffective when it comes to gaining any information on something like this. And this is coupled with the fact that any espionage that might be taking place is happening in a highly controlled, secure area. His presence there would immediately be a big warning to anyone spying. Radio shacks only allow limited access to personnel who have specific clearances and business in the shack. The second our Special Agent walked in the door, whatever espionage might be going on would be finished. Keep in mind all of this is coupled with the fact that we don't know with any degree of certainty whether or not there is actual espionage going on, and if so, how extensive it is. We are still in the theory stage of this investigation."

"So, how do we accomplish an investigation?" asked Berrycloth.

"LTCDR McNutt has an idea. I will tell you right now, I'm more than a little skeptical of it," said Fossate. "Davis, please give us an update on your solution."

"Actually, it was Special Agent Glasscock's idea," Davis replied, "But we've been giving it a lot of thought, and we think that if we can get HQ to approve it, this will be our only hope. We want to put someone undercover in the USS *Oklahoma City's* radio shack, and for all of the reasons we just discussed, we don't believe it can be one of our Special Agents. We think it needs to be an actual radioman." McNutt paused, taking a deep breath, knowing that this would be problematic, and met with opposition, which did not take long.

"That's just ridiculous," Berrycloth snapped. "You know as well as I do that the NIS does not use untrained people in this capacity. It's *policy*. Anyone undertaking an investigation with serious implications like this needs to have specific training and experience. I like the idea of putting someone in the radio shack, but it *has* to be a trained special agent. Can't we just send one of our Special Agents to Radioman "A" school and then send them in?"

Fossate chimed in quickly. "I understand the policy, Captain, but I can't imagine any other way to accomplish this. Davis, please explain why we can't use a Special Agent in this circumstance."

Davis paused, gathering up sufficient oxygen to give his best argument. "It would have to be an *actual* radioman. Only a trained RM would know that job and his way around the equipment, along with all of the complex protocols involved. There's no way a trained agent could pass themselves off as an RM. The job is too complex and varied. It would take several months to educate a Special Agent sufficiently to pass himself off as a radioman. Even then, there is so much inside knowledge that he would not convince anyone of his competence. It takes years to build the skills needed to establish confidence from his colleagues in the radio shack. Our person would need to be an experienced RM, at least a third-class petty officer, with enough knowledge, skill, and experience to be accepted and given responsibility from the get-go. We first and foremost need someone competent at the technical job."

"But what about investigative skills and necessary physical and weapons skills that he could be called upon to use?" Berrycloth inquired.

"We can send our person to NIS Special Agent Training in ONI Headquarters in Suitland, Maryland, for an abbreviated course," said Davis.

"But those skills, weapons, surveillance, etc., take time also." How could you possibly find an RM anywhere in the Navy with those skills?" asked Berrycloth.

McNutt paused for a moment. "I believe we do. Perhaps not the general investigation skills, but there is someone, right here in Pearl Harbor, who not only has those skills but has proven himself in the field."

"Hell, I hate to say it, but I find myself in agreement. I can't think of another way to handle this." Fossate asked the others on the call, "Anybody else have a better idea?" The silence on the line indicated they did not. "Unfortunately, I think you are right, LTCDR," said Deputy Director Fossate. "Let me run it up the flagpole to HQ. They are going to have a shit-fit when I ask for this," Fossate said. In the meantime, call in this RM. And I want to meet him personally."

"Aye Aye," said the group in unison.

"I sure hope you're right about this, LCDR McNutt," said Captain Berrycloth. "Your ass is definitely on the line with this one."

4

A CHANGE OF PLANS

Matt and Harry had settled into their racks no more than three hours earlier, after a raucous night of drinking and pool at their favorite Hotel Street dive bar, "Two Jacks." Two Jacks was a classic sailor bar with an amazing array of "interesting" people consuming far too much alcohol and behaving poorly. Hotel Street, nicknamed "Shit Street" by the sailors stationed at Pearl Harbor, was the red-light district of Honolulu, which Matt preferred to think of as the *entertainment* district. While it didn't come close to the entertainment value that Olongapo City outside of Subic Bay Naval Station had, it remained a place to have fun. Two Jacks was Matt's home away from home when he was in port. He loved the fact that there was no pretense in the bar, and as long as you minded your own business, you were relatively safe from direct confrontation. Collateral damage sometimes happened as a fight migrated into a neutral zone, but it was rare. Matt had taken several new people there over the months, which had become his welcoming tradition for new members of the radio shack. One reason Matt loved the bar so much was that they just didn't give a damn. Not about quality, not about façade, not about decorating, and not particularly about their customers. One incident that solidified his love for the bar was when he brought a new signalman, Howie Bran, who said he was from someplace called Kennebunkport, Maine, of which Matt had never heard. Howie was the epitome of affectation. Howie would go on and on about the wealthy family he came from and the privileged life in his hometown. And while he seemed like a nice enough guy, Matt felt Howie could use just a bit of perspective by having a drink at Two Jacks.

As they came to the entrance of the bar, Howie looked at Matt with a look of dread and said, "We're not *really* going in that place, are we, Matt?"

"Of course we are, Howie. It's a damn fine bar, and I thought I'd introduce you to one of the finer establishments on Shit Street."

They entered the small, dingy, poorly lit bar with Howie on guard for something terrifying pouncing on him. Two Jacks was about twenty feet wide, with a bar and stools on one side and tables against the wall on the other. In the very back of the bar was enough room for two pool tables. The patrons of the bar, however, were the bar's most entertaining feature. Understandably, most were sailors, but there were also merchant marines, locals, and even several drag queens. It might have seemed like an odd assortment of people, but that, to Matt, was one of the endearing qualities of the bar. As they took a seat at the bar, a huge man with a glass eye that was skewed upward at a very odd angle, looking a bit like a cartoon character who had just been hit over the head, wearing a t-shirt that read, "U.S. Olympic Muff Diver" with a rag over one shoulder came up to them. "Hey, Munchie, how's it going tonight?" inquired Matt.

The man sneered at Matt. "Ain't got all night. What's your poison?" said Munchie, without so much as a smile or an ounce of recognition.

"I'll have a Bud," said Matt. "What'll you have, Howie?"

Howie, trying to determine where on Munchie's face he should focus his eyes, said, "I believe I'll have a Vodka Martini, *very dry*, with two olives, my dear sir."

Munchie paused, looked at Howie with his one good eye, looked over at Matt with a "Who the fuck is this?" look, and without showing any emotion, said, "This is Two fucking Jacks, Mr. *Swanky Pants*. We got beer, and we got whiskey. Which will it be?"

With that, Howie tasted his first Budweiser, and Matt received personal gratification that lasted several months.

As Matt enjoyed sleeping off his beer, his consciousness gradually began recognizing someone shouting at him and shaking his shoulders. "Bert, Harry, get up! We got something big happening in the radio shack, and Chief Cheesewright wants you there on the double. I guess the Captain has called a meeting in the shack with all of the RM's in ten minutes.

Matt and Harry jumped up, donning their dungarees, and headed for the radio shack. They were the last of the RM's to arrive. RMC Cheesewright had recently transferred to the *Bob E.*, and Matt was already quite fond of him. The Chief asked them to come in and gather around. "There's something big happening, apparently, and the *Peckham* is going to be steaming tomorrow. I know we weren't supposed to be getting underway for several weeks, so we got some serious fucking work to do to get ready. The captain and communications officer have already briefed me, but Captain Stilton wanted to brief you himself." Just as the Chief finished, the captain of the ship, Commander Robert Stilton, walked in. Chief Cheesewright shouted, "Attention on deck!" and the Captain waved them at ease.

"Well, it looks like we are going to be having a little bit of fun in the next few days, men," stated the CO. "We've received intel that the Soviets are planning to test a new experimental missile. We just happened to have people in the right place to know precisely where that missile is going to come down, and the CNO wants us to do our best to try to retrieve that missile before the commie's do. In just about thirty minutes, our ship is going to be overrun with a bunch of spooks. Communication technicians, frogmen, intel experts, and others will be bringing something called a "quick van" to our helicopter hanger. I don't know what the hell is in it, but they will be running cables from the quick van to our radio shack and our radar array. We are going to head north with them to see if we can catch ourselves a missile. We're not sure of the exact day of the test, so we have to be there as quickly as we can. Now, these guys have all the stuff they need to do their job, and the only extra job you may have is sending and receiving some additional messages and possibly routing them to the spooks, just as though they were any other department on the ship. But other than that, we are just going to be their chauffeurs up to the landing zone. Give them every bit of cooperation they might need, but I think your job will mainly be to stay out of their way. Any questions? Good. Now turn-to." With that, the CO left the shack, and the RM's got busy getting ready to get underway.

Right on schedule, thirty minutes later, large trucks arrived at Bravo pier, and a crane placed a metal building on the helo deck. The building was just small enough to fit into the ship's helicopter hangar. Into the radio shack came numerous unfriendly and noncommunicative people. Other than asking to be shown where the transmitter room was and the other communications equipment, they said virtually nothing to the radiomen. Captain Stilton was right. Their primary job was to stay out of the way of these strange people.

The radio teletype traffic to the *Peckham* increased significantly, almost immediately, so the radiomen stayed busy receiving messages and relaying them to the Captain. They had the opportunity to see many Top Secret messages regarding intelligence on the missile and the Soviet's plans for the test. Unfortunately, the messages meant directly for the electronic spies went straight to them through their equipment. Most of the messages the radiomen were allowed to see were logistics issues, such as where to go, details of the journey, and updates on intelligence.

By the end of the day, the radio shack, which already housed a mass of wires in the ceilings and walls, was a completely chaotic mess with an exponential multiplication of connections and cables. So much so, some spaces were difficult to access for the radiomen.

Toward the end of the day, the Supply Officer called down to the radio shack. Everyone, including Matt, was moving at warp speed to get the shack ready to steam, so it was a surprise when the Supply officer asked Matt to come by his office immediately. The Supply Officer's job was to supervise the logistics of running the ship. They were in charge of ensuring sufficient supplies, including fuel and food, handling personnel issues on the ship, and payroll for the crew. Matt usually had little to do with supply other than picking up his wages on payday. As Matt arrived at the supply office, the ensign in charge of personnel greeted Matt. "Seaman Bertram," he said, "I received a call from the NIS office on base that you are to report there today." Matt gave the ensign a quizzical look. "Sir, why on earth would I need to go to the NIS office?" Matt asked.

"They said something about a routine update of your security clearance. But the person I spoke to did say you needed to go there today." The ensign handed Matt a chit, and without further concern, turned his back to his other work.

Matt checked back in with the Chief and gave him the news. Chief Cheesewright was not pleased. After erupting in a geyser of profanities, Chief shouted, "You're my only teletype repairman, and we are in a helluva hurry here. Why in the *fuck* is the NIS worrying about your clearance at this point? Get your ass there now and get back ASAP. We have a lot of shit to do before we get underway tomorrow."

Matt uttered a quick "Aye aye, Chief." He rounded up the duty driver to hitch a ride to the administrative offices at Pearl Harbor Naval Station. Matt walked up three floors and into the small, unadorned, drab office, let the secretary know he was there, and sat down. He looked around at the office and noted that it looked exactly like every navy office of any sort he had ever seen. Pea-green or gray metal desks and filing cabinets, a similar color of green or gray, with perhaps a bit of yellow-green on the walls, and fluorescent lights. On the wall was a picture of President Gerald Ford, another standard feature of pretty much any navy office.

As Matt observed his surroundings, it seemed odd that he would need to go through this. He had never even spoken with the NIS, and nobody he knew had ever had to do something like this. He knew that when he initially went through a background investigation for his security clearances, two "agents" had arrived at his hometown to interview teachers and friends, but that was the limit of his contact with them. He had never heard of anyone needing an "update."

An office door opened, and a Lieutenant Commander poked his head out. "Seaman Bertram?" he asked.

"Yes sir," said Matt. The officer motioned for him to come into his office. Matt was surprised that an officer with a high rank would perform administrative work on a security clearance for an E-3 enlisted man. "Sir, my Chief asked if we could do this quickly. Our ship is getting underway tomorrow on a classified mission."

"I know all about your mission, Seaman Bertram," said the officer. "We'll get you back as quickly as possible." Matt made a mental note that just because something was classified information, it did not preclude hordes of people knowing about it.

As Matt entered the officer's office, which he noticed shared the same decorating scheme and furniture as the reception room, he was surprised to see another man there. "Seaman Bertram, my name is Lieutenant Commander Davis McNutt. I'm the Special Agent in Charge of NISRA Pearl Harbor. I'd like you to meet Captain Bernard Fossate. Captain Fossate is the Deputy Regional Director of the Naval Investigative Service."

Matt could feel his heart rate increase and his breathing shallow. It was evident that this was *not* a routine "update" and that something much more serious was happening. He mentally reviewed his recent life for any trace of criminal activity. However, he felt reasonably satisfied that he had behaved himself passably since his dive into Subic Bay to try to retrieve Chief Boggs' dentures.

"I know that your shipmates call you Bert, Seaman Bertram. Would it be OK if we addressed you as Bert?" *Shit, everybody seems to know so damn much about me*, thought Matt.

"Of course, sir," replied Matt. "Sir, am I in trouble for something?"

"Bert, we'll tell you more about why we brought you in today in just a bit, but please be assured, it is not for investigation of any criminal activity," said McNutt. "Director Fossate wants to get to know you a bit before we talk about why you're here, so I hope you'll just breathe easy and consider this a conversation to get to know one another." *That sounds pretty weird and suspect*, thought Matt.

Director Fossate smiled. "Matt, we have been looking at your service record and talking with others who know you, and other than that little incident in Subic Bay with the Chief's dentures, you've done well for yourself in the navy. You're on track to make a third-class petty officer next year, you are a great teletype repairman, and we know that you have served on your ship's Landing Force Deployment Team with distinction. We also know a bit about the training you've received: Marine Combat Training, an abbreviated form of Naval Special Warfare School, Marine Force Recon Training, Jungle Survival Training, Survival Escape and Resistance Training, and Marine Scout Sniper Training. Finally, we do know about the incident in which your team played an integral part in Cambodia. We know that's not to be discussed, but we also want you to know that we know what happened and that you acted with bravery." *Shit, they really do know everything about me*, thought Matt.

"Sir, yes, but you've got to know that the training we got was pretty pathetic and very abbreviated. I don't think that the list of training activities really accounts for much," said Matt.

"Nonsense. It's unique. There's not another radioman in the entire navy that has had the training or experiences you have received, and you should be proud of them. May I ask you, son, are you considering making the navy a place for your career?"

Realizing that the politically correct thing to say would be something like *I'm giving it serious consideration*, or some such, Matt decided honesty was the best policy. "Sir, the navy has been really good for me, but I'm pretty sure that as soon as my commitment is up, I'll be heading on to other things as quickly as I am able."

"And it looks like you've got a good two and a half years before that happens, correct?"

"900 days and a wake-up, to be exact, sir."

Director Fossate paused to gather his thoughts, and staring into Matt's eyes, gave Matt a most serious look. "Bert, please keep this to yourself with the greatest of secrecy. We have a problem in Yokosuka.

Potentially a *huge* problem. Two RM's stationed on the USS *Oklahoma City* were murdered about six weeks ago, and their bodies turned up in the harbor. They had poison in their systems. There was a connection with the Soviets that we are still trying to piece together, but it looks like they decided to try to sell top-secret materials to the Soviets. It apparently didn't work out for them, as we are pretty sure they were murdered in connection with this scheme. Our investigation suggests that there was probably already some espionage going on onboard the *Okie*, and they may have been murdered to avoid exposing that espionage."

"Sir, that's pretty terrible and pretty scary," Matt said. "I'm just wondering what that might have to do with me?"

"Here's the thing, Bert," answered Fossate, "We have no idea at this point the extent of the espionage on the *Okie*, who is involved, and how they are involved. It could be one person who was doing what the two sailors attempted, and that's that, or, and we hope not, it could be a much larger conspiracy. We just don't know at this point. That's where you come in. We need a set of eyes inside the radio shack who can conduct a covert investigation of the shack's activities to help us understand who is involved and at what level. To do this without raising suspicion, we need an experienced radioman with enough rank to be given a higher level of access and responsibility. Our inside radioman's job *won't* be to 'bust' the bad guys. His mission will be to observe, gain evidence and report to his contact in Yokosuka so that the NIS can apprehend the spy or spies. We need someone who has proven himself in a challenging situation, who has enough experience to be credible, but who doesn't hold such a high rank that his presence would arouse suspicion. And, just in case things go south, our radioman needs to have the training required to defend himself.

"There isn't another radioman in the navy who can do that other than you, Bert. I'm saying we need you. But this will be completely voluntary on your part. From their actions with the two dead radiomen, whoever is involved is willing to use extreme measures to protect their operation, so I won't pretend that this will be a cakewalk.

We absolutely *won't* make you volunteer for this job if you choose to decline."

Matt sat back in disbelief. Less than six months before, he had found himself on a battlefield off the coast of Cambodia, involved in a fight where he lost two of his friends. When Matt joined the navy, he had no thought that something like that could happen. He had joined the navy for adventure, yes, but definitely *not* this kind of adventure. He had joined the navy for the travel, the drinking, the seeing the world part of the adventure. "So, sir, let me just get this straight because I'm having a little bit of trouble getting my head around what you are saying. You are asking me to go undercover for the NIS?"

"Yes, Bert, we are," interjected McNutt. I know it's asking a lot, but it's the only way we can understand what's going on and who is involved."

"I don't know the first thing about being a secret agent," exclaimed Matt. I'm a radioman, for godsake!"

"You already have quite a lot of surveillance and scouting skills, son. And we are going to send you to an abbreviated form of Special Agent training to give you the tools you need to carry out this mission competently," declared Fossate. *Oh God, not another bullshit 'abbreviated' school*, thought Matt.

Sensing what Matt was thinking, Fossate said, "It won't be some faux-schooling. It will be all the real classwork any special agent receives. We will eliminate the more esoteric information and the physical training. You have already had more weapons training than any of our Special Agents receive, so you won't need that portion of our cadet training. The classroom work will take three weeks, and then you'll head out to your new billet on the USS *Oklahoma City*, which is homeported in Yokosuka. And although you will remain enlisted military, you'll arrive as a third-class petty officer, which will get you more respect and responsibility from the get-go and a little more pay. And to sweeten the pot for you, we've gotten permission to take off 365 of those 900 days you have left in the navy for agreeing to volunteer."

Matt sat there, stunned. What he had just been told and requested to do, was quite an overwhelming amount of wacky and scary information for a young man, just twenty years old, to consume. Matt was having trouble formulating any words when LTCDR McNutt chimed in. "Unfortunately, Bert, we can't give you much time to think about this. We have a lot of work to do to get you the orders for transfer, the seat in training, and the billet in the shack on the *Okie* without arousing any suspicion. It's an opportunity to provide an enormous service to your country."

"Thank you, sir, I'll do it," stammered Matt. "I'll do my best, sir." Matt realized that he had just taken the same amount of time to decide to take this assignment as he had in deciding to join the navy in the first place. Thinking about it, it was also the same amount of time that he had taken to decide to "volunteer" for the landing force deployment team, which ended up being an utter fiasco. He made a mental note to work on this troubling trait.

"We know you will," Captain Fossate said, holding out his hand to Matt. "Now, you go chase that commie missile while we get every-thing in place to get you out of there. You can expect orders to arrive while you are on patrol. You'll need to act as surprised as anyone about the orders, I know I don't need to remind you, but I will: You will mention or discuss this with no one other than Special Agent McNutt, understood?"

"Yessir," mumbled Matt, "Understood completely."

5

HUNTING SOVIET MISSILES

A t 1300 hours the next day, the familiar three blows of the ship's horn indicated that the USS *Robert E. Peckham* was, once again, underway. Unlike the usual deployments of the ship to Asia and the South Pacific, this was a quiet departure. The sailors with loved ones had privately given their goodbyes at home; there was no assembly of ship's crew in their crisp dress whites standing at the rails and no fanfare. Instead, the *Bob E.* was headed on a "classified" mission to the Bering Sea, far to the north, where the ship had never before traveled.

The radio shack was hectic, which was good for Matt as he didn't have much time to dwell on the fact that he would soon not only leave his ship but would enter into yet another world in which he was in deeply over his head. Dozens of messages were arriving over the teletypes with continuous updates and constant changes to the minutiae of the mission. The electronic spooks came and went from the shack with a veneer of secrecy, isolating themselves both from the radiomen and the rest of the crew. They took their meals on the mess decks together and spoke to no one else unless absolutely necessary.

Matt was a bit fascinated by these electronic spooks, most of whom had the navy rating of Communications Technician or "CT."

Their lack of concern about cordiality or communication was a
ready-made challenge for Matt to attempt recognition and some
semblance of politeness from them. When he saw one in a passageway, he would say hello to them in a "hey buddy" sort of way. Unfortunately, he received little or no response, and when he directly asked
them questions, he rarely got more than a one-word answer. This
behavior on the part of these reclusive sailors encouraged Matt all the
more to continue to try to break through their protective *spook*
exteriors.

As the *Bob E.* headed north, the balmy tropical temperatures of
Hawaii gradually gave way to much cooler temperatures. The USS
Peckham had never been to the north before, and its deployments had
only been to tropical climates. Three days into their transit, it slowly
began to become uncomfortably cold on the ship. By the fourth day,
the engineers were very aware that the ship's heating system had
never before been used, and very troubling was the fact that apparently, no one knew how to turn the heat on. Regular dungarees began
to be covered by jackets, watch caps replaced ballcaps, and a few
people even broke out gloves and peacoats. The ship was becoming
colder by the hour, and the engineers, nicknamed *snipes*, were
working diligently to get the heat on. There were not nearly enough
blankets for the crew to double-up, and the chief engineer was
sending emergency messages to anyone and everyone who might
know how to get the heat on. The RM's were already used to colder
than usual temperatures in their workspace just because the mass of
electronic equipment in the radio shack required constant air condi-
tioning. But it was more than a little concerning when Matt came
back to his coffee cup an hour after pouring it, looked down at it,
looked up at Harry, and said, "There's ice on the top of my coffee!" As
the situation became dire, the engineers began throwing caution to
the wind to find an improvised solution. Finally, in part desperation
and part exasperation, one of the boiler technicians threw a giant
hammer at the thermostat, cracking the glass exterior. The BT stared
at the damage caused by the hammer, waiting for his CPO to start
screaming at him, for which the chief was visibly warming up, his

upper lip trembling. Just as the chief was about to let loose his usual string of obscenities, a rumbling sound started emanating from below their feet. The chief raised a finger to his lips as they recognized the sound might be steam in the heating pipes. The heat began flowing from the vents on the ship to their surprise and amazement, and the BT who pitched the wrench became an instant folk hero aboard the *Peckham*. As the vessel warmed, Matt had never been so grateful for that warmth in his life.

The USSR had been problematic for the US government since the end of World War II, when the "Cold War" officially began. Following the Cuban missile crisis in 1963, when the US and the Soviets both realized that they weren't willing to eradicate the world of humans to dominate the other, their antagonism toward one another became more focused on political, economic, and propaganda efforts. As the US government and the American public both became obsessed with Vietnam and the Indochinese conflict in the 1960s and early 1970s, the Cold War, by no means gone, was given much less attention by the American public.

As it turned out, the Cold War was an excellent opportunity to divert Americans' attention from Vietnam. The people elected to lead the United States government were in a pickle; the voters who elected them to high office were putting massive pressure on those officials to extract the United States from Vietnam. The problem was, they were in a catch-22; America, the "greatest" nation, couldn't possibly lose a war, yet it had become clear there was no way to win this war. In a masterful piece of sleight-of-hand, the government's propaganda machine kicked into high gear, declaring the US had "peace with honor," a euphemism for "we give up." At the same time, the government's marketing campaign began in earnest to escalate the publicity over the Cold War, transferring back to the USSR the honor of being American's most hated enemy. This distracted America's infuriated citizens' attention away from the process of slinking away from Vietnam with the USA's collective tail between its legs. A manufactured resurgence of the Cold War was particularly helpful to the US government in accomplishing this mission.

In addition to appeasing the public, and to maintain its implausibly generous funding from the US Congress, US military and intelligence establishments lent a willing hand in a disingenuous refocusing on protecting its citizens from what would be called by a future president the "Evil Empire." The Soviets' pervasive paranoia abetted these efforts and went a long way in the USSR's challenge to maintain its authority with its citizens. Having an enemy *outside* keeps the citizenry *inside* from focusing on their own adversity. As such, both the USSR and the USA remained steadfast in putting pressure on their primary adversaries in any manner they were able, short of actually firing weapons at one another.

As a radioman, Matt was privy to the Cold War each day during his radio watches. He saw dozens of messages each day on the fleet broadcast from other ships, submarines, and spy planes as to the locations of any mobile Soviet military asset. Military intelligence attempted to track every ship, submarine, and mobile warhead device globally and relied upon its navy ships and submarines to report any encounter on the high seas. Matt saw regular messages documenting the military's focus on keeping tensions high enough between the two countries. Both US and Soviet ships and submarines played a continual game of cat and mouse, trying to track one another and pretending to be a threat to one another. With some degree of frequency, the *Peckham's* sonarmen would spot Soviet submarines shadowing the ship, less than a hundred feet below their hull, matching the ship's movement turn-for-turn. Once the ship's crew detected such an incident, the Captain would often attempt to hard-turn one way or the other to expose the submarine. Other times the Captain would keep the sub under observation, trying not to tip the submarine's captain off that they were on to its game. The game would result in a flurry of messages to command about the size and type of submarine, which would then be compiled by military intelligence and put in a daily report to the fleet.

Russian trawlers, which intentionally looked like fishing vessels, yet contained enough electronic equipment to travel to the moon and back, would constantly encroach the *Peckham's* perimeter seeking to gather electronic communications information. The captain of the *Peckham* was often forced to divert course or even come to a standstill as a trawler would block its path while steaming.

Even with the daily reminders of the extent to which the two governments were attempting to keep tabs on and harass the other, the *Peckham's* current mission was exceptional. It was exciting to Matt to think that the navy would have the guts to attempt to actually *steal* a Soviet missile as it landed in the ocean. Matt was unable to imagine how the Soviets would let that happen.

As the *Peckham* came on station, it quickly became evident that the Soviets had no intention of allowing the US to come into possession of their weapon. As the Captain slowed the ship, Matt decided to go topside to try to satisfy his curiosity. As he opened the heavy metal water-tight door and exited the ship's interior, a fanciful scene presented itself. Multiple shades of grey had replaced the beautiful blue sky and deep cerulean ocean of tropical Hawaii. The atmosphere was covered with clouds of light grey, and the Bering Sea below was a much darker and more sinister grey. The air temperature was frigid, and Matt imagined the water was even more glacial in climate.

In addition to the environment, Matt saw an unbelievable assembly of ships within throwing distance. The *Peckham* was within 500 feet of at least three Soviet warships and several other ships that looked like trawlers, only much larger. As Matt surveyed this unbelievable scene, he saw that none of the vessels was moving. In a split second, one of the warships came about and launched full-steam, its trajectory aimed at the midships area of the ship. A second warship came about in front of the *Peckham* to stop any forward progress. A moment later, the first ship turned so that it was parallel to the *Peckham*. Matt watched with alarm as its massive six-inch gun rotated to face the *Peckham*. Almost simultaneously, from the doors on the ship's side came twenty or thirty men, each with AK-47's and what appeared to Matt to be submachine guns. Each man took position and aimed their weapons directly at the *Peckham*. Matt's immediate amazement at this sight soon turned to shock and disbelief, and not the least of all, fear. Almost as quickly, the first ship turned and headed away at full speed from the *Peckham* to the east, as the second warship did the same to the west.

This surreal exercise in intimidation happened several times a day for the next two days, to no avail. The *Peckham* stood its ground in each instance. When direct confrontation was unsuccessful, the Soviet ships attempted to draw the *Peckham* into a cat and mouse game in which one craft or another would race to various locations up to a mile or two from the *Peckham*, trying to draw the *Peckham* to follow in what appeared to be an attempt to lure the *Peckham* away from where they suspected the missile might land. Oddly, the Soviet ships would also come within 100 feet or so of the *Peckham* several times each day, behaving peacefully. Matt would watch Soviet Sailors playing volleyball on deck and recreating as though nothing at all was happening. For the officers attempting to put the *Peckham* close enough to grab the missile, it was a demanding and exhausting activity.

Toward the end of the second day on station, a Chief Petty Officer directing the CTs in their job came into the radio shack and approached Chief Cheesewright. After speaking together, Chief Cheesewright asked Matt to come over from his teletype repair bench. "Bert, this is Chief Spookman, er..., sorry, Spakeman, who works with our guests in the quickvan. He has a request of you."

Immediately on guard for more monkey business in his life, Matt advanced with some concern. "Seaman Bertram," Chief Spakeman cordially began, "We've got a little issue with one of our teletypes in the van, and, unfortunately, we don't have our own teletype repairman onboard. We would like to ask you to come up to the van and see if you can get it back up and running."

Matt could hardly contain his excitement. From the moment the spooks arrived, the *Peckham's* crew gawked outside the van and speculated about the mysterious and magical things that were going on inside the grey box. Multiple theories abounded, but none had been confirmed due to the taciturn communications the personnel yielded. "Of course, Chief, I'd be happy to help out. Let me get my tool bag, and we can take a look."

"Unfortunately, Matt, you need to be 'briefed' before you can go inside the van," said the Chief. LT FitzGourney is waiting for you on the helicopter deck to give you a briefing." This new bit of information had Matt even more interested in the adventure. Getting a 'briefing' sounded pretty damn spectacular. Matt proceeded with the Chief, and upon arriving, saluted the officer and introduced himself.

"Seaman Bertram," said FitzGourney, "Before we go in, I need to give you some information and warnings. Inside this van is the most sophisticated array of electronic surveillance equipment on the face of the earth. The men inside will be doing things that require a clearance *much* higher than you have. You need to know that you are not to divulge any information to *anyone* about the activities or equipment in this van, under penalty of court-martial. Do I make myself clear?"

Having heard similar warnings in the past, particularly upon returning from his mission in Cambodia, Matt had little visceral reaction and was all the more curious about the amazing things he would see. "Absolutely, sir. You can count on me."

With that assurance, the Chief and LT FitzGourney, with Matt following, went inside, Matt with his eyes wide. As the door slowly closed behind them, the lighting of the van was unlike any he had seen before. The lights emitted a very eerie purple color, making all of the crew in the van appear more like horror show characters than sailors. As he walked further into the quickvan, he observed two rows of desks along each side, each desk filled with completely unidentifiable electronic equipment. Most of the men sitting at each station wore headphones, and over a speaker inside was the sound of radio communications in Russian. There were strange scopes and an array of weird screens indicating something entirely foreign to Matt. They walked him down to the teletype, which allowed Matt to walk past each small workstation. Upon reaching the teletype bay, Matt opened the machine's cover, and watching it for a couple of seconds, grabbed a tension adjuster and a spring. He popped a spring on, closed the cover, and said, "Giver 'er a test, and we'll see if that's it." They tested it, and the teletype came to life, printing lines of what appeared to Matt to be garbled text. "Oh crap," said Matt, "it looks like we need more work," Matt said.

"Oh, no, Seaman Bertram, it looks to me like it's working perfectly," said Chief Spakeman, taking Matt by the arm and escorting him toward the door. "Thanks a bunch for your help." Amazed that one of the taciturn CTs would speak warmly to him, he walked alongside the chief.

As they were exiting the van, LT FitzGourney called Matt over. "I'm now required to de-brief you, Seaman Bertram," said the lieutenant. The contents of the debriefing sounded to Matt to be remarkably similar to the briefing. *Wow, a briefing, de-briefing, and a tour of the bridge of the Starship Enterprise, all in ten minutes*, Matt thought to himself.

As Matt anticipated, upon returning to the radio shack, he was accosted by his fellow radiomen about the fantastic sights he must have seen in the van. "Guys, they threatened me not to talk about the specifics," Matt said, "But I will tell you this. I have no clue what I saw or what they were doing. Pausing for effect, Matt finished by saying, "...but it was amazing!" Matt threw the 'amazing' part in to bathe in just a few minutes of fame among his shipmates. It was, however, the truth. If he had been tortured over what he saw, the answer would be the same: No *fucking* clue. But it *was* pretty amazing.

Three days after arriving on station, about an hour after sunrise, the combination of electronic intelligence and radar granted the spooks the realization that the missile test was on. Matt, by coincidence, was on the signal deck gossiping with the signalmen when the ship came alive with activity. The Soviets were ramping up their strategic 'tag' games, and it made sense to believe it was an attempt to lure the *Peckham* away from the landing zone of the missile. The Soviet ships, however, with all of the dramatic strategic maneuvers, were not successful in their attempt to distract the *Peckham*. The Americans, at this moment, were on top of their game. The officers on the bridge were frenetic with orders to 'come about,' 'hard to starboard,' 'all ahead,' and numerous other very naval-sounding commands. Out of the fantail hatch came combat divers, who were preparing their inflatable boat. Observers with powerful binoculars were aiming their lenses at the sky. Anyone who was not focused on a job specific to the task at hand had his head raised in anticipation of seeing the spectacle of a missile falling out of the sky.

And then, there it was! Out of the clouds was falling a depleted rocket with a mockup warhead, and in amazement, Matt saw that the *Peckham* was by far the ship closest to the missile. The *Peckham's* engine came to full throttle, steaming in the direction of the missile's ultimate collision with the sea, straining with every ounce of speed to be the first ship to the catch. With a colossal splash sending spray hundreds of feet in the air, the missile punched the surface of the water, disappeared, and then rebounded to the surface. Incredibly to Matt, the *Peckham* was no more than a hundred feet away when the missile hit, the sound booming from the impact with the water. Over the ship's side went the divers, and within five seconds, they were on the missile, diving out of their inflatable boat looking almost serpentine as they entered the water. Matt mentally counted the seconds as the divers struggled to harness the rocket. They had great difficulty getting the straps around the missile, and the nose appeared to be submerged. The more they tried to lasso the missile, the further it dipped, until finally and quite frustratingly, the missile, which was most likely engineered to do so, sank below the surface and disappeared into the abyss of the Bering Sea.

The divers had returned to the ship with faces revealing great disappointment. Almost like magic, all of the Soviet vessels had scattered, disappearing back to their domain, successfully keeping the Americans from capturing their prize.

6

UNDERCOVER AND OVER HIS HEAD

With its mission over, the USS *Robert E. Peckham* began her journey home. As expected, a message soon arrived containing orders for Matt's transfer to the USS *Oklahoma City*, CG-5. As Matt expected, Chief Cheesewright was not pleased with the news. "What in the *fuck* is the navy doing now?" he asked somewhat rhetorically. "You aren't supposed to have orders for another year, and we are going to be so fucking short-handed we won't be able to reach our own dicks!" Matt played the part of being surprised and threw out a couple of profanities, just to sound a bit more convincing. The Chief continued to fume for a few more minutes, throwing a stapler at the wall that missed its target, hitting and cracking the face of one of the high-frequency receivers. Breaking the radio simply fanned the flames of the Chief's epic pissed-offedness even more. Fortunately, Matt didn't have to do much acting throughout the episode. The Chief did not care to hear any input from Matt, preferring to be the soloist in his extravaganza of histrionic ranting.

The three-day trip back to Pearl Harbor was much more difficult for Matt than he expected as he had to say goodbyes to his shipmates, some of whom were the best friends he had ever had. It was tough to say goodbye to Harry, as he and Matt had grown quite close since Harry's arrival. Matt found that he was also having trouble saying farewell to the *Bob E.*, his home for the last year. A great deal of life-changing had gone on since his arrival, and he was more than a bit surprised at the feelings of sadness he had in saying goodbye to his ship. Even so, the day after returning to Pearl Harbor, Matt and his seabag were on a commercial airliner. The plane was heading for Washington Dulles International Airport, just a few miles from where he would be attending "abbreviated" NIS Special Agent Training at the Office of Naval Intelligence Headquarters in Suitland, Maryland.

Before leaving, Matt received instructions to go to Naval Support Facility, Anacostia and check-in to the Naval Lodge on base. His orders included information that he would be met for breakfast the following morning by a Training Supervisor from ONI. Curiously the instructions advised him to dress in civilian attire for the meeting.

The following day at 8:00 am, Matt was having breakfast with Special Agent Jake Nystings, one of the instructors at ONI. Special Agent Nystings was part of the new breed of Special Agents, a civilian, recruited from the US Marshalls to work for NIS. "Petty Officer Bertram," It's great to meet you. We've been kind of in a quandary about how to go about training you, however. May I call you Matt?" inquired Nystings. "You can call me Jake."

"Certainly, sir," said Matt. Apparently, they didn't know his nickname, but he certainly liked being addressed now as a petty officer. "People in the navy call me Bert, sir, if you want to call me that."

"I think I'd prefer to call you Matt," said Nystings. You are about to go through a metamorphosis of sorts, and it might be good for you to shed just a bit of your navy identity while you're with us. As I said, we're kind of in a sticky situation with your training. First, we've never done anything like this before. NIS just doesn't use undercover agents in this manner. We can't put you in the entire class because you've got to get to Yokosuka reasonably quickly, and your assignment is entirely confidential, so we can't have you mixing with our other recruits. Additionally, we're dropping the physical fitness portion of the training. We decided to keep the firearms training in, even though you're very familiar with weapons. You've only had combat training, however, and law enforcement weapons training is vastly different. Because of all of this, we've decided to give you a highly personalized and individualized course, meaning you'll have one person in your class: You and one instructor: Me. Other than the physical training, you'll get precisely the same training anyone else does. In addition, we'll spend most of the last few days going over protocol and techniques for counterespionage, which is typically a part of an advanced course, not usually taught to our new agents. We're going to have you stay here at the lodge for your stay, and I'll pick you up each morning to go to the NIS training facility. I guess I'd say you'll be getting an even better and more individualized education than any of our special agents."

Jake Nystings' words were music in Matt's ears. After his "abbreviated" (a metaphor for crappy) training for the landing force deployment team on his ship, he felt much more confident that he would be as prepared as possible for his assignment.

Other than worrying about the daunting duties in Yokosuka, Matt thoroughly enjoyed the training. He received private tutoring from an experienced special agent, which allowed him to ask questions whenever he wished and benefit from extraordinary attention. At the end of the three weeks of training, Matt felt much more prepared for his mission. He enjoyed Jake's company and thought he was a gifted instructor. Over the three weeks, the two became close and often spoke during breaks about the challenge ahead. Matt sensed that Jake was genuinely concerned about his welfare and was doing his best to contribute to Matt's safety.

As the training finished, Jake offered to buy Matt a beer at the club on base. "You've been an outstanding student, Matt. I would put you up against any of the new agents I've trained over the years. I wish I could give you the NIS badge because you certainly deserve it," Jake said with what Matt thought was genuineness.

"Thanks, Special Agent Nystings," mumbled Matt. "Any parting wisdom for a guy who is in *way* over his head?"

"Just this, Matt," answered Nystings, "The essence of undercover work is patience. Don't be in too much of a hurry with things. As they come to trust you, you'll naturally find opportunities to do your work. Just behave exactly the same way you would have had you transferred to the *Okie* to just be a radioman. Everything will fall into place, including opportunities to accomplish your mission."

"Good advice. Thanks," replied Matt. Matt had no idea of the "opportunities" that would soon be coming his way.

The following morning, Special Agent Nystings met Matt at the Naval Lodge with coffee to go and drove him to the Naval Air Station for his trip to Japan. Matt would be flying into Narita International Airport on a Military Airlift Command C-130 Hercules. Narita airport was about a three-hour drive from Yokosuka. His orders were to proceed to the Military Liaison in Terminal One. Unlike the other sailors who were heading to Yokosuka on the flight, however, Matt would be met by Special Agent Randy Glasscock, who would drive him to Yokosuka. That would allow Matt the opportunity to meet and get to know his "handler" (Matt supplied that term, which he had learned from his John le Carré books), and they could discuss the logistics of the mission and how they would work together.

Unlike most MAC flights that had a reputation for delays and cancellations, Matt's plane arrived at Narita early. Being in a Japanese airport was a frenetic and fascinating experience, so Matt decided to park himself in a seat in front of the military liaison's booth and people-watch. Matt was enjoying the experience, drinking a Japanese Coke with some sort of strange rice candy bar, when he spied what he considered to be a stunning young Caucasian woman with auburn hair, walking in his direction. Much to his surprise, the woman walked right up to him. *My lucky day* thought Matt. The woman sensed Matt was examining her, and her cheeks began to redden. Matt could see that she was blushing, but as quickly as it came, it vanished. The woman looked Matt in the eyes and said, "Petty Officer Bertram?"

"Yes, Ma'am," Matt replied with a slightly dazed look. "Are you here to take me to Special Agent Randy Glasscock?" Matt asked.

"I *am* Special Agent Randy Glasscock," she snapped. "Grab your stuff, and we'll talk in the car." Randy proceeded to practically sprint in the direction of the parking lot, quickly leaving Matt lagging several steps behind in the dust of her ire.

The two walked to the parking lot without speaking, and it was only after they were buckled into Randy's NIS-issued 1973 Datsun 510 that Matt gathered the courage to speak. "I'm sorry about assuming you worked for the person who was picking me up," Matt said with a look of shame, "I didn't even know there were female special agents in the NIS, not to mention ones who look ..." Matt realized he was going from the frying pan into the fire, and thought it best just to shut up.

"I understand, Petty Officer Bertram," Randy responded, "I get that all the time, and I apologize that I overreacted just a bit. I guess having the name Randy suggests a male. Anyway, we've got about three hours to get to know one another and to discuss how we will communicate and how I will direct your work on the *Okie*. She handed Matt a handwritten business card with the name "Randy" with two phone numbers and containing no other information. "We want you to simply get to know your new shipmates and superiors over the next few weeks, Petty Officer Bertram," Randy said as she gradually calmed down.

"Please feel free to call me Matt," he implored, "or Bert, which is my nickname. It will be much easier that way."

"And you can call me Randy, also, if you like," she replied, now back in control of her emotions, the anger draining from her.

Matt enjoyed the drive to Yokosuka. He had been in Japan several times on deployments and always appreciated how different the country was from where he grew up. His conversation with Randy, once she regained her composure, was enjoyable and informative. Randy explained that she was 28 years old and had been with the NIS for just under a year. She was one of only two female Special Agents in the NIS in 1975, and both because of her name and the fact that in

1975 the first assembly of gutsy women had barely broken through the "thin blue line" into law enforcement positions, she faced barriers each day on the job. Even a massive organization like the FBI had not allowed female Special Agents until 1972, and it was natural for people, primarily men, to assume that it was a role for men. Coupled with the fact that Randy was both physically attractive and relatively awkward socially, Randy had already experienced several hard-fought battles with both individual and institutional sexism in the NIS. The pervasive sexism in law enforcement only encouraged women like Randy to work diligently to excel in their duties to rise above the fray. Yet, she had a sensitivity to being the target of sexism, which Randy felt was a weakness and one that she didn't want co-workers to exploit.

"So, Matt, the first phase of the operation will simply be to begin 'fitting in' to the radio shack on the *Okie*. Start making friends, get to know your supervisors, and develop some trust from them in your skills. Keep your eyes sharp but also keep your nose out of anybody else's business and avoid attracting any suspicion. Once you build enough trust, we'll begin to talk about strategies for discovering any nefarious behavior among your shipmates. Keep in mind that we don't even know if anything is going on anymore, but this is probably an established espionage effort due to the risk the Soviets took in assassinating two sailors.

The phone number on the card is mine. There are two numbers on there, one is my office number, and the other is my beeper number. If I don't answer, I have a brand-new tape answering machine connected to my phone that will allow you to record a message. I'm still trying to figure out how this tape answering machine works, so after you leave a message, call my beeper, and I'll get to a phone within five minutes of your call, and then you can try again.

"I'll be your lifeline to the world outside. If you find yourself in any kind of trouble, or question what decision to make, call me. In addition, we'll meet at least once a week for an update when you aren't at sea. Now that you're a petty officer, we can meet at the petty officer's club on base. I'll get non-NIS credentials so that we can meet without arousing suspicion. I think that's about it unless you have questions."

Matt really could not think of any questions at this point. He had never heard of something called an "answering machine," but he did remember some doctors having beepers that always seemed to go off when they were at the movies. As far as his instructions on proceeding, things seemed pretty simple and obvious. As the silence became uncomfortable, both settled into a conversation about their lives and families. Matt learned that Randy had grown up with five older brothers, and she related that she had acquired considerable survival skills from that experience.

"So, Matt, I know something of your past from your file. You grew up in Los Alamos, New Mexico, 'The Atomic City.' That must have been interesting. What was it like? Were your parents' scientists?"

"Yeah, everybody asks that question. No, my Dad worked in personnel, and my mom worked in the lab's library. It was interesting. Have you ever read Michael Crichton's book, *Westworld*?" Randy shook her head. "Well, it's an interesting book about a company that creates this entertainment park for adults where there are robots that are characters in a western theme. Anyway, sorry, that's too much information, but Los Alamos felt a little like *Westworld* when I read the book. The government created a town hidden in the mountains of Northern New Mexico, built all the houses, roads, schools, and a hospital. It was all part of a government-managed town. No robots, but very strictly controlled."

Randy chuckled and said, "Yeah, I get how it would have been weird."

"Don't get me wrong; it was a great place to grow up. There was no crime, no poverty, no entry or exit without permission. And my classmates were mostly children of scientists, which meant that the school system was the best taxpayer money could buy. I was in the bottom half of my class with a 3.6 GPA."

"Wow, strange!" Randy said.

"Yeah, that's putting it mildly!"

Matt could not help feeling that he could trust Randy, and by the time they arrived on base, Matt had developed a genuine liking for her. On the other hand, Randy was all business, but every so often in conversation, Matt sensed a tell that perhaps she at least didn't *hate* him.

7

WELCOME TO OKLAHOMA!

Randy dropped Matt off on the far side of the naval base to avoid suspicion, and Matt grabbed a base bus across the expansive Yokosuka Naval Station where the USS *Oklahoma City*, CG-5, was berthed. Yokosuka was an important strategic location for the US Navy, as the ships homeported there were 17 steaming days closer to Asia than US-based ships. It would have taken five times the number of ships to rotate back and forth on deployment had the US not had Yokosuka. About 50 percent of the vessels in the fleet based in Yokosuka were underway on any given day, so there was a lot of coming and going in the busy harbor. Because the Indochinese war was in the area and the Soviets were very close, it made great strategic sense to have a large naval base in Japan. The Japanese did not have a say in the plan due to the terms of surrender they had signed 31 years earlier.

As the bus pulled up to the stop closest to the *Oklahoma City*, Matt was impressed with the ship's size and the intimidation its profile exuded. Nicknamed the *Okie*, the ship was nearing the end of its life, or, more specifically, lives. She had seen unparalleled service since her commissioning on December 22, 1944. She had seen combat missions in World War II, Korea, and Vietnam. The *Okie* had gone through several face-lifts, conversions, and updating, the last of which had just been that year when the navy redesignated her from a Light Guided Missile Cruiser (CLG) to a Guided Missile Cruiser (CG). In addition to her regular duties, she also served as the flagship for the Commander of the Seventh Fleet, Vice Admiral Theodore (Teddy) B. Howard. Admiral Howard commanded over 60 ships in the Seventh Fleet, most of which operated from Japan and Guam.

Okie was a much larger ship than the *Peckham*, and as such, Matt was not looking forward to navigating his way through the maze of decks and compartments. The *Peckham* had been only 300 feet in length with a crew of about 200 men. The *Okie* was double that length with a crew, including the staff of the Seventh Fleet, of about 1400 men. The radio shack was very different also. On the *Peckham,* there were a total of nine to eleven RM's, depending upon the day, and there was one space for the radio shack. The *Okie* had over 75 radiomen and occupied eight different spaces on the ship, including separate spaces for teletype repair and crypto equipment. The Communications division personnel were from both the ship and the staff of the Seventh Fleet.

Unlike the *Peckham*, the *Okie* was built for fighting. While the *Peckham* had one propeller, the *Okie* had four and could travel well over 32 knots. *Okie's* weapons systems were far more formidable than the *Peckham's*. The *Okie* boasted a 6"/47 triple turret (3 guns) on the main deck, a 5"/38 dual mount (2 guns) on the O1 level, a Mark 7 Talos missile launching system with a compliment of 48 Talos missiles and a Mark 7 dual-arm missile launcher also on the main deck. It was a pretty badass ship, in Matt's opinion.

As Matt approached his new ship, he thought back to the challenge of his first few moments on the *Peckham*. He was fresh out of boot camp, and had no idea what to expect. The memory brought a smile to his face as Matt relived his inability to find the right way to request to come aboard the ship, and the officer of the deck's condescending attitude, making Matt suffer on the gangplank for what seemed like hours. As Matt anticipated, coming aboard the *Okie* was a much more routine event, and before he knew it, he was walking with an escort to radio central. Waiting a few minutes while the radioman who accompanied him went to find the leading Chief, Matt was astounded at the almost exponential increase in radio equipment in the space. The ship was a communications masterpiece, as well it should, considering they were responsible both for the ship's everyday communications and the Seventh Fleet's, which coordinated traffic between 60 ships and the upper-level command of the US Navy. Matt guessed it would be a perfect place for a spy to gather intelligence on the navy.

Through the door walked what he supposed would be the leading chief, who approached Matt, jammed out his hand, and said, "Petty Officer Bertram? I'm Senior Chief Lester, and I'll be your supervisor here in the radio shack." Senior Chief Morris Lester was a diminutive man who, unlike most navy chiefs he had met, was in excellent physical shape with considerable biceps. Lester had been in the navy for 20 years, and at 38, was one of the "old" guys. Senior Chief Lester, nicknamed " Moe, " was well-liked and highly respected on the ship with a winsome smile and an unending energy supply. Most of the radiomen aboard considered the senior chief to be the most knowledgeable radioman in the radio shack. More importantly, he had built quite a reputation throughout the Seventh Fleet as a virtuoso of poker. The radiomen enjoyed telling others that he earned more money playing poker than he did from his navy salary. Perhaps more remarkably to those of the sailor class, Lester was notorious among his shipmates for his staggering flatulence. His men often timed the long and reeking farts the Senior Chief could unleash, and the rumor was that he had, on several occasions, exceeded the thirty-second mark.

The Senior Chief was one of four CPOs in the communications division. "So my friend and your old boss, Chief Cheesewright says you're a stand-up radioman, you know what you are doing, and he's incredibly pissed off that I have you now," Lester said, smiling. "Amazingly, the confirmation of your security clearance arrived before you did, so we don't have to worry about a delay getting you on watches. I understand you're a teletype repairman, but we have an unusually high population of them right now, so I'd like to start you out just on-call as a teletype repairman. We'll get you oriented and up to speed here in radio central with the everyday activities. That way, I can work with you for a few weeks, see where your talents lie, and we'll go from there. Sound good?"

"Yes, senior chief, that sounds great to me," said Matt.

"Alright, let's get you a rack in communications berthing, allow you get settled in, and we can meet back here after lunch for introductions. By the way, Chief Cheesewright said your nickname is Bert. Is it OK if we all call you that?"

Matt gave his consent as he headed out the door, escorted by another radioman, to find a rack in berthing, not relishing the fact that he would have to learn to navigate inside a large ship with a labyrinth of decks, compartments, and ladders.

After lunch, Senior Chief Lester gave Matt an orientation of the radio shack, introducing him to some of the sailors with whom he would be working. One of the sailors he met, Mike Petit, another third-class petty officer, seemed like a friendly guy and invited Matt to have a beer "or ten" with him after work. He offered to bring along some of his friends so that Matt could get to know them.

Radio Central was one of the eight spaces the radio gang occupied and the largest. The *Okie* had the same essential radio equipment as the *Peckham*, except on a massive scale. Rows of banks of HF receivers, UCC-1's, and patching boards lined the large room. The number of teletypes was astounding. There was an entirely separate space for the transmitters and a third space for the crypto equipment. Traveling forward from radio central and into the crypto room, Matt felt a sudden sense of panic in the sheer quantity of equipment. Still, as he looked at the staggering array of equipment, he realized that he knew how to operate pretty much everything in the space. It was comforting to know that Matt would have a dozen or more other radiomen standing watch with him, including a senior petty officer or CPO. Forward of the crypto room was the teletype repair shop, which made Matt smile when he reminisced about his teletype "shop" on the *Peckham*, which consisted of a small workbench tucked away in the corner of the radio shack. This shop had five workbenches and a fantastic collection of parts. Matt thought that if he could have had half of these parts on the *Peckham*, he would have been in teletype repair heaven.

The senior chief invited Matt to the mess decks for coffee and to chat about how the shack operated on the *Okie*. After the discussion, they sat and got to know one another just a bit. "So, how do you know Chief Cheesewrite?" Matt inquired.

"We were both seamen apprentices, just out of radioman school, and stationed on the USS *Gearing*. It was the 1950's so the job was very different back then. It was your chief who taught me how to play poker. I was a pretty shitty poker player but became fascinated with the game. The more I played, the more I realized that poker was underrated as a complex game of strategy. To me, it's much more complicated than playing chess. You don't have just one opponent, but four or five, each with different strengths and weaknesses. You not only have to be a student of math, odds, and have a memory for cards played, but you also have to be a student of people. You have to learn to read people, and not just to sense when they are bluffing or not. You have to learn tells and habits and what they do when they are nervous or confident. You have to learn that people always reveal when they are lying. You just have to know what to look for. It's a game of wits, deception, balls, and odds, and plain old fucking luck. It's the best game in the world. Once I learned how much skill goes into the game, I dedicated my life to becoming the best player possible. I lost a lot of money in the process, but once I truly understood the game, I made it all back and a good lot more in no time."

The senior chief, looking a little uncomfortable, lifted one of his butt cheeks and farted a back-end blowout that could have melted steel. Lester acted as though he had not noticed, and his monologue continued without pause. As Matt tried to keep the senior chief from seeing the tears in his eyes, Lester continued, "I have to admit, I'm the best poker player I've met, and I've met some good ones. It's partly because I'm smart and partly because I have some rules that I live by. For me, it's not gambling; it's applied science."

"I played a little poker in my life, too," Matt said. "I think I'm pretty good myself."

"Is that right," Lester said with some enhanced interest. "Where did you learn to play?"

"Well, actually, my grandmother taught me," said Matt, a bit sheepishly. "She would come to visit for a few weeks each year when I was a kid. Granny was a pretty cool lady. She took up smoking at 70 when my grandpa died and always had a cigarette hanging out of her mouth. Unfortunately, she never remembered to flick the ash off. My mom would find three-inch cigarette ashes around the house for weeks after she left. Anyway, she loved to play poker, so she would get all the neighborhood kids together when she visited and would have them bring all their loose change. She'd put on one of those visor hats, light up a cigarette, and play poker with us for hours. She taught me a lot about the game."

"Granny, huh? That's a pretty fucking great guru, I'm sure," Lester said sarcastically. "Ever play No Limits Texas Hold 'em?"

"I think I have heard of it," said Matt, trying to sound more experienced than he was. "We mostly played five-card draw and seven-card stud with grandma."

"Both good games, but Hold 'em is the game I pretty much play exclusively now. It's a hell of a ride. Grandma might just want to be dealt in. I'd be happy to teach you. It's a straightforward game with a few basic rules that takes a lifetime to master."

"I'd like that," Matt said, trying not to show his discomfort.

"Well, let me know any time you're interested in losing your paycheck," said the senior chief. "I'll be happy to take your money."

After a dizzying afternoon of orientation, Matt was looking forward to getting off the ship, getting a beer, and getting to know some of his shipmates. Matt, Mike, and two other sailors met on the fantail of the Okie at 4 p.m. in their civvies, ready to go ashore. Mike quickly introduced Matt to the two, RM2 "Long Dong" Gander and RMSN "Kit" Carson. Matt made a mental note to ask Gander how he received his nickname, but he was pretty sure his anatomy played a part. Matt was relieved that nicknames were as standard on this ship as on the *Peckham* and was privately grateful that his nickname was transferrable and not disgusting. He had served on the *Peckham* with Teacup, Blumpkin, Gizz, Dumpster, and others. Matt was just fine with his nickname.

As they were about to leave the ship, Senior Chief Lester passed them, wearing his civvies and carrying a gym bag. "Why don't you come work out with me, Bert? That beer will give you a gut!" said the Sr. Chief, in a friendly way, walking away without waiting for a reply.

Lester headed down the gangplank and opened the door of a corvette, throwing his gym bag in the passenger seat. "Wow, he's got a Corvette?" said Matt, with amazement. "I didn't know that you made that much money as an E-8 in the navy!"

"Oh, he doesn't," said Mike, "He doubles his income playing poker. Don't *ever* get in a poker game with that guy!" Mike said, obviously a victim of the Sr. Chief's prodigious poker playing.

Matt had been to Yokosuka several times while on WestPac cruises but had not spent much time off base. Most of their stops had been for a few days at most. Matt's new drinking buddies decided Matt needed an *authentic* Yokosuka experience; hence, they were flagging down a taxi to head to the Yokosuka district of Honchô. This area, known to sailors as "The Honch," was the bar district catering to US servicemen. Much like Olongapo was in Subic Bay, there was no shortage of bars, restaurants, and vice. The Honch was a bit less circus-like, existed on a smaller scale than Olongapo, and had its Japanese touch.

Nevertheless, there were still plenty of opportunities to find trouble. And the search was on for precisely that. The guys' favorite bar was the *New San Diego*, a dive bar with all the usual sailor services, including bar girls, music, plenty of beer, and raucous entertainment, and it made an excellent first stop for the evening.

As long as a person is somewhat likable and outgoing, making friends in the navy is a simple thing. Each sailor is a long way from home and even though they come from disparate backgrounds, he instantly has something in common with his shipmates: the navy. Matt was discovering this with his new group. Mike was the most outgoing of the three and was a genuine connector. He orchestrated the early conversation to make Matt feel more comfortable with his new shipmates. Both Long Dong and Kit seemed nice, although Kit came across initially as a complete space-cadet, often contributing to the conversation with statements that revealed he was not quite following the train of thought or, more likely, his train had derailed. All four made it safely back to the ship, Matt already feeling more at home than when he arrived.

Christmas passed on the ship, and as was the tradition when onboard over the holidays, Matt and several of the other single guys volunteered to trade or take extra duty so that the married guys could have Christmas day at home. The *Okie* would be in port over the holiday. As soon as the holiday was over, the *Okie* would be steaming on what seemed like Matt to be a frantic at-sea schedule. On January 5, 1976, they would head to Keelung, Taiwan, with four days in port, then they would travel to Subic Bay for almost two weeks in port. On the 24th, the *Okie* would participate in a multi-ship exercise called MULTIPLEX, then to Sattahip, Thailand, Singapore, and then home to Yokosuka on February 14th. Matt was starting to see that one great thing about being homeported in Yokosuka was that they would have the opportunity to see various ports without being gone from Yokosuka for five or six months at a time.

On January 2, Matt left the *Okie* at lunch break and walked to a bank of pay phones on the pier to contact Randy Glasscock to arrange their first meeting. When he called, he heard an answering machine greeting for the first time in his life. Matt was so uneasy trying to leave a recorded message that he hung up and tried again, this time leaving a rambling, partially coherent message when the voice said to speak. He hung up and then called Randy's pager. He waited the agreed five minutes, called back, and Randy answered. They set up a meeting for 5 pm the next day at the Petty Officers' Club on base.

The next day Matt walked to the club, arriving early. Matt's parents raised him to value the habit of promptness. Actually, habit was a bit of an understatement. Promptness was more like *obsessive-*

compulsive-earliness. Matt's parents had been gripped with the concept and treated tardiness as sinful, on par with adultery. While Matt was not quite as fanatical about being on time, it was at the very least an entrenched inclination. The result of this inclination was that Matt was almost always the first one to a party or virtually any other engagement and would sit in waiting rooms for extended periods long before his scheduled appointment. He had been late only a few times in his life, and the experience had been arduous and unpleasant. However, in a situation like this, Matt benefitted by adjusting to his surroundings and preparing for his meeting. Not that there was much preparation to do. He had only been aboard the *Okie* for four weeks and had pretty much zero to report.

Matt watched as Randy came through the door. Matt felt a momentary feeling of exhilaration at seeing her, not to mention a subtle tingle in his nether regions. His memories of their first meeting reminded him that he was a twenty-year-old sailor who had few, if any, interactions with attractive women outside of the professionals in the bars during liberty.

Randy spotted Matt in the corner of the club, giving him a smile and a wave. She sat down across from him, saying, "Good choice of tables. I doubt anyone who knows you will even see you back here. So, bring me up to date. How was your first month of assignment, Matt?"

"Pretty uneventful, I'd say," Matt responded sheepishly, "I'm really just getting to know the ship, my fellow radiomen, and my supervisors. It's a big change from the *Peckham*."

"I can understand. I know that you weren't supposed to be doing any surveillance this month, but did you see or hear anything that caught your interest regarding our operation?"

"No, everything looks on the outside to be good. My supervisor is a senior chief who is very diligent and a great guy, and the classified materials security looks to me to be as good or better than the *Peckham's*. I haven't encountered anyone suspicious or doing any activity that made me wary. By the way, do you have the ship's schedule? You know we are going to be gone for the next six weeks or so, don't you?"

"Of course, Matt, I'm keeping close track of your schedule." Randy lowered the volume of her speech just a little. "Just so you know, we now have confirmation that there is, indeed, a leak of classified material from the Okie. We sent several "bait" messages to see if anything would turn up, and the spy on your ship relayed the messages to the Soviets. So, the need for our mission is confirmed and has gone from speculative to real. I think it's a perfect time for you to up your game and begin the process of observing the others in the CR division with a different eye. It would be best if you didn't go overboard. Um, sorry for the pun; I do want you to start observing the people who have the most access to classified materials. Shift your thinking to put observation and surveillance as your highest priority. Hang back after watches for just a bit, observe what those people do during their off time. Don't follow anyone, but simply put your surveillance eyes on. It would probably be helpful if you made notes and looked for patterns as you review them. Especially look for people going off on their own or meeting people outside of the ship."

"Kind of like we are doing today?" joked Matt.

Randy paused and smiled, "Yes, a lot like this. A meeting like this might tend to arouse some suspicion among those who are involved."

Matt swallowed. He made a note to be more careful in orchestrating the next meeting.

Randy then gave Matt a mini-lecture on the art of finding patterns in people's behavior and following up on them. Remarkably, when describing the job of surveillance, she sounded much like the senior chief describing poker. "You need to not just watch what people do, Matt," Randy said, "You have to look at their gestures, listen to their words and watch their eyes. Eyes are the windows of the soul, and they will confirm or refute the words coming out of the person's mouth." Randy gave it a moment to sink in. "Now, don't go cowboy on us," she said, "As I say, no following people, no going through their stuff, but *up* the observation game. The next six weeks will be good practice. Keep building your relationships with the other radiomen and your superiors. Continue gaining their trust. This time should not be dangerous for you at all as all you will be doing is observing. I know you won't be able to call for the next six weeks, so give me a call when you're back in port. We'll see how you fostered your surveillance skills and make plans to step it up even more at that time. Keep in mind this will take time, and our directors understand that, so don't rush your work."

"That all makes sense to me, Randy," said Matt, pausing to work up some courage, "Can I buy you a beer?"

Now Randy paused, looking at Matt, which gave Matt hope, just for a second, that she was considering accepting. Portions of words like "Um, well, gosh" started coming from Randy and her face reddened until she gathered herself together a bit, ".... I'd love to, Matt, but I'll have to take a raincheck. Got a meeting to get to." Randy stood up, and smiled, saying, "You be careful out there, Matt, and let me know when you get back." Matt sat and watched as Randy left, feeling like an idiot.

As Matt walked back to the *Okie* from the club, a realization began to hit him for the first time, that while he was still Bert, the radioman from New Mexico, he was *also* Matt, the undercover agent from the NIS. He was two different people in real life. The NIS insisted on calling him Matt, and his shipmates only knew him as Bert. He thought to himself that perhaps that was a good thing that would help him to fit into each of those roles. Although he had taken quite a lot of time to come to grips with the fact that he was now an undercover agent, he somehow failed to allow it to be a reality until now. He had a *new* identity. He had not lost the prior identity, but he had now added the identity of a counterespionage agent, which meant he now had to lead a life as a liar and a thief. He couldn't help recalling a quote from *Tinker, Tailor, Soldier, Spy* by his favorite author, John le Carré, "The more identities a man has, the more they express the person they conceal." *Well, Matt*, he thought, *you took on a doozy of a new identity.*

8

SOUTH PACIFIC HERE WE COME!

T wo days later, at 0800, three blasts of the ship's horn on the USS *Oklahoma City* informed all that the ship was under-way. With the *Okie* being the admiral's flagship, the fanfare in leaving was even more extravagant than on the *Peckham*. With four or five hundred sailors in their crisp, freshly pressed white uniforms lining the decks at parade rest, the navy band playing "Anchors Away" on the pier while families of the sailors aboard waved and blew kisses to their husbands, lovers, and fathers, the *Okie's* departure would have been moving for all but the most insensitive person. Matt would ordinarily have been excited to be steaming again, mainly because the ship's destinations included three ports he had never visited. But as the radio day watch began that morning, a different set of eyes and ears were at work, and the job of seeking out a spy was paramount.

Once the Okie left Kaneda Harbor, Matt reported for his watch in Radio Central. He sat at a large Model 28 teletype, one of thirty onboard, typing outgoing messages. The teletype had multiple uses in the radio shack, and the machine was the radioman's workhorse. The machine could be used to receive messages, which would be typed onto big rolls of paper, copied and distributed. In addition, it could create teletype punch tape, which was essentially paper tape with holes punched into it, which would then be run through a tape reader, translated into something similar to morse code, and transmitted to other ships or shore stations. Morse code, which had been the primary means of communication on ships for the past 75 years, had, for the most part, been replaced by teletype communications. Matt appreciated the fact that he had learned to type in high school, as he was one of the fasted typists in the shack. However, he had to chuckle to himself, thinking about the fact that the only reason he had learned to type was that he had a significant crush on the typing teacher, Mrs. Whipple, and took every class she taught just to be close to her and her luscious hooters. While nothing ever transpired with Matt and Mrs. Whipple outside of Matt's vivid imagination, Matt did become a hell of a typist.

There was a great deal of mindless typing of messages in any radio watch, including status reports, navigation reports, supply messages, scheduling messages from the mundane to the urgent. In addition to the ship's messages, the radio shack served the commander of the seventh fleet, which quadrupled the messages sent and received.

As Matt was busy typing, he pondered the first steps in his mission to find the spy in his radio shack. He decided he would start with the guys he worked with the most and expand his observations. His supervisors were primarily RM1 A.J. Bunker, a sizeable, easy-going man from Kentucky, and Senior Chief Lester. A.J. and Senior Chief Lester worked together as a team, and Lester had Bunker in charge of the Cryptography room and supervising the watch. He and the senior chief mostly worked during the day unless something extraordinary happened, while the less senior radiomen managed the evening and night watches. The *Okie* had enough radiomen to set radio watches for eight hours each: A day watch from 0800-1600, an evening watch from 1600 to midnight, and a mid-watch from midnight to 0800. RM's were rotated among the watches weekly so that each would have the opportunity to have some semblance of a regular life a few weeks each month.

As Matt started making mental lists of the RM's, he decided he would make a chart of who hung out together and seemed to be friends, who were loners, and whether anyone had an unusual schedule or went off alone much. Unfortunately, when the ship was steaming, homeport life ceased to exist. The only friends one had were on the ship, and families and outside relationships were put on hold. There were no phones with which to call home, and the old-fashioned handwritten letter was the primary means of communicating with the outside world. Because of this, Matt could only observe the relationships among the RM's and their behavior onboard ship. Perhaps, when they were in other ports, he could see where they went and what they did if he had suspicions about anyone.

As Matt began observing the radio shack operations from his new perspective, one of the RM's immediately garnered his attention. RM2 Scott Mearey was, if nothing else, creepy. He was about five feet five inches tall, as skinny as a match stick, with skin that lacked any color other than pale white paste. He had no sense of humor and rarely participated in any conversation with the other guys on watch with him. Additionally, he had a habit of going to the head for extended periods, several times per watch. The guy simply gave Matt the creeps, which set off what he was now calling his "spy-dar" in a big way. Matt decided he needed to keep his eyes on Mearey very closely.

Of all of the people Matt worked with on watch, he was most suspicious of Mearey and RM1 Bunker. It wasn't that Bunker set off Matt's spy-dar; it was that the senior chief gave Bunker a preponderance of responsibility for highly classified items. Bunker managed the crypto room, acted as a courier for the monthly shipment of crypto cards for the devices, and was primarily responsible for destroying classified material. It was clear that the senior chief trusted Bunker, but Matt reasoned that any successful spy on the ship would have to garner the trust of his superiors.

Matt decided the first order of business was to follow Mearey to the head on some of his many trips to see what he was actually doing. After four visits to the head, Matt ruled it out as suspicious activity and realized poor Mearey had a genuine bowel problem.

The *Okie* docked in Subic Bay for a two-week stay, and Matt sensed this was an excellent time to keep an eye on Mearey. Matt had noted in previous ports that Mearey always seemed to go on liberty alone, and Subic was no exception. Mearey left the ship, seeping surreptitious behavior. As Matt left the naval base a safe distance behind Mearey and crossed the bridge over what sailors had dubbed the "Shit" River, he reminded himself how unique Olongapo City was. The Shit River was not, in fact, a river. It was a drainage channel from the Santa Rita River, and it was appropriately named. As soon as one started over the Shit River, the local source of both water and sewer, poverty was palpable. He watched small children swimming in it, sitting in small boats and calling to the sailors to throw a peso or two to them. He remembered his first time crossing the river with Chief Boggs and the chief intentionally throwing a peso far enough from the boat to force the child to dive after it. He found that to be grand entertainment, much to Matt's chagrin.

After entering the city, Magsaysay Drive, the main street in town, was lined with hundreds of bars, each one catering to different tastes and filled with girls anxious to provide "dates" to the sailors. An assembly of Jeepneys, old World War II-era Willy's jeeps that the drivers had converted into transportation-for-hire, swarmed the streets, each one painted with a clash of colors and decorated with plastic saints and tasseled tops. It was indeed an abstract sensory overload.

Matt tailed Mearey off the ship on several occasions, each time watching Mearey enter a particular door in an alleyway, a block off of the main street of Magsaysay Drive. Above the nondescript, almost invisible door was a sign in Tagalog, the native language of Filipinos, but otherwise, there was no indication of the nature of the business. One had to be looking for that specific place to see it. After following

Mearey there three times, Matt decided he needed to peak inside, but *not* when Mearey was there.

The following day, Mearey had watch, and Matt had the day off, so he headed to the alleyway and the unadorned door. As he walked in, to his surprise, he could immediately see he was in a bar, but quite unlike the typical bars that brand Subic Bay. There was no live band, and, more importantly, there were no bar girls. He sat down at the bar, ordered a San Miguel beer, and looked around the dimly lit establishment. There were pictures on the wall which, upon studying them, were all of men, many of them with no shirts on, and as he scanned the customers, he noted there were only men in the bar. A young man strolled up to Matt at the bar and said, "Buy me drink, sailor?" With a gulp, Matt quickly realized that he was in a gay bar. He took a great breath, put his money on the bar, smiled and gave the young man a polite and stammered *no thanks*, and headed for the exit. It looked to Matt that this, perhaps, was the cause for Mearey's veiled socialization on the ship and most likely ruled him out as the spy.

The six weeks of steaming went quickly for Matt. As their short deployment ended, the ship and crew were preparing for arrival at their homeport, cleaning spaces, swabbing decks, and preparing mooring lines. At noon on a sunny Sunday, the *Okie* entered Kaneda Bay and steered toward the naval base. Matt watched the scenery as the ship steamed by the beautiful skyline of Yokosuka, passing Kuriama Flower Park and its magnificent arboretum, Kannonzaki Light House, painted with a dazzling array of colors, and finally the island of Sarushima, before entering the harbor. Japan was far different from Hawaii, but he enjoyed the culture and scenery of Japan very much. He was settling into his watches and received more responsibility as his supervisors came to trust his work ethic and skills as a radioman. Matt enjoyed working with the senior chief and felt that they were creating a firm bond.

The *Okie* would be home until March 15, which meant that Matt could do more observations during the next three weeks before they left port. Matt could not help but notice the senior chief's almost daily routines. Like clockwork, at four in the afternoon, the man was heading to the parking lot, gym bag in hand. It seemed a little odd that the senior chief would be heading to the gym on a Sunday, the first day they arrived in port, and not run home to be with his wife. He did recall a couple of the radiomen saying the senior chief and his wife had "issues" off and on, with a gang-buster fight on the pier a few months ago. Most of the guys thought his wife had a drinking problem, and a couple of them claimed she had hit on them at one of the senior chief's famous barbeques. Matt decided that maybe going to the gym was a way of working off any tensions before heading home. "Hey, Matt," shouted Lester as he was walking toward his car, "Let's get a beer while we're in port some time, and I can get to know you on a more social basis."

"That would be great, senior chief," shouted Matt, "How's tomorrow?"

"Nah, I got a big poker game tomorrow after my workout," replied Lester. How about I have you and A.J. and a couple of the guys over to the house for a barbeque on Saturday? It's a bit chilly, but we'll have a good time."

"Works for me, senior chief," replied Matt, and each headed in separate directions. Matt thought it would be an excellent opportunity to watch RM1 Bunker more closely and get a feel for whether he merited further surveillance.

Matt walked to the pay phones repeating the same steps he had before to contact Randy: Phone call, awkward message on the answering machine thing, call the beeper, wait five minutes, then call Randy's main number again. They arranged to meet the following day at the same place and time. Matt had been keeping a spiral notebook with all of his observations, had made charts of the connections the RM's had with one another and wanted to show Randy his notebook to see if he was on track with his reconnoitering.

Randy reviewed the notebook, occasionally nodding, while Matt sat sipping his Asahi Gold in silence, hoping he wasn't too far off track. "You have been hard at it, Matt," said Randy, showing approval. "I'm guessing that you aren't going to get too far when you are at sea, though," she said thoughtfully. "This three weeks in port is going to be an important opportunity to gather more information, and it feels like it's time that we take a few riskier steps to increase our information-gathering. Do you feel ready for it?"

Pausing for an instant, Matt said, "I guess so. I'm not really sure what that means, though."

"It means you are going to have to get *much* snoopier on the ship. It looks like you've ruled one person out for the most part, but RM1 Bunker sounds worthy of more investigation. Also, keep in mind that our spy probably will *not* look like a spy. On the other hand, just because someone seems creepy doesn't mean they aren't a spy, or, something like that. It's kind of like that saying, *just because you're paranoid doesn't mean someone is not out to get you*. Awkwardly, I guess what I'm saying is to keep your eyes and mind open to any possibility and don't allow your prejudices, likes and dislikes, and personality issues to hold you back from putting someone on your watch list.

Additionally, while you're in port, we will install a hidden camera in radio central to send us some closed-circuit TV. Our agent afloat, whom you have not met, and probably will not meet, will be handling that surveillance. On the other hand, you need to find an opportunity to search Bunker's rack and locker and any personal spaces he uses and continue to look for other people who might be our guy. When you find someone who deserves a closer look, you'll need to do that. I know you can find opportunities when nobody is around."

Matt felt his stomach gradually rising and a feeling of anxiety well-up in his chest. "OK, I'll do it." They agreed to meet in a week to discuss anything found on the camera and what Matt had discovered in his groundwork.

"And if anything comes up before, feel free to contact me. Oh, and, don't do anything stupid and get caught, OK?"

Matt became dizzy at that. *Hell, I don't know what's stupid and what isn't*, he thought.

As Matt walked back to the *Okie*, he realized he had reached another turning point and was committed to moving forward with this whole undercover agent thing, despite an increasing wave of anxiety. He thought about that old saying about the difference between being involved and being committed. *It's like a chicken and a pig in a bacon and egg breakfast. The chicken is involved, and the pig is committed.* "And I'm the pig," Matt mumbled after they parted.

9

BUNKER

Returning to the ship, Matt headed for the communications berthing, which was three decks below radio central, amidship. The berthing compartment was much like the *Peckham's*, with sailors stacked three-high on narrow metal bunks. The *Peckham's* berthing compartment held a total of 55 men from all of the operations department, unlike the *Okie's,* which was home to 80 men, all of whom were radiomen. The bottom two bunks had their lockers built into the bed. When a sailor wanted to open the locker, they would simply lift the top portion of the bed and use a rod to hold it open, much like the hood of a car. Each locker had a hasp welded onto it, and sailors would padlock their bunks. The top bunk did not have a locker, so there were upright lockers squeezed into available spaces for the occupants of those bunks. Matt decided he had to find a way to get into A.J. Bunker's locker.

A.J. Bunker was a large man standing about six and a half feet tall and well over two hundred pounds. He had what to Matt's ear was some kind of eastern accent, perhaps New York or New Jersey. He seemed friendly enough, but Matt had seen Bunker's temper and impatience a couple of times with some of the newer RM's. He wasn't a guy that Matt would have sought out as a friend, but he also was not an asshole, of which there was a fair share onboard.

Bunker's rack was a middle bunk one row down from Matt's. The first-class petty officers and more senior radiomen got the best bunks in the darkest parts of the compartment, and they usually chose middle racks, as they were easy to get into, and it took less effort to access their lockers. As Matt hung out in the compartment, he pondered how to get a peek inside Bunker's locker without Bunker or anyone else spotting him. As radiomen were nearly constantly in the compartment, this was a delicate task. He thought, perhaps, he could keep an eye on RM1 Bunker's patterns in coming and going and bide his time waiting for some opportunity. Matt had no skills to pick the padlock, and he certainly couldn't cut it without a significant fray, so he was unsure how he would get into the locker.

Observation for a couple of days, however, paid off and exposed an opportunity. Bunker, unlike many of his grubby shipmates, took a shower every single day. Matt discovered that Bunker would enter the compartment each day, unlock his locker, undress, and set out for the head to take a shower, leaving his locker unlocked. That was the opportunity. He now had to access Bunker's locker without being seen by one of the eighty radiomen who came and went throughout the day.

A few days later, Matt's patience paid off. As was his habit, Bunker arrived right on time, followed his routine, and left for the shower, locker unlocked. In a rare moment, Matt was the only person in the compartment. Matt jumped on the opportunity, opened Bunker's rack, and quickly started searching. At first glance, there was nothing suspicious: A couple of Penthouse magazines, several science-fiction books, a letter-writing tablet, and clothes. Just the usual. No top-secret messages, crypto cards, or anything else that would have incriminated Bunker. Matt realized he didn't have much time and was rushing. In one corner of the locker, he found a small notebook. Opening it quickly, it didn't seem to reveal much, simply dates and an amount of money next to it. The amounts were pretty small in the

$100-$500 range with a name, "Makarov," at the end of the line. As Matt was scrutinizing the notebook, trying to decipher the meaning of the entries, he heard steps coming down the ladder. He quickly put the notebook back in its place and stepped out in the small passageway between racks, bumping Bunker squarely in the chest. "Hey, butthead," said Bunker with some nastiness, but much to Matt's relief, no sign of suspicion, "Watch the *fuck* where you are going!"

"Sorry, Bunker," mumbled Matt, "I was distracted," as he exited as quickly as possible.

The senior chief followed up on his suggestion to have a barbeque on Saturday and gave Matt the address. Matt would be attending with RM1 Bunker and two other radiomen, one of whom was a tall, lanky Texan who sounded like he just came off of a cowboy movie set and named, quite appropriately Matt thought, Clay Young. To Matt's mind, Clay was the *classic* Texan, calling any elder "sir" or "ma'am," much to the chagrin of the CPOs who hated to be called sir. Matt loved the "y'alls" and the colorful Texan colloquialisms like, "He's brave as the first man who ate an oyster," or "It's so dry my duck don't know how to swim." Matt had a regular watch rotation with Clay, an RM3, and was getting to know the easy-going Texan reasonably well. He was an interesting guy, and while on watch, they had bullshitted with one another during quiet times.

During one of their first watches together, Matt asked Clay to tell him about his background. "Well," Clay said, "I guess you might say I had a little bit different life than most of the guys I meet here in the Navy. My Daddy and I never got on very well. He thought I was lazy. He used to love to say to me, 'You're like a blister, Clay. You don't show up till the work's all done.'"

Matt soon learned that Clay's statement that he was a "little bit different" was an understatement. Clay was an anomaly among navy enlisted men. He had a bachelor's degree in electrical engineering from the University of Texas and had attended UT on a baseball scholarship. He was recruited out of college by the Minnesota Twins and spent a year in the minor leagues before being brought up to the majors. The odd thing was, Clay *hated* baseball. He related several times that he had a very rocky relationship with his father, whose ambitions for Clay had placed his son exactly where he did *not* want to be. Clay wanted to be a country musician and played the guitar pretty well, although his voice sounded to Matt like an unpleasant combination of Willie Nelson and Ozzie Osbourne. One evening in the off-season, Clay and his father had a colossal argument when Clay informed his father that he did not plan to return to the team the next season and hoped to join a band in Austin. His father threw such a fit that he smacked Clay over the head with Clay's guitar. Clay walked out of his father's house and joined the navy the next day as an enlisted man. "Why on earth did you do that?" Matt questioned on watch one evening.

"I just tried to think of the one thing that would piss-off my daddy the most, and the navy seemed like it would do the trick. It did. He's still got his tail up to this day." Matt was still amazed that he had even met a former big-league pitcher, and the story was one of the most entertaining reasons he had ever heard as to why someone had joined the navy.

"I'll tell you something, Bert, that I'm not too proud of. The other thing that keeps my Daddy dancing in the hog trough is that I had a girlfriend, and, unfortunately, she went and got herself pregnant -- with my help. The navy doesn't know about it because they'd kick me out or worse if they did, but I send every cent I can back to her in Fort Stockton so that she can raise that baby right. The two of us never really got along that well. She's two sandwiches short of a picnic. But I own up to what I did, and I'm paying her as much as I can so she don't go to CPS. I'm doing my best to do what is right. It's just really hard to know that I probably won't ever know that kid. In the meantime, Bert, I'm so poor the wolf won't even stop at my door."

If everything Clay had done had not impressed Matt, which it did, Clay had another talent that amazed Matt. Clay had a photographic memory. When Clay mentioned it, Matt thought he was just trying to be funny. "No, man, I really do. I can't forget anything I see, and I can recall it ver-fucking-batim."

Matt remained skeptical. "I'm serious, man. Give me anything I haven't seen before, and I'll recite it back to you."

Matt, remembering they kept a World Almanac in the radio shack to kill time during long mid-watches, pulled it out and opened it to the names of movie stars and their original names and birthdates. There were probably sixty names on one page. Matt handed it to Clay. Clay read the page, then handed the book back to Matt.

"Page 364. Actors and Directors born in 1930. John Astin, March 30, 1930; Polly Bergin, real name, Nellie Burgin, born July 14, 1930." Clay proceeded to give at least thirty more names and dates of birth before Matt had to admit, the guy actually did have a photographic memory. It was a source of constant entertainment for Matt. He could give Clay a page of a novel to read, and then hours later, Clay would recite it word for word.

On Sunday, Matt rode along with Clay to the senior chief's home in Clay's navy surplus 1963 Chevy pickup. If Clay's voice was terrible, his pickup was even worse. Neither door locked; a hasp and padlock were welded to the door, not that anyone would want to steal it. The floorboard had rusted out in places, and when Matt looked down, he could see the road passing beneath his feet. The truck had a garbage can welded to the truck's bed, which was a ready target for empty beer cans thrown from the cab while driving. Of course, with Clay's baseball talents, he hit the garbage can every time. Matt felt fortunate when a can made it into the bed rather than along the road. Clay had a gallon jug of used motor oil in the cab and put a couple of quarts in the engine each time they stopped for gas. It was great to see the looks the Japanese civilians gave as they passed. A pickup truck itself was unusual in Yokosuka, and this truck, in particular, was a source of interest and humor to people they passed on the street. However, Clay kept to the base as he never knew how many more miles the truck would give him.

As they pulled into the senior chief's housing, Matt was surprised to see high-rise condos. In Pearl Harbor, base housing was the typical duplex or triplex. Still, at Yokosuka, the navy had taken its cue from the area in general and provided condos primarily to the married enlisted men. Like any other base, however, the quality and location of the housing varied and improved based upon rank and seniority. Even so, Matt was impressed at how nice the condo was and the fantastic view the senior chief and his wife had of Kaneda Bay. As Matt and Clay walked into the apartment, the senior chief introduced his wife, Maddie, who already appeared to Matt to be about four sheets to the wind. She grabbed and hugged both Matt and Clay with a cigarette in her mouth and ushered them into their living room with an attempted Spanish welcome that sounded more like "mi case ese sus caysa." Maddie had dyed blond hair, long in the back and feathered with curls in a failed attempt to emulate the popular 70's disco look. Maddie appeared a bit haggard. Clay privately told Matt, "She looks like chewed twine."

The senior chief grabbed the two sailors out on the balcony, showed them a cooler with beer, pointed to three pitchers on a table saying "mojo" to them, which gave each sailor big smiles. Clay gave a little Texas-style whoop. Mojo was a magical drink the sailors adopted from Subic Bay. Made in various ways, it usually contained some approximation of 151 rum, cherry brandy, beer, Coke,7-Up, orange juice, and pineapple juice. The magic was the punch it packed while tasting like punch.

Although Matt kept a close watch on Bunker, he was now highly suspicious of everything he did, no matter how trivial. Matt enjoyed being off the ship, eating good old American burgers and hot dogs and perhaps drinking a bit too much. After gorging themselves on the food, the senior chief entertained them with stories of what it was like to be in the navy when he was young. They all traded sea stories of their most exciting experiences in liberty ports around the world. Matt was a bit surprised at how well Maddie kept pace with the drinking that was going on, but it was evident by her increasingly slurred speech that she was falling behind.

The senior chief and Bunker headed downstairs to play some pool, and Maddie went out on the balcony to smoke. Matt decided it might be an excellent opportunity to chat with Maddie to see if he could get more information, hopefully incriminating, about Bunker.

"You have a great husband, Maddie," said Matt trying to get the conversation started. "He's been great to work with and knows his stuff."

"Yeah, Moe's tolerable, I guess," muttered Maddie, "He makes sure I've got walking around money," she added. "If it weren't for the money he makes doing extracurricular activities, I'd be sayin' "hasta la pasta," if you know what I mean." It was strange to hear her call senior chief "Moe." He knew that his first name was Morris, for the first time, realized the connection of his nickname to his last name. *Shit, Moe-Lester?* Matt once again gave private thanks for having a tolerable nickname.

"Extracurricular activities?" Matt inquired.

"Um, yeah, you know, his poker playing and shit," Maddie managed to squeak out.

"So, it looks like Bunker and the senior chief are pretty tight. Do you see A.J. very often?" questioned Matt.

"Oh, off and on," burbled Maddie, "But they mostly go off and do boy things together, I think. I'm not really sure what they do, but I think that A.J. is a sleaze. He always seems to be skulking around, and I think he's got a little side-gig going on. I wouldn't be surprised if he were running whores or loansharking or something. He seems to have a bit too much money for an E-6."

Matt was about to ask another question when the two came back from downstairs. Matt was teeming with the thrill of perhaps being on to something and couldn't wait for his next meeting with Randy to report this tidbit of information.

Matt, encouraged by the information he had uncovered about Bunker's supplementary income, decided to see if Clay knew anything on the drive back to the ship. "Have you noticed anything strange about Bunker?" Matt queried.

"What do you mean?" asked Clay. "Like sexual stuff, or what?"

"No, just like anything," replied Matt. "Maddie just suggested that A.J. was into something outside of the navy that gave him extra income, and she suggested he might be into something illegal."

"Aww, that's a bunch of bullshit," Clay responded. "Maddie is an alcoholic, and I wouldn't trust her any further than I could throw her. Last time we had a get-together, she got drunk like today and grabbed my doodle-dasher, right out in plain sight."

"No shit," replied Matt with his mouth hanging open.

"Yeah, stay the fuck away from that flagrantly accessible tramp," suggested Clay, "She's wilder than an acre of snakes."

Matt decided to divert the conversation, musing at how many euphemisms people have for their manhood and how eloquent Clay could be for a Texan.

At their next meeting, Matt relayed the surveillance results he had carried out, the conversation with Maddie, and the notebook he had found. Randy let him know that the closed-circuit hidden camera had been installed and was working.

Randy paused, thinking things through before she spoke. "I think you are following the right path, Matt. I have no idea what the notebook would be about or what 'Makarov' might mean, and I hate to say it, but I think we need some pictures of it. I'm going to need you to get back into his locker one more time, Matt."

Swallowing hard, Matt sighed. "It was a pretty close call last time, Randy. And what do you mean, take pictures of it?"

Randy pulled out a tiny camera, and Matt's eyes lit up like fireworks on the fourth of July. "A spy camera?" Matt said with a bit too much enthusiasm.

"Yeah, pretty much," she answered. It was a very small rectangular camera and looked to be about four inches long. "It's a Minox C," Randy said with the sound of awe in her voice. It's the latest thing. It has an auto-focus, so you don't need to focus it, it takes good low-light photos, and one film cartridge will take 36 pictures. You probably should have had this before, and I'm sure you'll need it again. Just don't get caught with it. Oh, and you should probably get some practice with that camera so that you can use it easily when the time comes. Here are a couple of extra film cartridges. Go out and take some tourist shots, and when we meet next time, I'll get them developed to see if you are getting it. Got it?"

"Yes, got it. I'll get some practice and then do my best to get back into Bunker's locker and get some pictures as soon as I can." Matt was losing motivation the further he went into this investigation. The danger was beginning to become palpable, and he was, for the first time, genuinely regretting his decision to take this assignment.

Randy, watching Matt, guessed that he was starting to become more apprehensive about his job. Sensing that he might need a pep talk, she smiled and said, "Hey, if your offer of a beer is still open, I'd take one."

Matt's mood instantly changed, and he beamed a big smile back. "That would be great," he said as a smile replaced the frown he had moments earlier.

As the beers arrived, their conversation became more relaxed and informal. "I can't help but wonder how someone ends up being a Special Agent in the NIS," Matt mused.

"I guess I wonder that, also, sometimes," Randy replied. My father and three of my brothers are cops in Chicago, so I grew up in a cop family. I'm the only daughter, so I guess I ended up always having to play cops and robbers or war with my brothers. The regular girl stuff wasn't interesting, and it just seemed natural to want to wear the blue.

"I was in the selection process myself, as the Chicago P.D. was a little ahead of its time in hiring women police officers. I think the first female officers came on in the early 1900s. Granted, it was mostly office duty then, but female officers had become a mainstay by the time I applied. The same week I received approval to enter the police academy, someone in the NIS approached me who said they were looking to hire their first female Special Agents, and they thought I had a great profile. I didn't even know what the NIS was, but I checked it out and decided I would be given more responsibility more quickly that way and might just have a chance to travel a little bit. I was right on both counts. I earned more responsibility quickly, and here I am, working in Japan of all places. So what about you, Matt?"

Matt smiled and said, "I think you have a file an inch thick on me, so I'm not sure I can tell you anything more than you already know. I'm from a small town in Northern New Mexico and joined the Navy basically because I had no ambition to do much of anything else."

"Your record would say that a young man with no ambition has done an amazing job of turning that around," Randy said with a grin. "I think that you have risen to the occasion, not just with us, but with your landing force deployment team in Cambodia. I know that's not officially a part of your record, but it was an important consideration in choosing you for your current assignment. And – you're doing a great job." Matt couldn't help but feel a bit embarrassed by Randy's praise.

One of Matt's favorite songs, *I'm sorry* by John Denver, came on the jukebox. Feeling a bit more confident that Randy might have a slight interest in him beyond business, Matt swallowed hard and said, "I love this song. Would you like to dance?"

Randy had not anticipated doing anything more than having a beer with Matt, but she was still hoping to assuage some of his anxiety, and besides, she kind of liked the tall, skinny New Mexican boy. She smiled, nodded her head, and they stood and walked the short distance to the dance floor. Not a good dancer, Matt nevertheless did his best to keep pace with the rhythm of the music as he reached around Randy's back and pulled her a little closer to him. Randy laid her head on Matt's chest momentarily until her relentless sense of duty eclipsed her desires. "I'm sorry, Matt," she said, looking up at him. Dancing with you is really nice, but we just have to keep things on a professional level."

Matt took a deep breath and then looked into Randy's eyes. "I understand, Randy," Matt said with more than a hint of disappointment. "Maybe when this is all over, I can have a dance?"

"I'm sure that's a possibility," Randy said softly. They walked back to the table, finishing their beers with inane small talk. When her beer was empty, Randy stood and said, "You can do this, Matt. You are smart, brave, and well-trained. Don't worry, OK?"

As Matt watched Randy walk out of the club, a greater sense of optimism outflanked his fears. *Maybe I can do this after all.* Feeling a fool for the instantaneous mood change, he thought about all of the potential heroes in history who crashed and burned trying to impress a woman.

10

SPYING ON THE SPY

The *Okie* spent the first two weeks of March 1976 in port in Yokosuka. Matt was developing friendships, among those, Clay Young, of whom Matt just couldn't get enough. The laid-back Texan had no shortage of delightful Texas colloquialisms. Matt and Clay hung out several evenings a week. They enjoyed going to the base movie theater for 75 cent popcorn, "B" movies, and a little escape from navy life.

Following a movie one evening, Clay and Matt were walking back to the Okie from the theater after seeing *Bring Me the Head of Alfredo Garcia* for the fifth time. Clay, unlike practically everyone else in the world, absolutely loved the movie. Clay seemed pensive. "You know, Matt," said Clay, with the look of Aristotle on his face, "I think Bennie got a raw deal in all of that shitshow. He sure wasn't born under a lucky star, that hombre. I would have kicked that El Jefe's ass from the get-go and cashed in quick. That's what I'm going to do in life. I'm going to make enough cash never to have to worry about paying bills or child support or any of that shit again. I should have stayed with baseball. I'd have millions socked away by now."

Matt didn't respond to Clay's frustration. He knew Clay was sending most of his money home to the mother of his child, but he had a bed and three squares a day right now, so he wasn't exactly living like a hobo. *Hell*, thought Bert, *we're making $459.30 a month. That's more than I've ever made in my life!*

Matt was also getting to know Senior Chief Lester better, and he seemed to have taken a shine to Matt. As a third-class petty officer, Matt would have been watch supervisor on his old ship. With 75 other radiomen in his division on the *Okie*, he found himself relegated to more mundane activities. Even so, the senior chief had Matt working the crypto room several days each week and allowed him to share duties with Bunker. He and Bunker had made several trips together to the naval communications station to pick up the monthly crypto cards. While Matt remained suspicious of Bunker, he was also enjoying his company. Bunker, like the senior chief, was a very skilled radioman and a good mentor. Matt had felt very comfortable with his proficiency when he had arrived on the *Okie*. Still, he was learning skills from Bunker just about every watch.

In addition to enhancing his skills as a radioman, Matt was also working on his skills as an undercover agent. Matt would take practice shots with his camera on breaks and even worked on taking some surreptitious photos of other sailors without being noticed.

While his work in the radio shack was going well, Matt was having little success on the undercover side of his life. He had tried several times, with no luck, to get back into Bunker's locker. He had come close to being caught on two of those occasions. Fortunately, Bunker kept his routine, which allowed Matt to relax and take his time, waiting for just the right opportunity. Fortunately, that opportunity came a day later when, almost magically, Bunker left for the showers, and there was not one other person in the berthing compartment; a literal miracle. As Matt searched, once again, for anything suspicious, which he did not find, he was particularly interested in seeing the notebook once again. As he looked where he had found it once before, he was discouraged to find it missing. In a panic, Matt went through each compartment one more time, realizing he was pushing the time envelope. Just as he had decided to give up, he spotted the edge of the notebook buried under dirty magazines and dirtier laundry. He quickly took out his camera, opened the note-book, and snapped shots of as many pages as he could. He put the notebook back and returned to his rack just as Bunker returned. Without warning, Bunker gave a "What the fuck?" and came around the corner, holding his padlock in his hand. "Matt, did you see anyone in my space?" he inquired. "My fucking lock was on the deck."

Trying to think quickly, Matt grabbed at the first thought he had. "I think there might have been a couple of guys down here, but I was reading, so I didn't pay any attention."

"Well, fuck," said Bunker, again. "Maybe it just took itself off the locker," he said with a measure of irritation in his voice. "There better not be anything missing, or I'll go apeshit around here." Matt could hear Bunker going through his locker, checking to see if anything was missing. Not finding anything amiss, Bunker dressed and headed out of the compartment with Matt working hard to slow the rapid beating of his heart. He took a few moments and then gave himself a metaphorical pat on the back as he took the camera out of his pocket and stashed it in his locker.

The crew of the *Okie* was preparing for what they considered to be a long deployment of three months. Matt had to smile as his shortest deployment on the *Peckham* had been five months, so three months seemed pretty brief from his vantage. Matt was looking forward to this deployment as their first port would be Perth, Australia. Matt had never been south of the equator. Besides looking forward to seeing Australia, which he was over the moon about, there would be an ancient ceremony and right of passage as the *Okie* crossed the equator. To the best of anyone's knowledge, the tradition had originated when ships used sails instead of steam or nuclear power. It was hazing of the highest magnitude. Those who survived received the title of "Shellback," which was more coveted than any medal.

The three-month deployment, however, presented some issues concerning his communications with Randy. Before deployment at their usual meeting spot, they met for the final time. Over the last couple of meetings, Matt had taken the liberty of ordering a beer before Randy arrived, and it was quickly becoming a routine part of their meetings. As Randy walked up to the table, she very subtly flipped her hair back, and Matt's heart skipped a beat. Matt had to admit that he was slightly smitten with Randy, her auburn hair, and, well, everything else. As she sat down, she gave Matt a big smile, picked up the beer, and took a sip. "How are you doing, Matt?" She queried. Matt smiled, and rather than saying anything, pushed the film cartridge across the table to her. Smiling a broad smile, she said, "You did it! Well done, Matt!"

Matt, mentally patting himself on the back, attempted to display what was false humility. "Nothing to it," he said with a smile, both of them knowing it had placed Matt in some danger.

Randy grabbed the cartridge and put it in her purse. "I'll let you know what we find, Matt. I've been very concerned that you will be on deployment for three months, and it appears the investigation is making some headway. The *Okie* is going to be in Subic Bay several times during your deployment. I've gotten permission to meet you on base in Subic Bay when you are in port there. I will have our special agent afloat on your ship provide you with notes indicating where and when we will meet. You'll find them under your pillow in your bunk. I know that's taking a little bit of a risk, but we can't seem to think of another way to communicate. It's too bad those Dick Tracy wrist phones are just fiction."

As the two were getting up to leave, Matt saw Clay Young saunter into the club. It was the first time he had seen anyone he knew there at this time of day. They sat back down, hoping he didn't see them, but from the broad smile on his face, Matt could tell Clay had spotted them and was making his way over to their table. "Well, Matt, you sly *chupacabra*, you! You've been holding out on me!" Clay declared.

Randy, much more composed than Matt, held out her hand and said, "Hey Matt, introduce me to your handsome friend," to which Clay gave her a flash of his best Texan smile.

Matt, unable to speak, began muttering something incoherent.

"My name is Clay Young, ma'am," said Clay, with his most acceptable and friendly West Texas accent.

"Well, Clay, good to meet you. I'm Randy. I'm guessing you're one of Matt's shipmates from the *Okie*?"

"Sure am, ma'am," affirmed Clay, who was simultaneously turning in Matt's direction. "I thought we were friends, man," Clay said, pretending to be hurt, then turning back to Randy, said, "Pardon ma'am, but you wouldn't happen to have a sister here on base?"

Randy smiled her best flattering smile. "Unfortunately, not. Matt and I just met, and we were just chatting. I work in the administrative offices on base, and Matt was kind enough to offer me a beer." Standing and turning to both Matt and Clay, she said, "Thanks for the beer, Matt. I hope to see you again, but I've got to get going. Clay, nice meeting you, too," and Randy left quickly, hoping to minimize the interaction.

"You son of a bitch, Matt," Clay said with a smile. My respect for you just went up about a thousand degrees! She is all sweetness and light!" Matt smiled back, trying not to show his concern that someone from his ship had seen him with Randy. She had handled it much more calmly than Matt, but it was also kind of nice that Clay thought Matt was appealing to the girls.

Matt and Clay decided to get a six-pack at the Navy Exchange liquor store and head out on the town for the night. Clay's old pick-up was the subject of bewildered interest from the local Japanese people who were more used to seeing little Japanese cars than Chevy trucks. Especially a rusted one with hasps on the doors and with a garbage can welded to the bed.

The Japanese drove on the left side of the road like in the U.K., and the more beer Clay drank, the less he remembered this fundamental traffic rule. After several close encounters with other cars, the two decided to find a place to park and finish their beer. Mikasa park was a favorite of theirs. They could park in the parking lot, look across the harbor at the ships, and after dark, nobody ever seemed to have any interest in being in the park. Matt and Clay sat listening to a cassette playing Clay's brand new album, *Wanted: The Outlaws*. As they listened to Willie, Waylon, Tompall Glaser, and Jessie Colter, they chatted about home, the adventures they would have in Australia, and life in general. Despite the great conversation, Matt could see that something was bothering Clay, but he just responded with an "I'm good" and changed the subject when he queried Clay. Deciding not to probe further, Matt relaxed and listened to the lyrics of the songs. Matt had never been much of a country kind of guy. He much preferred B.T.O. and the Doobie Brothers. He had to admit, though, that country was growing on him, and especially the Texas version of country music on this new album. Matt fell into the soft rhythms, and poignant lyrics of *My Heroes have Always Been Cowboys*, his mind drifting. Matt was genuinely enjoying the big Texan's company, and Clay was the closest thing he had known to a cowboy. Sometimes Matt wondered if Clay was in that same situation the song described: *Sadly in search of, and one step in back of, himself and his slow-movin' dream.* At that moment, Matt felt as though he had found a lifelong friend in Clay. Clay seemed to feel the same.

Liberty call was almost always the two of them, looking to find some trouble. They were both looking forward to heading out on deployment and the experience of crossing the equator, becoming trusty Shellbacks, and seeing Australia.

11

THE ANCIENT ORDER OF THE DEEP

The following day the USS *Oklahoma City*, in full regalia with sailors in their dress whites lining the rails, left for deployment. The process of both departing from ports and arriving in ports was a great pleasure for Matt. Leaving meant they were going somewhere new, and arriving meant adventure. The kind of adventure Matt had hoped for when he joined the navy.

Things were a little dull in the radio shack. Knowing how much Matt liked to watch the ship get underway, the senior chief gave him a ten-minute break to go topside and witness the activity. When Matt returned, things had picked up, and Matt was assigned a teletype bank to gather messages and send to routing so they could go to the various departments of the ship. Just a few minutes into this watch, an interesting message began to arrive on one of his assigned teletype printers. He watched as the printer slowly tap-tap-tapped out the contents onto the paper in the machine. As it gradually revealed itself, Matt saw that the message was for the Admiral and labeled "Top Secret," which was a common classification for messages that came through the radio shack. However, Matt read the message, his eyes focused on the subject, which was *not* routine.

The message was detailing position information for three US

Navy nuclear ballistic missile submarines. He instantly became attentive to the contents of the message, as the actual positions of submarines was a subject he had not seen before. He was aware that the nuclear submarines in the Pacific were homeported either in Pearl Harbor or Guam and had two crews who alternated deployments. A boat would load a crew in Pearl Harbor, dive deep into the ocean, and would not surface again until it reached Guam. The rumor was that the only people who knew the actual positions of the subs while they were underwater was the crew of that particular submarine. The purpose of the secrecy was to keep the Soviets guessing their locations. If the Soviets knew where the subs were, the boats would be vulnerable in an actual war. This level of secrecy discouraged the use of nuclear missiles. The positions of the boats were only known to the Soviets when they resurfaced in Guam. After re-provisioning and a little rest, the sub would turn around and do the same thing back to Pearl Harbor. Nuclear ballistic missile submarines known by the acronym "SSBN" were the United States' most powerful weapon and the most potent deterrent to nuclear war. As such, they were the target of persistent surveillance by the Russians.

As Matt was reading the message, he abruptly sensed someone behind him. Looking over his shoulder was RM1 Bunker. As the printer finished printing the message, Bunker muttered, "Interesting. That looks like a message we need to treat carefully. I'll take that and process it, Matt. Always good to work as a team."

Matt watched as Bunker took the message into the crypto room, the opposite direction of the message processing center. Bunker shut the door behind him. After a moment, Matt realized that the heavy door had not entirely shut all the way. The hair on the back of Matt's neck raised in unison with Matt's suspicions. Matt knew he had to have a look through that crack. Carefully, he approached the door. Although it slightly obstructed his view, he was confident that he saw Bunker hunching over the desk, reading the message. As Matt watched with astonishment, Bunker reached into his pocket and drew out what appeared to be a camera, not much different than

Matt's, and snapped two quick pictures of the message. Matt's heart jumped into his throat as he turned to race back to his teletype. *I've got to let Randy know as soon as possible,* Matt thought. *I think I've got my guy.*

Without warning, the door suddenly opened, hitting Matt in the forehead. Bunker paused for a moment and discernably struggled to decide how to respond. Bunker looked past Matt, taking a deep breath, and seeing no one near, grabbed Matt by the collar and shoved him against a teletype bank. "What in the *fuck* are you doing, Bertram?" snarled Bunker, as quietly as possible so the other radiomen wouldn't hear, "Were you spying on me?"

"Of course not, A.J.," stammered Matt, "I was ... I was just going to the head. Really. I didn't even know you were in there!"

"Get back to your fucking watch, Bertram," growled Bunker, "I need to get this message to flag staff."

The following morning, Bunker did not speak to Matt. However, several times during his watch, he would catch Bunker looking at him with an intensity that sent Matt's adrenaline into high gear. The next morning, Bunker's focus on Matt seemed to intensify.

The journey to Perth would take ten days, with a full day lingering on the equator for the ceremony of the "ancient order of the deep." At least 400 years old, the ritual was partially a test, a substantial hazing, and an event never forgotten by its participants. Matt thought back to his old chief, B.S. Boggs describing it: "Legend has it that King Neptune and his representative, Davy Jones, require any sailor, before crossing the equator, to prove themselves worthy of transitioning to the bottom of the world, and to do so, a not-so-fair trial and a guaranteed negative *fucking* judgment are required."

In 1976 the shipboard navy was entirely male. Political correctness had not entered the lexicon of society. Hazing was simply a part of any male right of passage. There were rumors of maimed sailors and even deaths during the ceremony. However, no one could name any of the deceased sailors. Technically, participation was strictly voluntary, but there were covert consequences for anyone who did not volunteer to take part in the ritual.

The afternoon before the ceremony was the obligatory "Miss Pollywog" beauty contest. A junior person, always one of the uninitiated, known better as *Pollywogs*, was chosen from each division on the ship for the competition. Fully prepared divisions had collected bikinis, evening dresses, wigs, and make-up before departure from Yokosuka. Sailors lined the helicopter deck for the festivities. Each of the chosen beauty Pollywogs attempted to convince the other sailors to vote for them. The prize for winning was the opportunity to forego the hazing and to sit on the throne with King Neptune and Davy Jones (in drag) as their arm candy. Matt, preoccupied with his mission and a sense of impending danger, tried to enjoy the shenanigans. However, he was having difficulty letting go as RM1 Bunker was fraying Matt's nerves with his constant penetrating staring and scowling.

The choice of Miss Pollywog from the communications division was none other than RM3 Clay Young, now with the moniker *Candy*. Clay was probably the most unlikely choice in Matt's mind, as Clay was the epitome of the masculine cowboy. He had a full beard that seemed to cover not only his face but his chest, arms, and back. As the Miss Pollywog contestants entered the arena, cat calls, whistles, and an array of profane name-calling erupted from the sailors. Unlike most other events on the ship, even the officers submitted their entry, a young ensign fresh from Annapolis.

As the event began, Matt gradually let go of the anxiety from Bunker's stares and the growing belief that Bunker suspected Matt of spying on him. Matt watched with great anticipation for the entrance of Clay on the deck. Completely surprising to Matt and all of his fellow RMs, Clay entered with all of the flamboyance and flourish of

Flawless Sabrina. Clay wore a string bikini with water balloons in the cups, spike heels, and a blond 70's style wig with hair that cascaded down to the middle of his feather boa-covered back. Matt realized with a bit of self-consciousness that from just the right angle, and if you blocked out the beard, Clay was slightly sexy in drag. With his greatest hip-sway possible, Clay embraced his newfound alter-ego, yukking it up with the other sailors, blowing kisses, and giving a lap dance or two during the competition. Just to sweeten the pot a bit, someone had written "Blow Jobs: 5 Cents" in magic marker on Clay's back. Much to Clay's chagrin, he only made runner-up. Still, his shipmates called him Candy for several days after, until Clay finally grabbed a persistent sailor by the shirt and threatened to "Tip over his outhouse." Matt wasn't quite sure what that meant, but the inference was clear.

At 0530 the following morning, the ship's intercom came to life with the sound of a boatswain's whistle, shrilling the call for reveille. Trusty Shellbacks, those who had already survived the ceremony in the past, paraded into the berthing compartment. They roughly rousted Pollywogs out of their racks and into their uniform of the day: Trousers on backward, both legs rolled up above the knees, shower shoes on the wrong feet and no belts. One of the Shellbacks shouted that skivvies were allowed if they wished to spare their dungarees rather than their buttocks. One person in their division, SMSN Guilder, had opted out of the ceremony a few days earlier. Unfortunately for him, he woke up that morning tied into his rack by twenty or thirty rolls of dental floss, and he would remain there for the remainder of the day.

The entire group of low and slimy Pollywogs, with Matt and Clay in tow, were mustered on the ship's forecastle and allowed final prayers. All of the Pollywogs were required to cry out in unison, "We are doomed, for surely the misdeeds of our wretched souls shall be visited upon us this day. Please have mercy, most benevolent King Neptune!"

The condemned were then given a hearty meal, represented as "Blood of red-eyed seadog, selected portions of seaweed, last year's hard tack and salt water." It looked a bit more to Matt like creepy-looking jello and tasted worse than it looked. Nevertheless, all were required to finish it—those who didn't throw it up, anyway.

Following breakfast, the Wogs were given a bath with a firehose, a most unpleasant experience. Then the now soaking wet, low and slimy Pollywogs were put on their hands and knees and made to crawl to the ship's fantail. For weeks before the event, Shellbacks had been creating shillelaghs. These two-foot lengths of firehose had electrical tape on one end as a handle. Shellbacks decorated their instruments of torture with graffiti containing such niceties as "Death to Wogs!" The Shellbacks used the firehose to smack the backsides of Pollywogs along the route. Radarmen were posted on watches and shouted "RF, RF, RF," listening for echoes. In contrast, Pollywog sonarmen called "Ping, Ping, Ping," and were required to quickly put an ear to the deck to listen for echoes. Pollywog radiomen were required to shout out international morse code for SOS constantly.

The final and most important watch was the toilet watch. The Pollwog toilet watch was required to flush the toilet twice a minute to observe the reversal of the flush swirl as the ship crossed the equator. He was to shout "all's well" when the rotation reversed. That signaled the beginning of the baptism.

Upon word from the toilet watch, the Pollywogs would crawl, in line, toward the fantail on 600 feet of non-skid decking. The long crawl was torture, but the belittling and physical hazing the sailors received along the way dwarfed the crawl. Anytime a Shellback would ask a Pollywog, "What are you?" the Pollywog was required to reply, in the most pathetic tone possible, "I'm a low and slimy Polly-wog." Insufficient groveling yielded a smack on the buttocks by any and every Shellback in the area.

As Matt crawled with the rest of the Pollywogs, he, too, endured the same level of name-calling and smacks on his backside. Suddenly, without warning, however, he was caught off-guard by what felt like a baseball bat on the back of his head. The strike velocity caused Matt's arms to buckle underneath, and he went down, chin-first onto the non-skid decking. All of the color in his vision momentarily turned brown. He pushed himself up and looked to his rear to see Bunker sneering above him, shillelagh in hand. One of the other Shellbacks shouted at Bunker, "Hey, man, that's way too much."

"Shut up, Leary," said Bunker, "This one's a special case."

Additional tests and hazards befell the Wogs along the way. One particularly cruel ordeal involved a twenty-foot-long canvas shoot filled with rotting leftovers from the mess decks. The Shellbacks required the Pollywogs to crawl, roll and exit the far side. Dozens of eggs were utilized as humiliation devices as the Shellbacks smashed them on the Pollywogs' heads. "Special cases" were made to wear dog collars and be led about by Shellbacks.

After repeatedly saying only, "I'm a low and slimy Pollywog" hundreds of times, it became an automatic response by the Wogs. As each Wog approached the fantail, they passed the "Royal Baby," a CPO with a considerable belly smeared with grease. Each Wog kissed the Royal Baby's belly, coated with grease, which painted the Wog's face and head. A dead pig's head also required a kiss before ending up at the judgment table, at which point each Wog would be summarily pronounced "guilty."

The final phase of the ordeal was the royal baptism. A tri-wall that had been somewhat waterproofed to hold water, about three feet deep, was placed on the fantail. Each Wog, face covered in grease, with eggs smashed on their head, was required to climb in, and several Shellbacks would push the Wog's head underwater. When the Wog came up, Shellbacks would say, "What are you?" The natural response to almost everyone was, once again, in a most pathetic voice, "I'm a low and slimy Pollywog!" That was the wrong response, and as such, the Wog would receive another dunking. This ordeal would continue until the Wog finally realized their habitual mantra was the incorrect response, which very often took three or four dunkings. When the Wog came up and shouted the answer, "I'm a Shellback!" the ceremony was over, and the low and slimy Pollywog was now a member of the Ancient Order of Shellbacks.

During this last stage of the ceremony, Matt was only vaguely aware of the ceremonial goings-on. Bunker's behavior confirmed that

Matt was in trouble. He struggled to formulate a plan on how to protect himself, thousands of miles from anyone who could help.

Matt had the evening watch that day, and much to his relief, Bunker was nowhere in sight. As the evening progressed, Matt gradually calmed down some, yet to have any plan to protect himself. He debated going to the Special Agent Afloat. The SAA was the only person on the ship who was aware of Matt's actual purpose. He had not even met the man and did not want to compromise the mission further, so he decided to keep that idea as a backup.

When Matt finished his watch, he decided to go topside to get a bit of air and think. The weather had become much rougher than it was in the morning, with substantial waves pummeling the bow, and the ship was beginning to rock side-to-side in response. Although it wasn't raining, the wind had increased, and it was evident they would soon be in a storm. The angry weather felt like a confirmation that Matt was in serious trouble. He figured that if Bunker was the spy, he could expect similar treatment to two sailors found dead in the harbor. Matt reasoned that there was a possibility that Bunker didn't suspect him of being undercover but might have just been upset that he was sticking his nose where it should not be. Matt had to admit that the only realistic answer was that Bunker had pegged him for what he was. The violent behavior toward Matt was far beyond what that sort of minor infraction might have provoked.

Matt took a big breath and decided he would head below and try to get some sleep, hoping he would have some strategy to deal with this in the morning. He began approaching the passage that would take him back below decks and found the right water-tight door. Lifting the large lever to open it, he froze, realizing that he stood face to face with Bunker, a look of sinister delight on his face. "There you are, you little snoop," said Bunker with a horrific emotionless calm. "It seems I might have been found out. Tell me the truth, are you a plant or just an idiot?"

"I just don't know what you're talking about, A.J.," squeaked Matt, "I really don't!"

"That's fucking bullshit, and even if you are just an idiot, you are a problem that needs to go away." Bunker looked past Matt to the side of the ship. He smiled and growled, "And it's a perfect night for you to take a swim." With that, Bunker launched a right-hook into Matt's jaw, which sent Matt reeling. Bunker propelled his fist once again into Matt's abdomen, which doubled him over. Seizing the opportunity, Bunker grabbed Matt by the torso and lifted him off the ground, staggering towards the rail. As Bunker gave a heave, Matt's body fell helplessly over the railing. Matt looked down, seeing only the ocean below. As he fell head-first, he began bracing himself for what now appeared to be an inevitable impact with the water. As he was falling, however, he felt his foot catch between the two fence wires. The entrapment of his foot in the wires stopped his fall momentarily.

When Bunker realized that his victim's fall had stopped, he grabbed Matt's leg, tugging and pushing. When that did not extricate Matt, Bunker began shoving Matt's head with violent force, attempting to disentangle Matt from the wires so that he would continue his fall into the angry waters below. Much to Bunker's surprise, the effort backfired as Matt's entanglement in the wire rails became a slingshot of sorts. With a forcible recoil, Matt shot back towards Bunker, slamming into him. The force of Matt's body back over the railing knocked Bunker to the ground. Matt staggered to his feet and started running. Bunker caught Matt's ankle with his outstretched fingers and sent Matt back to the deck with remarkable speed. Dazed, Bunker started to lift himself back up. Matt turned again to run. As he did, out of the corner of his eye, Matt saw a fire extinguisher on the bulkhead. Almost as a reflex, Matt grabbed at the fire extinguisher, shaking it out of its restraints.

Matt swung the extinguisher in a roundhouse with every ounce of effort possible, providentially striking Bunker squarely in the head. The impact caused a cracking sound that Matt could hear over the howling of the wind and the waves. Blood gushed from Bunker's nose and ear as his eyes rolled up into his head. Simultaneously, the ship's bow hit a massive wave, driving it upward like an out-of-control teeter-totter. The momentum caused Bunker, still on his feet, to stagger back toward the fence. As the ship's bow fell under the wave's crest, it sent Bunker momentarily into the air. The ship disappeared below Bunker's feet as his body became weightless. In a moment, Bunker disappeared into the angry brine below.

Matt fell to his knees, his nose bleeding, his chin throbbing, and his gut burning. He peered over the rail into the sea, scanning for any trace of Bunker. All Matt could see was dark foam and white-capped waves. He stood for a moment, finally grasping the reality that his adversary was gone. Matt felt a flash of relief for a moment, which was quickly replaced by an overwhelming sense of dismay. Matt choked back tears, then vomited until there was nothing left in his stomach.

At 0800 the next morning, the CR division mustered, had rollcall, and were given the orders of the day. As Matt arrived, Clay gave him a surprised look. "What the hell happened to you? Looks like you've got on the wrong end of an angry Bozo bop bag!"

"No," replied Matt, trying to think of an acceptable reason for his black eye and bruises, "I got on the wrong end of a wave during the storm last night and went head-first into a pipe."

At the beginning of muster, each division holds a rollcall. CR division completed rollcall, and Bunker was absent. "Has anybody seen RM1 Bunker?" the senior chief asked, to which no one answered. Senior Chief Lester sent two of the other CPOs to berthing, then the mess decks, then to the radio shack, none of which turned up Bunker. The officer in control of the bridge sent numerous requests on the 1MC, a loudspeaker that reached every ship's space. When Bunker did not respond, the division officer sent a search party to scour the ship for Bunker, to no avail. Thirty minutes later, over the ship's speakers came the dreaded words, "Now hear this: This is not a drill. Man overboard. Repeat, man overboard! All hands to general quarters." Three hours of searching the ocean resulted in no sign of RM1 A.J. Bunker, and the captain reluctantly called off the search.

That evening, two sailors sat whispering at a table by themselves on the mess deck, one in dungarees and the other in a khaki uniform. "So, did he fall overboard, or was he pushed?" one of the men said.

"I don't think we have enough information to say with certainty at this point," said the man in the khaki uniform. I think we need to be safe and assume it was *not* an accident. Let's keep our eyes open for anything out of the ordinary, and follow-up."

"I agree the first man said. One thing I've already noticed is that RM3 Bertram looked pretty beat up this morning, and yesterday, during the Shellback ceremony, Bunker laid into him pretty bad with a shillelagh."

"It's fairly obvious that there will be an investigation," said the man in khakis. "If Bunker was murdered, it risks exposing everything. We need to figure this out before they do, and we can't take any chances. We have a lot to risk."

12

MAN OVERBOARD

Men falling overboard at sea happens occasionally. It has been an occupational hazard for sailors since men first built boats and went to sea. In the navy of 1976, the risk of going overboard was much less than it had been in the past, but it still happened from time to time. When such a mishap occurred, it usually happened during the daytime when work was going on, such as refueling or maintaining exterior equipment. The unfortunate sailor was ordinarily fished out unharmed. It was uncommon for someone to go over the rails at night. It was even more infrequent for a sailor with a dozen years in the navy to do so.

Losing a sailor at sea is of great concern, from the lowest rank to the highest rank in the navy. With the admiral aboard, the CO was anxious to know whether or not it was an accident and determine how it happened. The *Okie* was fortunate to have a "Special Agent Afloat" from the Naval Investigative Service aboard. SAA's were assigned to the largest of the navy's ships; the nuclear aircraft carriers and the flagships of the fleet commanders. The aircraft carriers were small cities with commensurate crime. The USS *Nimitz*, the world's largest aircraft carrier in 1976, commissioned the previous year, had almost 6,000 sailors and airmen aboard when the air wing was attached. The SAA's job was to investigate onboard crimes, including sabotage to government property, and generally act as an onboard detective. The SAA position was very competitive as there were very few seagoing spots, and it gave the Special Agents an opportunity to travel and work independently. They were given better quarters in officer's country, ate with the officers in the wardroom, and given their own office onboard their ship. Because of his investigative skills, the captain requested the SAA onboard to assume responsibility for the investigation.

Special Agent Leon Capelli was the Special Agent Afloat assigned to the USS *Oklahoma City*. Leon was a former navy officer and an Annapolis graduate. When Leon was a young officer, he received an offer from a very quiet organization within the navy, the Office of Naval Intelligence, to train to become an agent. In 1966 the Naval Investigative Service officially received its name. NIS had been instrumental in counterintelligence during Vietnam, and many of its operatives were civilians. During the early 1970s, the NIS began switching to an all-civilian force of Special Agents, and Capelli promptly resigned from the navy and re-joined the NIS as a civilian.

Leon considered himself married to the NIS and liked the freedom that having no other family gave him in his career. He had traveled the world and had held a variety of posts in exotic and sometimes dangerous places. Capelli had served in such disparate places as Vietnam and Bahrain. As such, when the opportunity to be assigned to shipboard duty came his way, he was free to experience a year at sea. Leon was enjoying his assignment on the *Okie*. It was much smaller than the aircraft carriers that most of his counterparts were assigned to, which meant less crime and a much more laid-back work day. Being far from the bureaucracy of an NIS office was precisely where he wanted to be, and being a former naval officer, life onboard a ship was a familiar one.

When Special Agent Glasscock had contacted Capelli to tell him about the investigation onboard the *Okie* and the details surrounding their placement of an undercover agent in the radio shack, Capelli was first a bit disgruntled that they had brought in an outsider when this was *his* domain. Any special investigations, in his opinion, should have been handled or at least supervised by him. Randy was careful to explain to Capelli the reasons for this. Leon kept hope that there would be a role for him at some point.

Capelli's supervisor gave him two tasks that fueled his hopes for participation in this operation just before this deployment. First, he would need to identify the undercover radioman and keep a clandestine "eye" on him and would be the go-between to relay messages to the sailor at certain times. Second, he was to place a hidden, closed-circuit camera in the radio shack. The first task was the most enjoyable. Each day, he would seek out RM3 Bertram to check in and make sure he appeared safe without actually contacting him. The second task was much more mundane. He spent innumerable hours reviewing videotaped footage from the camera, a mind-numbing job at best. The day before crossing the equator, he spotted something that captivated his interest while studying the hours of mundane activity. Two men, one in dungarees and one in khaki's, were going through key cards for the crypto machines, and it appeared to him that they might have been taking photographs. He instantly became excited and marked it for further review. The Camera did not capture very high-resolution images. It would take a bit of work to identify the men in the video.

Four hours after the captain called off the search for RM1 Bunker, he summoned Capelli to his stateroom. The senior officers briefed him on what they had learned since discovering Bunker had gone overboard, which was not very much. "All that we really know is that he went overboard. We don't know if the cause was nefarious or accidental," said the CO, "But that's your job. I won't tell you your job, Agent Capelli. Still, if it was not a suicide or accidental, the most likely perpetrator is someone that Bunker worked with or was associated with closely. You have my authorization to interview any and all potential witnesses and suspects and report to me as soon as you have something."

Capelli was instantly intrigued by this development. He finally had an investigation he could sink his teeth into. And yet, Leon mused that it would be a rare coincidence for the same radio shack that held both suspected spies and an undercover agent to be unrelated to Bunker's demise. He was also entertaining the idea that this would allow him to meet RM3 Bertram in person due to this investigation.

Capelli started by building a review of Bunker's life from a few days before his death until the present. While at sea Capelli had limited resources and had no way to investigate much of Bunker's background, other than anecdotal reports from the sailors he interviewed. Capelli also had no way to contact his supervisor while at sea. Capelli decided he would call when he arrived in Perth for a background investigation to be completed and update his supervisor. In the meantime, he decided he would start with Bunker's watch supervisors and the communications officer and work his way down to the RMs, Bunker's co-workers.

Bunker's watch supervisor, Senior Chief Lester, gave a glowing description of Bunker. He remarked that Bunker was a "model sailor and a helluva radioman, with good prospects for making CPO later in the year." Other radiomen Bunker stood watch with gave similar reports. None of his interviewees felt Bunker was depressed or a suicide risk.

Capelli cobbled together a timeline of the days prior to Bunker's disappearance. There was nothing amiss and there were no apparent conflicts with anyone until the morning he went overboard. That morning was quite interesting and started with Bunker throttling RM3 Bertram during the equator crossing ceremony. Several witnesses mentioned that Bunker went beyond the usual hazing of a Pollywog. The rest of the day seemed normal, but another detail quickly emerged from several of his interviewees that Bertram reported for muster in the morning, looking as though he had been in a fight. Each told Capelli that Bertram brushed it off as a slip and fall into a bulkhead steampipe during the rough seas the night before. Had Bertram not been the undercover agent onboard, Capelli would have put Bertram at the top of the suspect list. Capelli was beginning to suspect that Bunker's death was *not* an accident, but interviewing RM3 Bertram was the next and most obvious task in the investigation. It also allowed him to get to know Bertram without arousing the suspicion of the other RM's.

Senior Chief Lester entered the CR division's berthing compartment and found Matt resting in his rack. Upon seeing Matt's face, the senior chief exclaimed, "Wow, Bert, you did get beat up, didn't you?"

Becoming instantly defensive, perhaps obviously so, Matt gave the senior chief his version of how the bruises occurred. "Well, that being said, Bert, the SAA wants to see you in his office to see if you know anything about Bunker's disappearance. It will be good for him to understand that Bunker was a good guy, *won't* it?"

"Of course, senior chief," Matt said softly, "I'll head up there right now." Matt dressed and set off for the SAA's office. As he was walking, he was having similar thoughts to those of Capelli. It would be good for them to meet in person, and even more importantly, Capelli was the only person onboard the *Okie* to whom Matt could tell the truth.

Special Agent Capelli opened the door of his office for Matt and ushered him in. Capelli offered Matt coffee and a donut, which Matt gladly accepted, a rare food on the enlisted side of the ship. "Matt, it's good to meet you finally. I know that you know I'm in the loop on your mission and purpose onboard the *Okie*. Special Agent Glasscock and I talk each time the ship is in port. What you don't know is that I've been looking in on you to be sure you're doing OK from time to time."

"Thanks, Special Agent Capelli," smiled Matt. "I sure wish you would have been looking in on me last night ..." Matt's voice drifted off, and he choked back the urge to cry, more out of relief than angst.

"Please, Matt, call me Leon. We are peers in this setting. Why, um, why don't you just bring me up to date on what has been going on?"

As meticulously as possible, Matt outlined his discovery of RM1 Bunker, apparently taking photographs of Top-Secret Materials. Matt then related that Bunker had discovered Matt watching, the violence that ensued, the attack during the equator crossing, and finally, the attack that resulted in Bunker's death.

Capelli sat stunned, taking a moment to wrap his head around the facts Matt had outlined. "Oh my God, Matt," stammered Capelli, "that's got to be really tough for you. How are you doing with all of this?"

"Better now that we have talked," said Matt. "But I guess I'm still in a state of shock myself."

"Do you think Bunker was it? Was he our spy? And more importantly, do you think he was acting alone?"

"I'm sure he was a spy, Leon," Matt said with firmness. "I don't know if he's alone, but I think probably so. I haven't seen anyone else who has acted even remotely suspicious."

"I hate to be the bearer of bad news, Matt, but he might not have been acting alone," Capelli said glumly. I'm not sure, but as you know, we have a camera in the radio shack. Just before this all blew up, I believe I saw two people in the radio shack with crypto cards on a table, and I'm pretty sure they were taking photographs. I can't say this for sure as I haven't had the time to review the footage thoroughly. Still, I think we should operate under the premise that Bunker was not acting alone, and we can hope we are wrong."

Matt sat, stunned. His head began spinning as anxiety once again welled up inside his chest. "What should we do?" Matt inquired.

"We reach Perth the day after tomorrow. Once we can leave the ship, I'll call Special Agent Glasscock and update her. I will have had time to review the footage more completely by then, so we might have more information. In the meantime, I think you should just try to be your normal self overtly. Go about your watches and leisure time just as though nothing has happened, and talk to no one about this. Get in your brain that you cannot trust *anyone* on board this ship except me at this point. We won't speak again until I get some direction from Glasscock. Still, it seems that we need to label this an accident to allay any suspicion quickly. Agreed?"

Matt walked out of Capelli's office feeling pessimistic that this was going to end well. By the time he reached the radio shack, he had found enough determination to follow through on Capelli's direction. Matt entered the radio shack, reported in, and headed to the teletype repair room. As he sat down at his workbench, Senior Chief Lester walked in. "How did it go with the SAA, Matt?" inquired Lester with a voice of compassion.

"It went well, senior chief," Matt said. "I did just what you told me and let him know that Bunker was a stand-up guy."

"Good. I'm glad to hear that, Matt. Now let's get back to business and put this mess behind us, eh? We'll have a beer in Perth and catch up, OK?"

Matt was glad to accept the invitation. At this moment, he was happy to accept the assurances of the senior chief. Even though Capelli told him not to trust anyone, he was certain the senior chief was a good man.

13

TUCKER, SANGAS AND NOSH

Matt returned to his duties with a watchful eye on his surroundings. Matt reasoned to himself that if there were at least two more spies in the shack, Bunker could have easily revealed Matt's snooping. The bruises and gashes on Matt's face were difficult to explain in such proximity to Bunker's death. However, a source of comfort was that Clay and the senior chief seemed to have taken Matt under their wing. Matt sensed that one or the other of them was always close by him. Matt felt some relief from this and appreciated the effort the two made to keep an eye on him. He realized that he would not hear anything from Randy or Capelli until they were in Perth, yet he kept a watchful eye for notes tucked under his pillow.

The second morning following his meeting with Capelli, the *Okie* steamed westward, out of the Indian Ocean, past Garden Island, and Kwinana Bay's outer harbor. They would be mooring in Fremantle, a city adjacent to Perth. This was where the Australian Naval Base was, with piers large enough to accommodate the 610 foot long *Okie*. The scene passing before them was breathtaking. The land was lush, and the color of the water was a beautiful emerald green. The air was warm but not too warm. The city smelled fresh and clean, unlike many of the Asian ports Matt had experienced. Those ports often reeked of sewage and stale, humid tropical air.

As had become their habit, once the ship completed its mooring and shifted to shore power, and the officer of the deck announced liberty call, Clay and Matt set out to explore the area. They had heard how great the beer was in Australia, and were enthusiastic about giving it a try (or ten). The area surrounding Fremantle's port was primarily industrial, so the two began hailing one of the numerous cabs that had appeared on the pier. Both sailors had learned from being in various ports overseas that cab drivers were a great source of information on the entire array of entertainment venues available locally. They flagged down a cab and jumped in the back.

"If you have never been in Fremantle, mates," the driver said, "Then you've got to go to *Percy Flint's Boozery and Eatery*. Been there since the 1930s, and they have the best beer and tucker in the area." Both looked at the driver with questioning looks regarding the word "tucker." The driver saw from the sailors' faces they were not tracking him. "You know, sangas? Nosh?" The questioning expressions on their faces continued, and the driver finally gave up and said, "chow!" Looks of recognition came upon their faces until the driver added, "You might find some nice Sheila's, too!" The sailors decided not to confirm their ignorance and just raised their thumbs and left it at that. With a quick affirmation, they were off to explore Australian libations.

Both sailors were amazed at the welcoming attitude and genuine affection the Aussies had for American sailors. Once the locals identified the sailors, they showered them with attention, affection, and free beer. This kind of treatment was an unusual experience for them. Both in Yokosuka and Pearl Harbor, sailors in the mid-1970s were treated with negative and even hostile behavior from the locals. The activities of numerous sailors justified some of the mistreatment. Even so, the navy brought more revenue to Honolulu and Yokosuka than the tourist industry, and most sailors behaved themselves while off the base. Now, in Australia, they were being treated as heroes and honored guests, which, while a bit disconcerting at first, was a delightful experience. Both Matt and Clay continued to discover that speaking Australian was something to learn to avoid trouble. Clay had an incredibly challenging time communicating with the Aussies, who were flummoxed at Clay's colloquial Texan sayings. Clay had a close call when they were watching a rugby match on television, and he asked one of the men at the bar, "Who are you rooting for?" Instead of slugging Clay, the Australian explained that "rooting" was a synonym for fornicating and not be used in the context of sports at any time.

The two also learned that the word "pissed" meant something entirely different than the American definition. The two were, once again, sitting at a bar, which had come to be their primary recreation in Australia, when a man next to Matt looked at him in the eye and said, "Boy, am I pissed!"

Matt thought he was in trouble and said, "I'm sorry, what did I do?" That was when he learned that if you were pissed, it meant you were drunk.

That being said, being drunk was rarely obvious among the Aussies. Clay voiced this observation as they were walking to the ship one evening. "I've never seen guys who can consume such massive quantities of beer and who pretty much do so constantly. What amazes me is that even with all that beer, they function better than a Baptist preacher on Sunday even though they are drunk as Cooter Brown!"

Two days after arriving in Perth, a man arrived in Australia, by plane, from Yokosuka. Dressed to blend in with the locals, he sat down with the American in a pub at the Perth Airport. Speaking with a distinctly Russian accent, the man addressed the American parsimoniously. "You have this Bertram under surveillance, yes?" the Russian inquired.

"He hasn't left our sight since Bunker went overboard," said the American. And we've seen nothing suspicious up to this point."

"And Bunker said nothing to you or your associate about Bertram?"

"Nothing of which we are aware. But I fear that if there was an encounter, it was rather spontaneous and not well-thought-out. Bunker tended to have a quick temper and was always a bit too independent for me. Your instructions, Makarov?"

"Blue," said Makarov, using what was a code name for the American, "We have a very good arrangement going here, which dates back almost ten years if I recall?"

"Yes sir, it does," said Blue, "and I think it's been good for both of us. We are very close to my retirement, and I'd hate to see things end badly."

"Blue, I think this Hombre is a bad egg." It always made Blue feel uncomfortable when the Russian was trying to sound like a cowboy. Blue had resigned himself to the fact that everyone had their quirks, and this was Makarov's. Yet the cowboy sayings, coming from the mouth of a Soviet KGB agent, were incredibly distracting.

"Well, I'd like to take the shootin' iron to the young radioman just out of caution. I'm afraid that because of what's going on, it would cause more suspicion, rather than less," Makarov said dolefully. "We still have little evidence the radioman has any involvement in counterintelligence anyway. Let's keep the surveillance going. Please don't allow him to be out of your observation here in Perth. In the meantime, it might be fitting for you to befriend him, let him get to know you. If he is involved in this, he may let his guard down with you, and if not, you may have a recruit for your efforts. If you find anything that confirms his involvement, let me know when you arrive in Subic Bay. Don't take any action on your own unless it is evident the sailor will bring this down before arriving in Subic. Also, let's don't assume that he is acting alone. Even if he is uninvolved, there may be someone else who is less obvious, who is at work against us. Understood?"

Blue affirmed Makarov's directive, adding, "By the way, Bunker's things were searched, and we recovered his camera. There's used film in it. I hope it will be useful."

"Your information is almost always useful, Blue," acknowledged Makarov. Let's keep it that way."

The *Okie* was to be in Fremantle for a total of six days before departing for Subic Bay. Although Clay and Matt had daily radio watches, they both recreated in town as much as possible. The day before departure for Subic Bay, Senior Chief Lester came along on one of their excursions. The senior chief spent the day with them at Kings Park, one of the largest city parks in the world and located in the center of Perth. After the park, they headed to Percy Flint's to introduce the pub to the senior chief, have dinner and drink beer on the senior chief's dime. The three laughed and drank while feasting on chicken parmigiana, barbecued snags, and meat pies, which they learned, was the national dish of Australia, to the surprise of all three.

"Let me tell you, you young sparks, the navy is very different from the one I joined," mused the senior chief. He pushed back the last of his food and took a long quaff of his Swan Stout. A thunderous belch soon followed the senior chief's pull on the beer. He simultaneously liberated an air biscuit from his back end. Matt could have sworn they were harmonizing.

Matt, trying to diminish the smell overtaking him, duplicated the chief's pull on his beer, swallowed, and inquired, "What was different about it, senior chief?"

"I joined in 1956. My first duty was the USS *Gearing*; a classic 'tin can' out of Norfolk. Christened in 1945, it was anything but a comfortable ship. We slept in hammocks, ate *shit on a shingle*, rather than this mamby-pamby food, and our job as radiomen was to send and receive morse code. We typed those messages out on a manual typewriter. There were no fancy *selectrics* and no teletypes. We would spend eight fucking hours with headphones on, tapping out and listening to morse code, and tuning and re-tuning our receivers trying to get any semblance of a signal. There was no coddling or wet-nursing the crew. You stood on your own, or you got knocked down. You got promoted on your merit, not a written test, and you didn't have to wait for an opening to make rate. If the navy was still that way, I'd be master chief now, no doubt. Now, I'll bet there aren't a dozen radiomen on our ship who even know morse code. And everybody whines about the conditions when they are the fucking Ritz compared to my day."

The senior chief took a deep breath and another pull of his stout, then continued, "Things were simpler then. We did our jobs, took home shit for pay, and lived to go to sea. It's more complicated now, and I, for one, can't wait to take my retirement. I've got plans to live in the lap of luxury, and I'm saving my stake money right now. Have you heard of this thing called the World Series of Poker?"

"Isn't that the big poker event in Las Vegas?" Matt inquired.

"You better believe it. I've been following it since it started six years ago. It's about a $10,000 buy-in for the final event, but last year a guy by the name of Brian 'Sailor' Roberts won 210 fucking thousand bucks. Even the preliminary events went for fifteen grand. I've been studying these guys: Johnny Moss, 'Amarillo Slim' Preston, Puggy Pearson. They are damn good. But they haven't seen me. I get the first prize of two hundred grand, and I'm set for fucking life! And now they play no-limit *hold 'em*, which I'm an afficio-fucking-nado at."

Matt was a bit startled at the enthusiasm with which the senior chief spoke. Wishing to have something to bond with him over, he replied, "Yeah, senior chief, you told me that you would teach me sometime. I'd love to learn. I think I'm a pretty good poker player already."

"Oh, really, Matt? We'll have to play and see how much you know about poker. I hope your granny was a good teacher because if not, I'll be making my Corvette payment with your paycheck." Matt realized he might just be in over his head, but it seemed to be the senior chief's passion, and he could lose twenty or thirty bucks if he had to.

As for the current quality of food on the *Okie*, Matt quietly disagreed with the senior chief's *mamby-pamby* comment. He thought the food was dreadful and couldn't imagine anything worse. To a young sailor like Matt, 1956 seemed like the dark ages. It was the year Matt was born. He imagined how antiquated life as a radioman must have been in those dark ages before teletypes.

As their evening wore on, the senior chief seemed to become more focused on Bunker's death, causing Matt's anxiety to surge. Lester must have asked Matt a dozen times throughout the evening if he knew anything more about Bunker's death. By the final inquiry, Matt became worried that the senior chief suspected he was involved in Bunker's death, creating mounting apprehension. Matt hoped he had a good enough poker face to avoid more suspicion.

14

DEEPER AND DEEPER

On the morning of the seventh day after arriving in Fremantle, the *Okie* set sail for Subic Bay. The ship and crew would be at sea for seven days. The senior chief had moved Matt to the teletype repair room as his full-time station. The move gave Matt mixed feelings. Being in teletype repair meant that he worked only during the day and was on-call for repair work on a rotating basis. The change in position gave Matt some semblance of routine, with regular working hours, meals, and sleep, which was a good thing. The drawback of the change meant that it was more challenging to keep an eye on any suspicious activity in the radio shack and crypto room. Matt purposely kept the door between the teletype repair shop and crypto room open whenever possible to provide more opportunities to monitor anything even vaguely nefarious.

By the time they had been back at sea for two days, Matt's apprehension was diminishing, and he was settling into his new routine. Matt had a chance to see movies on the mess decks or topside on the helicopter deck in good weather. His sleep improved with the absence of a rotation of watches between days, evenings, and midwatch.

On the fourth day at sea, Matt came down to the berthing quarters to find a note under his pillow, saying *Meet RG PO Club 3:30 Thursday. Watch for a tail.*

The *Okie* docked in Subic on Wednesday, with sailors spilling off the ship, heading for the pleasures of Olongapo like greyhounds after a rabbit. Matt had duty that day, which meant no liberty for him until Thursday. As Matt was cleaning up his workspace, the senior chief walked into the crypto room, his desk being just beyond the door to the teletype repair shop. Lester was also preparing for liberty. His attire signaled a trip to the Chief's Club to work out, carrying his customary black gym bag. As Matt watched unseen, the senior chief set the bag on his desk, appeared to scan the room for bystanders, opened a drawer in his desk, and placed two file folders into the bag. He shut the desk drawer and left radio central with Matt, cocking his head like a puppy, wondering what in the hell the senior chief might have put into his gym bag from the shack. A kernel of wariness crept into Matt's awareness. *Is the senior chief a spy?* Matt quickly pushed this thought out of his head. Next to his friend Clay, the senior chief was the least suspicious person in the radio shack. He told himself he was becoming way too paranoid and vowed to forget what he saw.

On Thursday afternoon, Matt headed off the ship, ostensibly toward Olongapo. He took a winding route toward the petty officer's club, trying to ensure, as Capelli advised, that he was not being followed. While Matt was in Special Agent training, he learned how to tail someone without being observed, but the class never discussed the opposite situation. He decided he would apply his tailing skills in reverse hoping to reveal any potential followers effectively. He wound around buildings, feinted in a direction opposing his goal, backtracked, and stopped to appear to be reading direction signs. He saw no one following and, after twenty minutes of zigging and zagging, decided it was safe. As he turned the corner on his way to the club, he smacked chest-to-chest into another sailor. "Wow, Bert, where you headed so fast?" It was Clay, appearing as surprised as Matt was.

"Hey, Clay," a startled Matt gabbled, "I'm ... um ... heading to the uniform shop to get a new pair of dungarees." Lame, he knew, but it was the best he could do under pressure.

Clay smiled, grabbed his shoulders, and turned him around. "It's that way, ole buddy."

"Oh, thanks, I ... knew I was a bit lost."

Clay slapped him on the back. "Well, when you're done, meet me at Swanky's, and I'll buy you a San Magoo!"

"You got it, Clay. I'll see you in a bit. Glad you came along to put me on the right path. This is a big friggin' base," Matt jabbered, waving over his head, traveling away from Clay.

As soon as Clay was out of sight, Matt took a deep breath and changed direction back to the club. Arriving a bit tense from his chance meeting, Matt ordered a beer and moved to a table as far from the few sailors getting a head start on liberty.

Matt was watching the door with anticipation of Randy arriving. Quite a lot had happened since they last met in Yokosuka. Quite a lot. He caught a spy, received two thrashings, and killed someone, albeit in self-defense. The experiences of the last few weeks seemed completely unreal as Matt reviewed them. Yet, he knew they were all true. And other than Special Agent Capelli, Matt had no one he could trust onboard the *Okie* to pour out his feelings. As Randy came through the door, he was surprised that his usual feelings of attraction and affection weren't there. A crushing sense of relief had replaced them, and now he would finally have someone with whom he could be candid. Choking up just a bit, he quickly swallowed the urge to cry like a baby, took a deep breath, and gave Randy a smile and a wave.

As he stood to greet her, Randy rushed to Matt. To Matt's surprise, she threw her arms around Matt and gave him a whopping hug. "Matt," Randy said, looking at him with a thoughtful expression of empathy and relief, "I'm so sorry for what you have had to go through the last couple of weeks. How are you holding up?"

Up until that moment, Matt had thought he was holding up pretty damn well. With unspoken permission to let it go, Matt folded back into his seat, his guise of tough spy-catcher gone, and as he slumped back, said, "All things considered, pretty shitty."

"I get it, Matt," Randy expressed, "But you did it, and we are all proud of your actions at NIS." Quickly changing the subject to the business at hand, Randy said, "Capelli brought me up to date on what happened with Bunker. Matt, Capelli also let me know that he reviewed all of the hidden camera footage, and he has confirmed that there are at least two others involved. One is an enlisted man, E-6 or below. The other is wearing a khaki uniform, which means he's either an officer or CPO. They were definitely taking pictures of documents, which makes their intentions pretty clear. We weren't able to see their faces or rates, however, so we don't know who they are."

"Shit," was all Matt could extricate from his throat.

Randy took a breath and slightly cleared her throat. "There's more," she said, "We analyzed the photos you took of Bunker's notebook. It does appear to be a ledger of sorts, but the mystery name in the last column, 'Makarov,' we have identified. Pyotr Makarov is the name of a Diplomatic Officer in the Soviet Embassy in Tokyo. We are very familiar with Makarov. He is, in fact, a Major in the KGB. Makarov has a position of authority in a division of the KGB that recruits people in countries the USSR wants intelligence from to spy against their own countries. It's pretty clear that Bunker was spying for the Soviets and working for Makarov."

"Oh shit," were the most articulate words Matt could squeeze out. At least he had managed two words this time.

"There's one more thing you need to know," Randy said. She stared into Matt's eyes, swallowed, and took a breath. "When we were going through the possessions of the two murdered radiomen from the *Okie*, we found Makarov's business card. The danger you are in is pretty clear. These people are serious about what they are doing and are willing to murder to keep it quiet. I'm ... I'm sorry to have to say this, but the stakes could not be higher."

Feeling the blood drain from his face, Matt began to feel nauseous and light-headed. He was breaking out in a cold sweat. "Well, it sounds like you've got as much as I can give. Can't you guys take it from here?" Matt said hopefully.

"I know this is really tough and scary, Matt," Randy said with empathy in her voice, "But you have done a great job to this point, and you are making the progress we had hoped for. Only you can get the evidence we need to take these people out. It's asking a lot, I know, Matt. We will provide you with as much protection as we are able, but it's going to be up to you to bring this investigation to an end."

Matt shook his head, looking down at the table. "I knew that was the answer. I just thought I'd ask."

As much as Randy wanted to change the subject, there were still a few thorny issues to discuss. "I know that you already know this, but we know there are at least two more spies on your ship. Well, actually in your radio shack. After what happened to Bunker, you could very well be under suspicion yourself. You need to be very, very careful." After dropping that issue in Matt's lap, she tried moving to a more manageable level of conversation. "Is there anything else you've discovered? Any hunches, suspicions, or anything else that you feel we need to discuss?"

"I can't really think of anything," Matt stammered.

"OK, Matt," Randy responded. "I'm going to be here in Subic the entire time the *Okie* is here. I'm giving you the number here at the local NIS office. Just let them know you need to talk to me, and they will track me down. I'll be close to the phone as much as I am able. Call anytime you need to, and we can meet, or if it's critical, we can send back-up. If I'm not there, they will get a message to me quickly." She paused and then put her hand on Matt's. "Matt, you are doing great. Just be careful, OK?"

"You can count on that," Matt said, managing to force something close to a smile from his lips. They stood to say goodbye, and Matt, mostly from his worry, said, "There might be one thing, Randy. Senior Chief Lester, my supervisor in the radio shack, did something yesterday that I had just a moment of concern about."

Randy stopped and turned toward Matt. "Tell me," she affirmed.

"I was in the teletype repair room after the ship docked, and the senior chief came into the crypto room in civvies with his gym bag. Looking a little suspicious, he put some folders into his gym bag before leaving. It's probably nothing, but I just thought it might be worth bringing up."

"It was, Matt. I don't know if there's anything to it, but I think you should follow up on it. We'll get his service record information sent here. I will take a look at his back story. I'm sure you have a lead that you need to track down."

"If you think so, I will," Matt said with some reluctance.

"I do. It's good seeing you, Matt, and I'm delighted you're OK. You did well."

When Matt returned to the *Okie*, his emotions were close to getting away from him. He hoped Randy was wrong about possibly being under suspicion, but his senses told him it was a good possibility. He decided that he should hide his notebook someplace else on the ship other than his locker, which he did. He resolved to keep his camera and film with him. He went to bed with his head spinning, wondering how a kid from a little town in Northern New Mexico could end up here, at this moment, in this place. If he told anyone the story, he would have been branded as the most fantastic sea storyteller of all time. Considering the talented sea storytellers in the navy, that was saying something.

Two hours later, two men sat on the mess decks, each with a cup of coffee. Senior Chief Morris Lester sat across from RM2 Clay Young. Anyone looking at them would have assumed they were just shooting the shit.

"Were you able to follow Matt today?" Lester asked Clay.

"Yeah. A strange thing happened that doesn't make sense," Clay responded, "I was following him and could have sworn he was trying to lose me like he was aware he was being followed. He lost me for a moment, and we accidentally bumped into one another as we each turned a corner. He said he was going to the uniform shop but was walking in the opposite direction. When I pointed that out, he headed out that way and then back-tracked to the Petty Officer's Club."

"OK, that's strange." Lester paused for a moment, considering this bit of information. "But it's not in and of itself enough to take action. It's just one more chip on the table."

"Well, how about this then," said Clay. "I tailed him to the club, and he had a beer with a lady-friend that works in Yokosuka. I met her there, and she said she was a civilian employee. I can't understand why she would be in Subic."

"Well," the senior chief pondered, "She could have a job that requires travel around the Seventh Fleet bases." He paused and thought for a moment before speaking. "OK, the chips are starting to add up." The senior chief sat silently for a moment and then smiled. "Let's just assume he's intentionally sniffing our assholes. Poker isn't just played at the table. It can be played here in real life. And I'm going to outplay him. Let's raise the stakes a bit. I think it's time for a compartment-wide locker search."

15

AN UNEXPECTED SUSPECT

Matt had mixed emotions about putting the senior chief into the 'suspect' category. Everything he had seen since arriving on the *Okie* indicated Lester was a stand-up guy, and Matt genuinely liked and respected him. Had he not seen Lester's behavior putting the documents into his gym bag, Matt would have resisted any probing. Still, he could not deny that Lester's behavior raised suspicions, and at the very least, was a clear violation of security rules.

Matt knew it was a long shot that he would find anything in the senior chief's desk, but it was a good place to start. Once he knew Lester was not in the shack and the crypto room was empty, Matt left his desk in the teletype repair shop and began a quick search of the desk. As expected, he came up empty.

The next logical step would be much more difficult. Matt needed to access the CPO quarters, look through Lester's locker, and hopefully search his gym bag. This task would be a challenge. The CPOs had separate quarters that included their bunks and lockers, a small kitchenette, and a large table. E-6 and below were restricted from access unless they were there on official business. There was only one entrance, the main door off of a public passageway.

Matt decided to wait until the daytime when he knew the CPO quarters were likely to be empty, and the senior chief was likely to be involved in matters in radio central. As Matt entered the CPO quarters, one CPO was sitting at the table in the living area, newspaper spread on the table, doing a crossword puzzle. The CPO looked up with a questioning look as to why an E-4 would be in the quarters. Matt put on his most nonchalant attitude and said, "Senior Chief Lester left his coffee mug on his rack and asked me to come get it for him."

"God knows Moe can't live without his fucking coffee, but I thought that mug was welded to his index finger." The chief gave Matt directions to the senior chief's rack and went back to his crossword.

Matt entered the berthing compartment and breathed a sigh of relief to find it empty. He went straight to Lester's locker and found it predictably locked. As Matt struggled to determine what to do next, his jaw dropped as he spied Lester's gym bag at the foot of the bed. Trepidation flooded Matt's brain. Matt knew that if he found something incriminating in the bag, his respected mentor was a spy, and it would cause him to be ruined and imprisoned.

On the other hand, thought Matt, *who would be dumb enough to leave incriminating evidence on their rack?* Trying to relax, Matt began searching the gym bag. As he rifled through Lester's belongings, he found everyday items: Gym shoes, shorts, a t-shirt, towel, a deck of cards, and a book, *Salem's Lot*, by an author Matt had never heard of named Stephen King. Matt was about to give up finding anything and quickly escape from the CPO quarters when he felt something at the very bottom of the bag. As he pulled the object out, he shuddered. It was a small film cartridge, just like the kind his own camera took. Attached to the cartridge was something even more chilling. In handwriting was a note, clipped to the cartridge:

Makarov
Edsa Plaza Hotel Manila
Room 1010, 8633 8888

"Oh shit ..." Matt involuntarily whispered. Makarov! Breath flowed from Matt's lungs in a violent gust, and he reeled against the rail on the side of the bed. It took every ounce of effort for him not to hyperventilate and put the things back in the bag. Staring at the film cartridge, he considered putting it back also. On impulse, he decided he had to keep it. If he could get it to Randy, it just might contain the evidence he needed, and he could retire from his life undercover. He tucked it in his front pocket and did his best to return the bag to the place he found it.

Matt made a poor attempt at gathering himself up so that he wouldn't leave the CPO quarters looking like he had just seen a ghost. He stopped for a moment and took in a deep breath, practicing a carefree look. Matt passed by the CPO doing the crossword, and, fortunately, the chief was too involved in his crossword to look up. Once out of the quarters, he leaned against the bulkhead, making every effort to calm down. Thoughts raced in his mind uncontrollably. *Shit! He's a spy! What the hell will I do? I need to get to Randy! Oh my god, this is REAL!*

Matt walked back toward radio central, trying to plan how to contact Randy and get her the film. He was sure that this would be enough evidence to persuade NIS to pull him from the ship. Special Agents could arrest Lester, and Matt would be out of danger. He decided the best course would be to get to SAA Capelli's office and involve him in the next steps. Matt changed direction, turning toward the passage that would lead him to Capelli. He reached the office with relief and knocked on the door. No answer. He tried the knob. The door was locked. Matt found some paper and started writing a note to put under Capelli's door. Before he could finish the note, over the 1MC came an announcement. The loudspeaker boomed with an ominous pronouncement: "Now hear this, all communications and radio personnel not on watch are to report to CR berthing immediately for a locker inspection. Once again, all CR personnel not on watch are to report to CR berthing immediately."

Matt stopped. He knew they regularly inspected berthing quarters, especially in countries where drugs were available, inexpensive, and plentiful. Sailors, particularly radiomen with higher security clearances, were also subject to frequent urine samples for drug use. After all, it was the 1970s and drugs of every sort were popular among sailors and readily available. Matt observed a whole industry of sailors who guaranteed themselves to be clean, selling urine to other sailors who might be a bit dirty on the U/A. Matt tried not to associate this inspection with anything going on with him but contacting Capelli would have to wait until after the inspection.

When Matt arrived in the berthing compartment, the communications officer and several senior enlisted men were going through lockers. As Matt entered the compartment, Senior Chief Lester said to Matt, "Just go over to your locker, unlock it and wait for us to get to you. Do not open it or remove anything, understood?"

It was probably the fact that Lester said this, now knowing what Matt knew, that sent shivers of dread from his head to his feet. He did as ordered and waited. As Matt was waiting, he felt a great deal of relief that he had hidden the notebook on another part of the ship. Matt was relieved to see that they were only checking lockers and not the sailors. Matt was reasonably confident that the film canister he took from the chief's bag and his camera and film cassettes in his pocket would be safe.

Lester finally reached Matt's area of the compartment. Lester opened the locker used by the sailor who slept below Matt, gave it a five-second look-over, and told the sailor to lock it up. As he came to Matt's locker, he smiled and said casually, "Hey, Matt, if you aren't doing anything this afternoon, let's go get a beer at the Chief's Club, OK?"

A bit startled by the comment and highly relieved, Matt smiled back and said, "I'd like that, senior chief!"

"Let's knock off today a little early. Let's say 1600. Get an early start on the weekend. I'll invite Clay to tag along."

The senior chief then inspected Matt's locker in a manner that resembled an archeological dig for King Tut's tomb, a blatant contradiction to the friendly invitation he had just given. Lester went through every square inch of Matt's locker, looking inside shoes, shaving gear, and even fanning books. When he finished with the locker, he stepped back and examined Matt from head to toe, a menacing look on his face. Matt quickly realized Lester was considering searching his person. Lester took a step closer to Matt. As Matt braced himself for a body search and the ultimate discovery of the camera and film, the glare in Lester's eyes quickly vanished. He flashed Matt a disarming smile and said, "See you on the quarter deck at 1600."

Matt nodded his assent. Matt needed to get back to the teletype repair shop as it was probably already noticed that he had been away for too long. He decided that as soon as he got off work, he would change into his civvies and make another stop at Capelli's office. It seemed, from the senior chief's manner, that Lester had no suspicions about Matt. Matt had no intention of getting a beer with Lester.

Unknown to Matt, the senior chief walked away from Matt's locker with a small piece of paper he had found. On paper were two initials: "RG" and a number, which appeared to Lester to be a base phone number.

16

CORNERING A MOUSE

Matt revisited SAA Capelli's office three times that afternoon, with no luck. It was getting close to 1600 hours, so he scribbled a quick note to him:

Found evidence in Lester's gym bag. Lester doesn't know I have it, I think.
He's taking me to Chief's club for a beer at 1600
Help!
MB

He slid the envelope under the door, hoping against hope that Capelli would be back in the office, and read the note before he had to leave with the senior chief.

At 1530 Matt had still not heard from Capelli. Matt grudgingly changed into his civilian clothes, hoping he could get to the pier to call Randy and return to the ship in time to meet Clay and Lester on the quarter deck. He finished dressing and headed toward the passage that would take him topside. Matt saw Clay coming down the passageway toward him and gave him a wave. "Hey buddy, you're moving faster than a prairie fire with a tailwind. What's the rush?" Clay said with a cheerful smile.

"Oh, just have a quick errand to do before we head out," said Matt, hoping Clay wouldn't notice the shake in his voice.

"Ah, come on, brother," Clay implored, "I got something I want to talk to you about."

"We can talk in a minute, Matt said. "I really have to get this done."

Matt walked on without further reply. The trek from berthing to the quarterdeck took a good five minutes with the stairways and winding passages. He walked out the topside door onto the main deck and back to the quarterdeck, stepping up his pace as he saw the gangplank. He approached the officer of the deck, gave him the usual "Permission to depart the ship," and started to head down the gangplank when the OOD said, "Hold on a moment, Bertram. Senior Chief Lester called up and asked me to keep you on the ship until he got here. Said he had something he needed to discuss before you left the ship."

Stunned, Matt looked from the OOD, down the gangplank, to the back of the peer and the bank of five payphones. He was fifty feet away from his call. A feeling of dismay welled up in his gut as he sat and waited for the senior chief.

A few minutes passed as Matt sat, dazed, waiting for the senior chief. Each minute felt like an hour to him as his mind raced, trying to formulate a plan to get to a phone. He looked back at the door from below just as the senior chief and Clay sprang out, Lester looking a bit tense and hurried. However, as soon as he saw Matt, his visage changed, and he gave Matt a big smile. "Hey, Bert, glad you waited for us," said the senior chief, "I didn't want you to get lost on the way to the club like you did the uniform shop the other day."

Shit, Clay told Lester about that? Matt thought. *Why the hell was that an essential topic of conversation?* Matt had no time to process that detail as Lester held out a hand to Matt to help him up, slapped him on the back, and the three sailors headed toward the club.

Along the way, the senior chief was all smiles, cracking some of his worst jokes, which every radioman in the division had heard a hundred times. When Lester told jokes, he was the first and loudest to laugh at them. Usually, he broke wind simultaneously, and, predictably, he gave several anal exhales during his monologue. Matt was starting to believe that the senior chief was utterly unaware that he was expelling gas, and either he didn't care about it or couldn't control the constant barn burners.

The more Lester talked, the more relaxed Matt became. Even in the face of the overwhelming evidence that Lester was a spy, Matt's mind began to create rationalizations that might vindicate his suspicions of Lester. If nothing else, Matt was comforted that Clay was along with them, as he knew Lester wouldn't try anything with his friend present.

When they reached the club, the senior chief signed the two lower enlisted men in as guests. They found a table and ordered San Miguels. Matt was completely off balance as Lester laughed, joked around, and told some of his best, or at least raunchiest, sea stories. "Ever been to Bangkok, Matt?" asked Lester. "It's a fucking carrousel of debauchery."

"No, we were supposed to go, but our ship came across a boat full of Vietnamese refugees who Malaysian pirates had attacked. We saved them but ended up going to Pattaya Beach instead of Bangkok."

"Yeah, we all heard about that one. Your ship and crew did well on that. That's where you got that UN humanitarian service medal you're so damn proud of. Well, it's too bad you missed Bangkok. The fucking city is in-*fucking*-credible. Texas street is beyond bizarre with hookers you can shop for in storefront windows. And any kind of sex you want is cheap and available! Ain't nothing like it!"

Lester and Clay laughed with a distracted Matt joining in, more than a bit preoccupied with his current fix. Matt's mind was racing, working to contrive a plan to get to a phone in the club. It occurred to him that there was a bank of payphones just by the head. Matt waited until they were on their third beer, and attempting to sound offhanded, said, "Well, got to see a man about a horse," and got up to go to the head.

Clay shouted at him, "Hey, man, that's my line! I might be making a Texan out of you!"

Matt successfully extricated himself, and as he was walking down the hall, took a deep breath. As he reached into his pocket to get Randy's number, he felt a sense of panic swell up as he realized that he had left it in his locker. *Hopefully, I'll have time to call base information and get the number*, thought Matt, as he grabbed a phone. Just as he lifted the receiver to his ear, Clay came around the corner. "Calling your girlfriend?" Clay said caustically.

"Uh ... no ... I ... I was just passing by, and the dang phone rang," Matt said. *That sounded like an idiot.* "Nobody there."

Without hesitation, Clay smiled and said, "I gotta knock the dew off the lily myself," slapping Matt on the back. "Come on, let's tap our kidneys. Senior chief has a great idea about what to do next."

Next? I was hoping 'next' would be to get back to the ship, Matt thought, as he preceded Clay into the head.

"Hey, there you are, sparks," said Lester upon their return. "I have a fucking *grand* idea. I don't know if you guys have ever been to the Whiterock Resort or not, but it's a great place, and I stay there a lot. All three of us have the next two days off, so let's grab some bourbon and cokes, get a room, party our asses off, and, Matt, you've been telling me you're a poker player, so we'll get us a good game going. I'll teach you how to play Hold 'em, and you can dazzle me with those practiced skills that granny taught you. How much money you got on you?"

"Well, um, I'd like to senior chief, but I don't have clothes or a toothbrush or anything. We probably should go back to the *Okie* first," Matt said, stammering. "And besides, most of my cash is in my locker. I only have a hundred bucks or so on me."

"No worries on the cash, Matt. Once I take your money, I'll stake you on the rest. You'll need a couple of paychecks to recover, anyway! And you don't need your shit. They got everything we need at the hotel. We're heading out, and that's final," Lester said fervently.

Matt gave a silent sigh of surrender, thwarted in his efforts to call Randy. He grudgingly walked, Lester in front and Clay behind, up Magsaysay Boulevard, out the front gate of Subic Bay Naval Station, and into the curious world of Olongapo City.

In the city of Olongapo, there were many ways to travel. The colorful jeepneys careened around corners and dodged in and out of traffic like a stampede of kitschy cattle. The jeepneys were old WWII era Willy's jeeps converted to hold six or eight people, decorated in garish colors, and operated more as small, private buses. The city also had public buses and taxis available. But, out of all of the transportation choices in the city, the most fun was to ride motorized rickshaws. These imaginative lorries carried two or three people, had a motorcycle front-end and a covered seat in the back. For a couple of pesos, the driver would take you anywhere in the city. The drivers were famous for their hair-raising thrill rides, winding in and out of traffic, giving the rider an amusement-park-worthy fright. A good rickshaw ride bordered on terrifying, with horns blaring, men cursing, and a noticeable lack of mufflers. The senior chief flagged one down, just past the Shit River bridge, and the three squeezed into a seat made for two, with Matt jammed in between Lester and Clay. The rickshaw launched into the busy street as though it was the only vehicle for miles, nearly colliding with a jeepney, both drivers swearing in their native Tagalog.

"*Putang ina mo!*" their driver screamed while the other equaled the profanity with something sounding to Matt like *tay*. Whatever they were saying to one another, some severe cussing resulted in a high-speed road rage competition. After the third near-miss, their driver ultimately backed down, realizing his tip was on the line. The driver headed up Magsaysay Boulevard, past the sailor bars, massage parlors, and the Filipino version of convenience stores, the ubiquitous sari-sari shops. The rickshaw made a hard right turn on Rizal Avenue, one of the main thoroughfares in the city. Matt watched the notorious red-light district of Olongapo gradually become more residential, as the bars gave way to businesses and everyday citizens going about their business. They crossed the Kalaklan Bridge over the Mabayuan River. Matt noted that it was picturesque and, unlike the Shit River, was not strewn with the poverty, trash, and sewage he saw near the naval base. They turned onto the National Highway and soon had a gorgeous ocean view to their left and the beautiful coastline.

While Matt would have ordinarily enjoyed the drive, at this moment, he was overwhelmed with near-panic as he struggled to formulate anything resembling a plan. The further they traveled from the naval base, the less hope he had for any opportunity to call Randy. As they pulled up in front of the Whiterock Beach Hotel, Matt had realized that he was entirely on his own. He was holding onto two bits of hope. First, his friend Clay was with them, which gave him an advantage in numbers if the senior chief tried anything nefarious. Second, there was still the possibility that the senior chief neither knew that Matt was working undercover nor had evidence against him. Matt hoped this was just a weekend outing for pleasure and poker. Considering the current situation, Matt realized that he had few options other than to see how things played out.

As the rickshaw stopped at the Whiterock Hotel's front entrance, the three sailors awkwardly extricated themselves from the small seat, paid the driver, and walked toward the door. Matt was actively observing each detail of the entrance, the other two sailors, and the street behind them as he struggled to formulate an escape strategy -- without success.

Before they could reach the front desk, a small Filipino man approached, a broad smile on his face and his right hand extended toward the senior chief. "Chief Moe," the man called out, "It is so good to have you back! Are the three of you staying?"

"Good to see you, Ernesto!" The Chief offered to the man. "Yes, we'll be staying. I trust you have my usual suite available?"

"We will make it available for you, Chief Moe," the man said with enthusiasm. "Poker this weekend?"

"Just a fun game for the three of us, Ernesto," said Lester, "But if your man Keanu is available, poker's much more fun with a fourth person."

Ernesto nodded emphatically and said, "I'll have him come up momentarily. Your usual bourbon and cokes?"

"Oh yeah, and we'll need at least a couple of bottles of your best. And of course cards and chips."

"Of course," said Ernesto as he moved behind the desk, grabbed a key, and handed it to the senior chief. "And because you want Keanu, I'll assume that you'll not want to be disturbed by pretty women this visit?"

"Right," said Lester. "It'll just be poker this weekend, and we will appreciate the least amount of disturbance possible."

"Of course, Chief Moe," Ernesto affirmed.

With that, the three headed up to the second floor of the hotel. The elevator and stairs were at the end of a long hallway, and the three walked the entire distance to the last room on the floor. As they entered the room, Matt was surprised at how nice it was. The only hotels he had stayed at in the Philippines had been in the sailor district and left much to be desired. The suite in this hotel was a clean and bright white with light blue trim and appointed with high-quality furnishings. It had two bedrooms, a wet bar, sofas, a kitchenette, a large table, and a television set. There was a sliding glass door that led to a large, covered lanai. Clay opened the door and stepped out with Matt. The view was stunning. Subic Bay and the beach were no more than three hundred yards away. A bucolic view met Matt's eyes as he saw people playing on the beach and swimming in the ocean. There were small sailboats, and several small motorboats lay beached, just out of the bay. Two floors down, just below their deck, was a large, lavish swimming pool. The pool had a swim-up bar surrounded by elaborate lounge chairs. Most of the chairs were occupied by people in swimsuits. They enjoyed service from waiters dressed in white jackets with bow ties and elegant trays that they carried above their heads, perched on their spread fingers.

As Matt searched for any possible path of escape, there was a knock on the door. A waiter brought in several bottles of bourbon, a case of cokes, playing cards, and poker chips, followed by a tall, broad, and unattractive man. Matt assumed it was none other than Keanu. Keanu might have been part Filipino, but he visibly possessed the genes of a Samoan. The man was huge. Keanu smiled at the senior chief, revealing a gold front tooth. One of his eyes drooped as though it was damaged. As Keanu came closer to Matt, he saw a long scar from the top right of his forehead, traveling down and across the eye, ending just below his nose. There was much about this man that set off alarm bells in Matt's gut. Keanu was going to be playing poker with them. Matt hoped that would be the extent of Keanu's job.

Special Agent Afloat Leon Capelli walked up the gangplank of the USS *Oklahoma City* and, after checking in with the OOD, headed toward his office after a fun day of relaxation on Grande Island, a small Navy recreation area just a short ferry ride from the base in the middle of Subic Bay. Casually checking his watch, he noted it was 6:00 pm, or 1800 hours military time. As Leon entered his office, he saw at his feet the note that Matt had slid under the door. Capelli's heart jumped into his throat as he read it. Having gotten to know Matt Bertram a bit, he knew that Matt would never cry wolf, and the situation was dire. The note Matt wrote stated he would be at the Chief's club at 4 p.m. Capelli grabbed his pistol and speed loaders from his desk and ran to the quarterdeck. Capelli used the quarter-deck telephone to call the NIS office in the hope of catching Randy before she left for the day. Fortunately, Randy was still in the office, reviewing the background investigation results on Senior Chief Lester. Capelli, with some degree of anxiousness in his voice, said, "He says in the note that he's found evidence on Senior Chief Lester. It sounds big, and it sounds like he's probably in trouble."

"Leon, it's even worse," said Randy. "We've uncovered records of exorbitant spending by Lester and his wife. It's far more than he makes as an E-8, and he would have to be winning thousands of dollars a month playing poker to explain this. It looks to me like he has another means of support, which is probably traceable to the USSR."

"I'll grab the car and meet you in front of the Chief's club as soon as you can make it," Randy replied. "I think we need to prepare for the probability that we will arrest Lester."

Capelli agreed, saying, "I'm out the door right now." Both Randy and Capelli arrived at the entrance of the club at the same time. Capelli suggested he go in and take a look as he would attract less attention than a woman. Quietly resenting the idea, Randy nevertheless agreed that was the best course to take. Capelli made a quick search of the club, and neither Matt or Lester were there. He came back and let Randy know. Randy asked one of the waiters if the two had been there. "Oh, yeah, Chief Moe and two other sailors were having beers. Looked like they having a good time!"

"Did they say where they were going from here?" Randy inquired.

"Oh, yeah, senior chief said they going to Whiterock Resort and play some poker," the waiter said.

Randy and Capelli looked at one another, thanked the waiter, and dashed out of the club to Randy's car, racing to the Whiterock Resort. Neither knew what sort of trouble Matt might be in, but both realized that they were probably walking into a shit-show.

17

A POKER LESSON

Matt stood sullenly on the lanai looking at Subic Bay, wishing he was one of the vacationers enjoying the sand and warm waves. As he turned to go back into the hotel room, Clay was mixing bourbon and cokes for everyone. Keanu was sitting at the table with the senior chief as Lester counted out chips and opened the cards, and said, "Come on and sit down, Bert, and I'll teach you the rules of Texas Hold 'em."

"The rules of Hold 'em are just about as simple as 'Go Fish,'" Lester said with a chuckle. "But learning how to play the game well is more complicated than chess. The dealer rotates with each hand. He deals two cards to each player, face down. The player to the dealer's left is called the 'small blind,' and he antes five bucks. The next player is the 'big blind,' and he antes up twice as much. The first player to bet is three from the dealer, and the betting rules are pretty much the same as any type of poker. Players bet on their two hole cards first round. The dealer then puts three cards face up in the middle, and we have another round of betting. A fourth card goes face up with another round of betting, then a fifth card goes face up and a final round of betting. You make the best hand you can with your two cards and the five that are up. That's about it. Simple, huh?"

Clay started passing out drinks to the men at the table. Lester grabbed his drink and downed it in one pull, handed the glass to Clay, and said with a pathetic attempt at a Texas drawl, "Fill 'er up, pardner!"

Matt was glad for the opportunity for some alcohol and took a drink, almost choking. "Clay, did you put any coke in this?" he asked. He realized that the only alcohol he had consumed for many months was a few beers, and the hard stuff felt like it went straight to his head. All four men finished their drinks, Clay poured another round, and Lester started dealing. Lester was his usual cordial self, giving Matt pointers with each hand and telling stories of great poker conquests and dismal losses in his card-playing life. As Lester told stories, Matt felt a strong buzz from the alcohol, and Lester's casual chatter began to relax him. Clay was the designated bartender and was diligently mixing and pouring as each man drained his respective drink. Matt marveled at the mass quantities the senior chief was capable of guzzling. He decided he had better slow down as he was starting to feel drunk. Clay seemed to have dedicated his afternoon to seeing Matt plastered, as his pouring was relentless.

While Matt won a couple of hands, it was apparent that his money would be gone quickly. When he was down to his last ten dollars, Lester laid the cards down on the table. The friendly, smiling face the senior chief usually displayed was suddenly replaced by something intense and sober. The entire atmosphere of the room palpably changed with Lester's dramatic change of expression.

"You're never going to win this game," the senior chief pronounced. Matt wondered if Lester was speaking about the poker game or the spy game. "Unless you learn something about how to play the game competently. And I think it's time that you received a lesson, Bertram." Lester finished his sentence and then gave Matt a big smarmy smile.

"First, you need to know the math of the game. There are only 52 cards in the deck. The same fourteen cards are duplicated four times. That makes for pretty easy math. The probability of certain cards showing at certain times can be estimated, if not exactly, within reasonable limits. Once you know the math, you need to bet on the cards with the highest likelihood of producing a winning hand, which means if you're dealt shit, you fold. I don't know if you noticed, but I fold four out of five hands, and I fold early. I play tight because I know the odds, and I wait for the hand to come to me. Once I have the cards, I'm not afraid to be all-in and raise like hell. On the other hand, you, Petty Officer Bertram, are a maniac, playing on the hope that something great will come up on the flop. That's your first mistake, Bert. You play too loose."

Lester looked at Keanu and motioned with his head at the door. Keanu stood up and walked to the door, standing in front of it. Matt felt the dread well-up inside of his gut as he slowly realized the game had changed.

"Sixteen years ago, I realized I had been dealt a great hand. The navy saw fit to put me in a radio shack. They gave me a top-secret clearance. Then they let me see practically everything there was to see about the military and its secrets. It didn't take a rocket scientist, just a radioman, to know that there was great value to others in that information. I met a KGB agent who put some beautiful cards in the flop, and I was off and running. I saw duty on three ships and three communications stations. I sold information to the Soviets that included crypto codes, ship's movement info, submarine locations, missile readiness, and even the status of the hemorrhoids on the admiral's butt hole. I even helped them build a prototype KWR-37 to use the cards to listen to the fleet broadcast. Been doing it for eight fucking years and made a shit-load of money, and until now, nobody suspected a thing. So I played my cards well, and it paid off for me."

Matt swallowed. He looked at Keanu and understood a boulder was standing in front of the door. Matt turned his head and looked at Clay, standing by the bar. He gave Clay an imploring look seeking help and support in Clay's eyes. Clay simply stood, immobile, not saying a word.

"Here's the second strategy you need to learn, Matt," said Lester. "Poker is a game of deception. I know, everybody understands a bluff in poker, but they don't realize that you can play the *whole game* using deception. You can make people think you have a bad hand when you have a good one, that you're a chicken shit and will back out at the wrong time, and that you don't know what you are doing when you actually do. When you're in the game, you want the other players' perceptions not to match reality.

Here's a great example: You didn't want to believe I was a spy. You wanted to believe that Bunker was the only one involved, and I kept you believing that. It wasn't reality. Bunker worked for me. You also wanted to think that Petty Officer Clay Young was one of the good guys and was your friend. It wasn't reality. Clay works with me."

Clay gave Matt a look that belied Lester's statements. Matt's heart skipped a beat when he realized Clay was a part of the espionage. While Clay remained silent, Matt saw that Clay's eyes revealed a deep sadness. Matt sensed Clay was not taking any pleasure in Matt's situation. Matt had trickles of sweat running down his back and knew his face was flushed and his forehead moist. His sense of dread was bordering on panic. The only person in the room he thought could help was batting for the other team.

"And while we're talking deception, there's more," Lester continued. "When I searched your locker, I found something I didn't tell you. It was a note with the initials 'RG' and a phone number. I called that number and found that it just happens to be the number for the Subic Bay office of the Naval Investigative Service. That, of course, was very upsetting as it suggested that you either are an agent with the NIS, or you're in contact with the NIS, presumably over what you know about our little operation. Well, son, I did some investigating myself. I have an old buddy who works at the Judge Advocate General's office on base, and they work closely with the NIS. He has access to employee lists, and since he owes me a great deal of money from poker losses, and he was willing to check you out in exchange for the debt going away. He discovered that you're not an employee of NIS and that there is nobody with the initials of 'RG' in the Subic Bay office.

"So, *what would that mean?* I asked myself. It pointed to one of two conclusions. First, you are working undercover for the NIS, or second, you are some rogue do-gooder who thinks he can save the world by bringing down a Soviet spy. I figure it's most likely number two. You want to know why, *Dudley Do-Right*?"

"Sure, senior chief ... why not?" mumbled Matt.

"Well, this comes down to another important poker strategy, *asshole*. You have to be able to read people. Suppose you are sitting across the table with someone who has a king and an ace in their hand, and there's a ten, jack, and queen in the flop. In that case, they sit quietly and don't move because they don't want anyone to know they have potentially an awesome fucking hand. They don't look at their hand at all, they don't smile, and they don't talk. Happens every fucking time. I've watched you from the start on the *Okie*, and you are a fucking wimp. You aren't smart enough or sneaky enough to have pulled off a successful investigation, and it's pretty obvious even to a brain-dead maggot that you obviously don't have the training to be a good investigator. If you were working with the NIS, they would have had enough evidence by now that I would be in shackles in the brig in Yokosuka. I know it because the last place on earth you would be right now is in a hotel room with an enormous Samoan guarding the door and a guy you thought was your friend about to draw a pistol and aim it at your head."

Matt looked at Clay. He was moving his hand to the small of his back, lifting his shirt, and extracting a .45 automatic from his waist. The terror welled up in Matt's chest, and he started trembling, the sweat now profusely dripping from his forehead.

As Clay aimed the pistol at Matt's teeth, Lester, now clearly enthralled with his lecture and gloating over his intelligence and skill, continued. "You know how else I know? I know you stole a roll of film from my gym bag in my quarters, and if that little piece of evidence was in the hands of NIS, they would have come down on me like a swarm of locusts. Do you see teams of NIS agents swarming this hotel? I haven't. So I know that they don't have the film, which means that you still have it. That number you had from the NIS was probably from when you called them and tried to convince them that a highly decorated senior chief petty officer was spying for the Soviets. They're probably still laughing about you. You're a fucking nut, plain and simple, *Do-Right.*"

Despite his dire situation, Matt took the tiniest moment to do a bit of mental gloating himself. Matt told himself *the senior chief thinks he is so intelligent, but he's not as good as he thinks. I'm still screwed, but at least he's wrong.*

"So, Bert, I know you think this is the end, but being a gambling man, I'm going to offer you an opportunity to walk out of here with your life." Matt had to process Lester's statement for a second. A tiny ray of hope?

"I need that film cartridge. If I get it, I know you have nothing on me, and I can let you go because you're no longer a threat to me or my business with the Soviets. Yes, I'll make sure your navy service goes down the fucking tube, but at least you'll have your life."

Matt sat motionless, looking at Lester. "How do I know that if I get it for you, you'll let me go?" Matt asked.

"Common sense, Bert." I'm not a killer. I'm a spy. I just want to preserve my enterprise and get to retirement.

Matt, though far from clear-headed, sat, staring. Lester gave Matt the same in return. Finally, Matt shook his head and stood up, saying, "I guess I have no choice. I'll have to take your word on that." Matt reached into his pocket and pulled out a small film cartridge. He held it in his hand for a moment and then extended his arm and dropped the canister into Lester's open hand.

"Good decision, Bert." Lester smiled at him and shook his head. "Unfortunately, you're not very good at reading people, and you've already forgotten what I told you about the importance of deception. One of the other significant rules of poker is, 'never drink when you're playing for high stakes.' You've been drinking since you came in. You're practically drunk, which means your decision-making skills are lacking. Your ability to perceive reality is diminished, and your reactions are for shit. On the other hand, I have been drinking pure coke all afternoon, thanks to my bartender. Just saying, Matt, you're a fucking gullible, drunk pushover.

"Now, my friend Clay and my other friend Keanu are going to

escort you from this room, take you up the road a bit, and shoot you in the head. Another unfortunate sailor, drunk on liberty, in a dangerous place who happened to piss-off the wrong person."

Matt was laboring to bring any bit of air into his lungs. His head was buzzing. The loudest sound in the room was that of his heart, struggling to burst through his chest.

As Lester was motioning to Clay and Keanu to grab Matt, there was a knock on the door. Clay and Keanu looked at Lester, questioning with their eyes what to do. "Who's there?" shouted Lester.

A momentary pause increased the spy's uneasiness. Then, from the other side of the door came a one-word reply: "Makarov."

Both relief and tension came over Lester's eyes. He motioned to Keanu to open the door. "Pyotr," Lester said, "I thought we were meeting tomorrow."

"I got the news that you had taken matters into your own hands concerning Bertram, Blue, and I came to make sure you didn't fuck this up. I told you you were not to take any action in no uncertain terms but to let me and my agents handle this. You are just a fucking spy, Blue. You don't know what you're doing when it comes to dispatching this situation. I am not understanding your disobedience and am more than a little angry." He turned his head to look Matt over, then walked over to Clay.

"Mr. Clay Young, you ol' sidewinder! It's good to see you, Texas! We got to chaw the rag when we have time! I've got to deal with Blue for now. He done loaded the wrong wagon." Makarov turned back to Lester, his smile melting quickly. "You know, Blue, I've always liked Mr. Young here. He's got common sense. I've got to visit that great state of Texas someday. But right now, I have to clean up your shit."

"Pyotr, look, I'm smarter than you think, and I have this well in hand." Lester, pumped full of adrenaline from his self-evaluated success in outsmarting the asshole, began shouting at Makarov. "You aren't the only one who can handle this!"

Matt watched the escalating anger between Lester and Makarov, then glanced at Clay and Keanu. They were also preoccupied with the unlikely commotion between the two men. Matt realized he would not have a better opportunity for escape now that the KGB was here. Out of pure panic, he turned and feinted toward Keanu. The move took him by surprise. Because of his mammoth size and facial disfigurement, he was unused to having anyone act aggressively toward him. At the last second, Matt put his head down and charged at Clay with all the energy he could muster. By a stroke of luck, his shoulder crashed into Clay's midsection. The impact caused Clay, as he was falling forward, to squeeze the trigger on his weapon, firing a bullet. The unexpected missile grazed Keanu in his right cheek, sending him crashing against the bar, dazed but still standing. Seeing just one small chance for escape, Matt continued running at full speed, out the sliding doors, and onto the lanai. Without pause, he jumped, feet-first, over the railing, hoping against hope he would hit the pool. Matt landed just inches from the swim-up bar but in deep enough water to soften his impact. Scraping both knees on the bottom of the pool, he swam as quickly as he could to the edge and pulled himself out. Shocked pool-goers were shouting and standing as Matt stood up. He glanced at the room above to see Clay and Keanu standing, with Clay aiming his pistol. Matt looked right and left and decided his best option was to dive over the hedge just beyond the pool. The thick shrubs acted as a buffer between the pool and the busy street just beyond. Once he had vaulted the hedge, he ran across the traffic toward the beach.

Looking out the sliding doors at an escaping Matt Bertram, Makarov slowly shook his head back and forth. He turned to Lester and said, "Your actions, Blue, will require us to go after him, now that you've screwed this up."

Lester, looking calm, said, "Relax, Pyotr. I haven't screwed anything up." He reached in his pocket and pulled out the film canister Matt had given him, handing it to Makarov. "I have the only evidence the kid has, and I confirmed that he's not working for anyone else. He's a lone ranger on a mission, and he has no solid evidence against us. We have all the time in the world because he's not getting back on the *Okie* without getting arrested."

Makarov looked at the film canister, turning it slowly in his hand, then shook his head slowly back and forth. He looked into Lester's eyes, holding the canister in front of Lester's face. "You are even more stupid than I gave you credit for, Blue," said Makarov. "This is not your film. It is made in America, not USSR."

The blood drained from Lester's face as he realized Matt had switched canisters. He stood, gaping at Makarov, his lips moving but no sound exiting his mouth. Lester had a moment of reluctant realization that perhaps Matt was more intelligent than he had suspected. He had just been a victim of the deception he was praising moments before.

Makarov shouted at Clay and Keanu to come with him, Lester following close behind. He looked at Lester and said, "We have to find Bertram and kill him, or it will be you who die, and 'dying ain't much of a living, boy.'"

The four men raced out the door, down two flights of stairs, through the hotel lobby, and finally the front door. Clay shouted to the others, "I saw him get out of the pool and jump the hedge on the other side. There's a road there. He's probably trying to get to that."

"Keep your guns hidden," Makarov said, "We can't shoot him in public."

The four ran to the hedge and climbed over in hot pursuit of Matt, who hoped the couple minutes of head start would make a difference in his survival.

18

A NEW VIEW OF SUBIC BAY

R andy and Capelli frantically sped through the streets of Olongapo, heading toward the Whiterock Beach Hotel as rapidly as possible. Fighting the traffic and pedestrians in the road made for less speed than either would have liked. Their final turn was onto Mojica Street and then into the hotel entrance. As they were pulling into the hotel driveway, they viewed a curious and concerning sight. Four men, including Senior Chief Lester and Petty Officer Young, ran through the parking lot and jumped the hedge on the far side. "What the hell is happening?" said Capelli. It was rhetorical. It wasn't apparent to either of them what was happening, only that it was grave.

"One of two things is going on," Randy said. "They could be running away from something in the hotel, or they could be chasing Matt." While there might have been more possibilities, those were the only possibilities they could investigate quickly. They decided the best thing to do would be to split up. Capelli got out of the car to go into the hotel and see if Matt was there, and Randy sped out the hotel entrance hoping to intercept the men.

Capelli ran into the lobby, flashed his NIS badge, which meant nothing to anyone in the hotel, but garnered a lukewarm response from the lobby manager. "We hear shot in room, a man jump out window into pool, and they run through lobby," was all the manager was willing to say.

"What room were they in?" shouted Capelli. The manager told him the room, gave him a key, and Capelli sprinted up to the second floor three steps at a time, down the hallway to the end room, only to find the door open. He drew his weapon and shouted, "Federal Agents! Hands up!" to which there was no reply. He quickly found the room to be empty. The sliding door to the lanai was open, so he went out, looked down at the pool, and then past the hedge. He saw the four men dodging traffic and running toward the beach. At the shoreline, he saw Matt, who was pushing one of the two motorboats on the beach out into the water, then attempting to start the motor.

Matt pulled the starting rope on the engine, hoping to hear it come to life, without success. He looked up and saw the four men about a hundred yards away, sprinting toward him. He shut his eyes, pulled the starter rope, and yelled at the engine, "Start dammit!" This time the engine sputtered to life. He twisted the throttle handle as far as it would go. After a few turns, the engine gasped and stopped. He took a quick glance up, and he saw the men had made half the distance toward him. In addition, however, another threat appeared. Two Filipino men with machetes were running into the water. Matt surmised that the angry men were the owners of the boat he was attempting to steal. Matt gave one more pull at the rope, and the engine came to life. The four spies were entering the water, but their attention was on Matt. They failed to see the two Filipinos, who, now that it looked like their boat was out of their reach, turned their attention to the four pursuers, screaming and waving their machetes. As the boat began moving out to sea, Matt looked back once again. Clay had drawn his weapon. The two Filipinos had their hands up. The momentary distraction had given Matt just enough time to get far enough into the bay that the men could no longer pursue him on foot.

Matt took a deep breath, which felt like the first in several minutes. He kept the throttle completely open and began to concern himself with where he was going to go. He considered making a straight line for the opposite side of the bay. It was not more than a mile across, so he could transit through the bay to the other side where he could disappear. He also had the choice to go north and find a beach there. South, however, seemed like the wisest direction. If he went south, he would eventually reach the naval base, which would provide safety. Either way, he was beginning to feel confident that he had successfully eluded the spies.

That moment did not last long. As Matt looked back toward the beach, his jaw dropped as he saw Makarov, Lester, and Clay snatching the second boat on the beach and steering it in his direction. Matt turned his attention back to the bow of his little boat, struggling to decide which direction he should go. Although it was further than the other side of the bay, he elected to turn south toward the naval base. The closer he got to the base, the higher his odds were of avoiding probable death.

Just as the three men launched their stolen boat, a dirty grey navy carpool sedan careened through bushes bordering the beach, launching its front wheels in the air and scattering dozens of beach-goers in all directions. The car continued moving until it almost reached the water, then came to a sudden stop. Randy peered through the windshield of the car, witnessing a huge Samoan man giving a motorboat a push as its motor throttled to full-speed. Riding in the boat were Makarov, Young, and Lester. Randy jumped out of the car and drew her weapon, but the three in the boat never looked back, failing to see Randy's dramatic entrance to the beach. After successfully launching the motorboat, Keanu turned to see a woman aiming a pistol at him. After considering taking her on, he decided to put his hands in the air. Perhaps a quarter mile beyond the three spies, Randy saw Matt heading out into the bay in another boat.

Capelli came running, struggling for breath, his weapon drawn. Although it was too late to catch the spies, they at least had the big man in custody. "What do we do now?" Capelli implored.

"Get cuffs on this guy, and we'll turn him over to the police until we can figure out his role in all of this." Just as she said this, a jeep with two Filipino police officers raced down the beach toward them. Capelli tried but could not make his cuffs large enough to close on the big man's wrists. After showing their badges and IDs to the police and explaining the situation, the police officers agreed to take him to their local jail and allow the NIS to take custody later in the day.

As the police officers drove off with the huge Samoan man in tow, Capelli said, "At the risk of sounding redundant, what do we do now?"

Randy stared at the disappearing boats, thinking. "We don't have much in the way of tools to use, Leon," Randy reluctantly said. "We have no helicopters, special forces, or much of anyone to help right now, and we've got to get to Matt before they do. Matt could go any direction, but he would be heading toward the naval base if I had to guess. It's his best hope to find safety. We can get on the National Highway heading south, and we just might be able to see him along the way and flag him down. I think it's our best chance."

The Filipino police officers drove their prisoner back off the beach. Instead of going to the police station, they drove the man back to the Whiterock Hotel. Upon arriving, the manager handed each of the officers 500 pesos, and they walked out, leaving Keanu behind.

19

RACE TO THE BASE

Subic Bay had been a flourishing ship refuge since the Spanish conquered the Philippines in the 1500s. It was not used as a port until the 1800s, as the Spanish had foregone Subic Bay and made Manila Bay the primary headquarters. Subic Bay captured the attention of the US Navy when the United States collected the Philippines as a prize in the Spanish-American war. The bay was known for its deep water and protection from the nastier weather in the South China Sea. It had been a primary strategic naval base ever since. Subic had played a significant role in the Vietnam War. Subic Bay's strategic proximity to Southeast Asia made it the perfect location to refuel, repair and reprovision navy ships and troops transiting to and from Vietnam.

The usually tranquil waters of Subic Bay were anything but serene as Matt raced to stay ahead of the boat following behind. Even though three men were in the boat, Matt decided he had made the wrong choice in which boat to steal, as the craft to the rear appeared to be slowly gaining on him. The voice of Matt's high school track coach, saying *look ahead, not behind*, kept resonating in his head, but he couldn't help checking to see how close the boat was to his own. Matt guessed the waves on the bay to be two to three feet high. The small motorboat tossed him up, down, to and fro, sometimes plowing the top of the bow perilously close to submersion. Wet top to bottom since his swan dive into the pool back at the hotel, he was, for the first time since being in Subic, happy that the temperature was in the 90's.

Matt kept sight of the land on his left as he headed south. With the gift of being a few minutes out of range of a KGB weapon, he tried to think through a strategy – *any* strategy that might gain him the ability to lose his pursuers. He knew that if he stayed south long enough, he would enter the waters of the naval base, which was his best bet for safety. Yet the base was still miles away, and that would give the spies time to catch up. For the time being, he decided to stay as close to the shoreline as he could so that he could make landfall if it became clear he could not outrun them.

Still at full-throttle, Matt passed the delta of the Matain River. He had visited the area once on liberty and remembered there were quite a few bars along the beach. It could be an excellent place to land and make a run for it if needed. Yet, he was still hopeful that he could outpace his adversaries and try to reach the base, if at all possible.

Randy and Capelli made it quickly to National Route 305, which, under various names, went all the way to the Subic Bay Naval Station entrance. From Whiterock Beach, the road veered away from the beach. For an excruciating amount of time, they were unable to see the shoreline of Subic Bay. Capelli had an unfolded map on his lap, attempting to help Randy navigate the circuitous route to reach Matt. The word "highway" was at the very least a stretch in terminology. It was more like a parking lot than a highway, filled with stoplights, vendors, traffic, people on bicycles, motor scooters, and pedestrians. "It looks like once we cross the Matain River, we'll be able to see the bay," Capelli said, sounding a bit unsure of himself.

"As soon as we can see it, let's pull over to the side of the road. I'm trying to calculate in my mind if we will be ahead of Matt or behind him when we reach that point, but at least we can take a look," said Randy. It was tough going, as the closer they came to the center of Olongapo City, the worse the traffic became and the more dense the obstacles. As they crossed the bridge over the Matain, they got their first peek at the bay. They continued further south and finally reached a point where they had a good view of the bay. They pulled the car over to the side of the road and climbed out. Neither had binoculars, so they hoped that Matt would stay close to the shoreline where they could see him. They were too far from the beach to be able to shout at Matt as he went by, but they could at least confirm that he was indeed heading toward the naval base.

In a few minutes, they heard the sound of a boat motor. From the north, heading south, they saw Matt, head lowered, apparently in an attempt to streamline his profile and keep the splashing waves from his eyes. Despite knowing that Matt was too far to hear their shouts, they shouted and honked the car horn. The cacophony of horns and noises from the street quickly absorbed their own.

Their shouts ended when they saw the boat pursuing Matt. "Oh my god, Randy, it looks like they might be gaining on him," Capelli suggested unhappily.

"They can't be more than three or four hundred yards away from being within range of their weapons," Randy muttered, slowly shaking her head.

Capelli looked at the map, trying to find a location where they could get close enough to attract Matt's attention. "OK, it looks like about two miles down the highway, there's a big curve. That curve looks like it comes within a hundred feet or so of the beach. I think that's our best bet for getting his attention."

The two watched as the two boats went by, then ran back to the car to find the curve.

In the pursuit boat, Lester sensed that they were making up some distance. Shouting over the sound of the waves, he said to Makarov, "Do you have a plan?"

Makarov smiled. "It looks like we are gaining on him. The bay would be a perfect place to kill him. No witnesses for miles! I think if we can get another hundred yards or so closer, I should be able to get a shot. Unfortunately, I'm carrying a *Samozaryadny Malogabaritny*.

Only good close-up, so we need to be as close as possible for me to be accurate.

"Anyway, I have a backup plan," said the Russian. "I gave Keanu a card with a number. Keanu will have called the number, and my comrades will be on their way." Makarov pulled a small walkie-talkie out of his coat pocket and began speaking Russian into the microphone. The radio buzzed back with another voice, also in Russian. Not short on ego, Makarov gave Lester a consummate look of ego-driven superiority. "You are *not* an agent, Lester. You are just a mole and, perhaps for a few minutes, a boat driver. Let me do the thinking, and I'll turn this hombre into buzzard bait." Lester scowled at Makarov, saying nothing. Clay, hearing what Makarov said, could not help but smile.

Randy and Capelli started the car and pulled out on the road. Just as they merged into the traffic, a black sedan with two men inside almost hit the back of Randy's car. The car swerved to the left at the first opportunity, opened the throttle, and passed the two NIS agents like they were standing still. "What the hell was that?" Randy asked.

"I don't have a good feeling about it, Randy. It was a *Lada*."

"What the hell is that?"

"Soviet sedan."

"Shit."

With the surplus of impediments on the road, the Russian car was not making much progress. Randy kept her distance as it did not appear they had aroused any suspicion from the riders in the car, and she wanted to keep it that way. Capelli continued to navigate while at the same time keeping an eye on the newest players in this dangerous game. As they rounded the turn out of the pocket of urban development and into a much less developed area, they could pick up speed a bit. "We're not more than a quarter of a mile from where we need to stop," Capelli said, "When we do, pull over, and we can run the hundred yards or so to the beach. We'll have to let the Russian car go where it will for now."

With wind and waves splashing his face and blurring his vision, Matt gave a quick look behind, reducing his already poor attitude to complete misery. The spies were gaining on him, and Makarov had his weapon drawn, as did Clay. Matt passed the mouth of another small river and noticed that the shoreline was becoming less urban, with trees close to the shore. He thought about turning in, but with the spies gaining on him, he calculated that he would be a sitting duck if he made landfall. At least if he kept them on the water, his chances of evading a successful shot from the spies were greater.

Matt noted that he was approaching a small peninsula jutting out into the bay about 50 or 100 feet. As he got closer to the peninsula, he could see two people on the beach, jumping up and down, shouting and waving their arms. The sight seemed curious to him, and so Matt steered a bit closer to take a look. He was within three hundred feet of shore when he gasped. He could not believe his eyes. Randy and Capelli were there! Up until this very second, Matt had no idea that they were even aware of his situation. With a shout of joy, he steered even closer to the beach. *This might be my chance*, Matt thought.

Just as a slight glimmer of hope stirred inside him, he heard the shot. A bullet hit the side of the boat. Then another. He knew he would not successfully make it to shore. He screamed as loudly as he could at the two, "Santa Rita River!" and then steered back out into more open water, twisting the throttle, trying to will the boat to move faster. As he entered deeper water, he felt his speed pick up, and gratefully, he started to create a modicum of distance from his malevolent hunters.

"Santa Rita River," Randy repeated. "Yes! He's going to head upriver on the Santa Rita. That's the river that is the outlet for the Shit River. He's going to try to hit the river, and if we're lucky, we can grab him on one of the bridges that go over the river. If not, he could turn onto the Shit River, which would take him practically to the front gate of the naval base."

Capelli studied the map. "The best way to go is just to stay on this road. When it reaches the Santa Rita, it turns and follows the river to Magsaysay Boulevard. There's a bridge across the river at Dewey Avenue. It looks like we could catch him there."

"I hate to ask the question," Randy said reluctantly, "But if those were Soviet agents in that car, what do you suppose their plan is?"

"They looked to me like they knew exactly what they were doing. I think we have to assume the men in the car are in touch with Makarov by radio, and my best guess is they are going to try to intercept Matt the same way we are."

"Look at the map, Leon." Is there a place they could get a shot off before Matt turns onto the Santa Rita?"

Capelli studied the map. "Shit. It looks to me like there is a perfect place they could do it: Kalaklan Point, which is exactly where the Santa Rita flows into Subic Bay. There's a lighthouse there, so it's on higher ground above the bay. They would have a clear shot for a thousand yards out into Subic Bay."

"With the speed at which they passed us, they could be there now," said Randy. "I think we have to try to stop them, or Matt won't have a chance."

"Can we stop them *and* get to Matt?"

Randy didn't have an answer. "We have to try," was all she could say.

As Capelli had conjectured, the two KGB agents turned off the highway at Kalaklan Point and radioed Makarov where they were. Makarov backed down on the boat motor's throttle to give Matt the impression he was gaining ground and dissuade him from changing course, which was perfect for a kill shot.

There was a dirt road that extended to the beach. The agents chose to stop well before the road, as the ground where they were at was a good thirty feet above the beach. It was a textbook location for a profitable sniper shot. The agents exited the car. One of the agents opened the trunk while the other scouted the area for bystanders. There were none. The agent at the trunk unwrapped a blanket. Carefully enveloped like a swaddled baby was a Dragunov SVD-63 sniper rifle with a 375mm PSO-1 telescopic sight. He grabbed two magazines, each containing ten 7N1 rounds. Depending upon the quality of ammunition and the shooter's skill, the rifle was capable of lethal accuracy up to 1400 feet. The agent using the weapon this day was quite proficient. Having the capacity to fire twenty rounds within a minute made the odds good that he would have a successful kill shot, provided his target came close enough. The agent would have also been pleasantly surprised to know that Matt would be passing no more than 75 feet from his position as he would be preparing to turn onto the Santa Rita River. The agent climbed into the back seat of the car, rolled down the window, and rested the barrel on a rolled towel placed on the bottom of the window. The other agent leaned against the car and searched the water with binoculars for the arrival of the boats.

As Randy and Capelli arrived at the turn-off for Kalaklan Point, they could see the black Lada, parked about fifty feet from the beach. They stopped for a moment, watching with horror as they saw the agents preparing for the ambush. From their vantage point, they could see Matt's boat just to the north, apparently still out of view of the KGB agents. "What the hell are we going to do?" Capelli growled.

Randy's response was to slam her foot on the accelerator and race down the road as quickly as she could force the government sedan to go. The agent with the binoculars looked up with complete surprise at the vehicle heading their direction and realized that the driver intended to collide with their car. The realization came too late for the agent to warn his partner or to take action. The agent with the rifle did not even see the car. He had spotted the motorboat, had taken aim, and had started to squeeze the trigger. "Der'mo!" shouted the other agent as Randy slammed on the brakes and rammed the side of the car. The force of the collision sent the sniper and his rifle out the car's window, also throwing the agent with the binoculars a dozen feet in the air.

Matt's first realization that anything was happening on the beach was the sound of a crack on the side of his boat. A bullet had pierced it. He looked back, but he had gained enough distance from the spies to recognize that it couldn't have been them. The sound of the collision on the shore brought his attention to Kalaklan Point. He saw Randy extracting her car from the side of a black sedan and watched as Capelli began shooting in the direction of a man getting up from the ground, drawing a weapon. Randy's car moved quickly in reverse, turned toward the road in a cloud of dust, the target of several shots from the agent.

As Randy drove back toward the main road, Capelli uttered a groan, doubling over in pain. His right arm was bleeding. He had taken a shot in the shoulder from one of the agents. "Ohmygod Leon! You've been shot!" Randy screamed.

"I don't think it's that bad, Randy," Capelli grunted, attempting to minimize Randy's panic. "Keep driving!" As they rounded the corner, the road skirted the left side of the Santa Rita River, they looked to their right at the river, and Matt was parallel with them. Capelli shouted, "We'll pick you up at the next bridge," to which Matt gave him the thumbs up.

The bridge over the Santa Rita was several hundred feet upriver, which took some time to approach. As Matt came closer to the bridge, he quickly looked back and saw the spies making the turn into the river. He saw the bridge coming up quickly and judged that he might not have enough time to climb the embankment and make it to the car. While Matt was driving the boat in the bay, he had become aware that the motor's twist hand throttle had no spring return to stop it if he took his hand off of it. He realized that this could work to his advantage. Matt steered the boat to the middle of the river. He quickly tied a piece of torn fishing net he found in the boat around the tiller on the motor to keep the boat moving in a straight line. He took one last clear breath and dove into the water, allowing the boat to continue its course on the river at full speed.

Matt swam underwater toward the shore, hoping his pursuers did not see him jump. He swam the remaining distance to a place on the shoreline partially hidden by the brush and climbed to the road. Randy opened the car door, and Matt jumped in, entirely out of breath from the climb up the embankment. Randy gave him a quick squeeze from the front seat. "I had no idea you guys were out there looking for me," Matt said, tearing up. "You are the best thing I've ever seen in my life!"

Wasting no time, Randy jammed her foot on the accelerator and turned onto Dewey Street. As she did, she updated Matt on what they had been doing since they learned the senior chief was taking him to the CPO Club for beers. Randy told Matt that they felt the best plan right now would be to get back to base with haste. As they crossed the bridge over the Santa Rita, the spies were just beginning to pass under the bridge, apparently at least momentarily fooled by seeing Matt's boat continuing upriver. Matt was watching out the window to see what they would do. Lester looked up at the bridge as Randy's car passed over and pointed up at them, obviously shouting. Makarov was putting his walkie-talkie to his ear, shouting also. Matt's heart sank as he realized the ruse didn't work. "They've seen us!" Matt shouted.

"All we can do now is get back across the gate to the base before they can," Capelli groaned.

"Shit, Capelli, you've been shot!" Matt exclaimed. He grabbed his handkerchief from his pocket. It was a very wet rag from Matt's swimming pool jump, Subic Bay and the Santa Rita River. Even so, it served as a makeshift bandage for Capelli.

Working hard to muster bravado, Capelli said to Matt, "You said in your note that you had evidence on Lester. Boy, I hope you still do because we've got very little hard evidence right now. We left word with the NIS office that Lester's our guy, and they've been building a dossier on him, but we need a nail to seal his coffin."

Matt reached in his pocket and wrapped in a plastic bag was a film canister. "I think I have what you need right here. I just hope it didn't get ruined from all the water I've seen today."

"That's going to be the most important evidence we have," said Randy, "so it's imperative we get that to base as soon as possible. I'm pretty sure that we disabled the KGB agents' car, so they shouldn't be a problem, and there's no way that the others can beat us back to base. I think we have clear sailing to get there."

No sooner had Randy finished her sentence when, in the rearview mirror, a black sedan with a crumpled side and missing a fender, moving at very high speed, appeared. In a split second, it was on their bumper. The driver was attempting to get to the side of

Randy's car, where it would, no doubt, attempt to spin the navy sedan. Randy banged her fist on the steering wheel. "Shit-shit-shit" was the most she could articulate.

She made a hard left onto an unmarked street, hoping it wasn't a dead-end. "You're doing good, Randy, just breathe," Capelli consoled her. Looking at the map on his lap, he said, "Go left at the end of the street. We'll be going the wrong direction, but we can double-back."

Randy made a hard left turn. Because the Soviets were so close to theirs, they lacked time to react and turn themselves, continuing down Dewey street, forcing them to make a U-turn in the middle of the road. Randy headed back on Canal Street and turned right on Dewey Street again, crossing the same bridge they had just crossed, going the other direction.

Moments after the navy sedan re-crossed the Dewey Street Bridge. The Lada also crossed and then stopped. Makarov, Lester, and Clay got into the car as it once again sped down the street, turning onto the National Highway leading into the sailor district of Olongapo. Makarov, speaking Russian, asked the driver where the second man was. The driver replied that a mysterious car had rammed his car, and the shooter was thrown out and killed. Makarov learned that his agent only saw the car when he stood up after being thrown to the ground himself and fired several shots at the vehicle as it sped away. The agent couldn't tell how many occupants the car had, but he was reasonably sure the driver was female. Makarov turned to Lester and said, "So, chief smart spy, Bertram was a lone wolf, huh? Who is helping him?"

As Lester attempted to stammer out an answer, Clay chimed in, saying, "I know that Matt has a girlfriend, and I saw her at the club in Subic. It must have been her."

"Well, hell," said Makarov. "This lady is as welcome as a porcupine at a nudist colony. The plan just changed. We can't kill Bertram just yet. We have to know who this lady is, and why would she be helping?" Makarov said rhetorically. "We need to snare them both before they get back to base. I don't want them dead until we know who they are and what they are doing. If they are working for an agency, then this operation is finished, and your life in the good old US, Blue, will be over. If the sailor is just a vigilante, then we kill him--probably both of them, and our operation stays intact."

"If he isn't working on his own, you'll live up to your promise, Makarov, and get me to the USSR and a happy retirement, right?" Lester tentatively questioned, nodding his head at the spy.

"Of course, Blue, not to worry," Makarov said, without making eye contact.

As the three Americans sped down the street, Matt shouted, with more than a bit of discouragement in his voice, "I think I see the car behind us a few blocks."

"OK, folks, it's time for a new plan, and quickly," said Randy. She looked at Capelli, the pain evident on his face, then at Matt in the rear view mirror. Neither said a word.

"So. We know that we need to get the film back to base as soon as possible. We know that Leon has to get medical treatment as soon as possible, and we know that these assholes are not giving up easily. I think if we have a fighting chance, we have to split up. Leon: Do you think you could walk a couple of blocks in your condition?" Capelli nodded his head. "Then, we'll do our best to lose them for a minute or two, drop you off, and you can get to the base and call in the cavalry. We'll lure them further away to give you the time you need to get through the gates without being shot, um, *again*."

"I don't like that, Randy. I think we should all get through the gates," said Capelli.

"It won't work. These are trained killers. They are too skilled and too close, and we know they include a sniper and a KGB major. They'll take us out before the marines can figure out what the hell is going on. We'll all be dead, probably along with several marines. No. We *have* to split up."

Capelli lowered his head, then gave it a slight shake. "OK, alright. I ... I can't think of another idea. How about you get somewhere safe? If you can get away from them, stay away from the base entrance because you know they'll have people watching for you. Let me know when you find a safe place, and we'll send the troops to get you."

"That doesn't sound like much of a plan, but it's as much as I can handle at this point. Matt and I will let you know where we end up. If you don't hear from us, you can assume the worst."

The three were traveling up the National Highway, which the locals referred to as Olongapo-Bugallon Road in that part of Olongapo. There was a bridge about a mile away that crossed the Santa Rita River toward the naval base. The black sedan was following closely, but other than tailing them, they made no threatening gestures. Randy suggested it was most likely because they knew they were heading to the base and were in the process of setting up a trap closer to Subic. If Makarov had two agents working with him, he likely could have more. They turned on Rizal Street, which would lead them to Magsaysay Boulevard, and then a straight shot to the base. Capelli searched his street map for the best possible place to try to lose them. "East Third is about three blocks from base. If you let them get close, then take a hard left on third; that should give me the time to jump out without them seeing me."

Randy picked up speed, trying to encourage the spies to follow her more closely, which they obliged to do. As they approached Third Street, Randy took a hard left, and as she hoped, the Lada missed the turn. She pulled over, and Capelli quickly got out. Staring at Randy and Matt, he tried to put on a brave face. "You'll do good. Call when you get someplace safe."

Capelli ducked into the alley, and Randy gunned the car, continuing down Third Street. It didn't take the sedan long to catch up. She turned right on Rizal Avenue. "I'm going to head back to Magsaysay," Randy said to Matt, who had climbed over the back seat and into the passenger seat, grabbing the maps and taking over Capelli's job as navigator. "Open the glove compartment," she told Matt, who complied. In it was a handgun with a shoulder holster. It wasn't just any handgun. It was the NIS Special Agent's standard-issue revolver in 1976: a Smith and Wesson Model 19 .357 Magnum with a four-inch barrel. "I'm sorry I don't have a badge to give you, Matt, but you are, in my mind anyway, a Special Agent now, and I thought you should have a proper weapon."

Matt smiled at the gesture of acceptance Randy offered. Still, his smile quickly turned to more of a grimace, as it was the first time he had considered that he might need to use a weapon in this assignment. A momentary recollection of using a fire extinguisher against Bunker forced him to admit to himself that he had already used a weapon. "Thanks, Randy. I hope it will stay in its holster," he said. He took off the short-sleeved shirt he was wearing, put the holster over his T-shirt on his shoulder, then put his shirt back on.

With a shake of her head, Randy said quietly, "I don't think there is any way we can outrun these guys." Our best scenario will be to lose them for a minute or two and then abandon the car." While it was apparent the car was vulnerable, it felt a good bit safer than the two of them exposed on the street. Yet Matt was unable to suggest an alternative.

The navy sedan, followed closely by the Lada, followed Rizal Avenue and turned right on Third Street. Third Street, while not as busy as Magsaysay, was still filled with traffic, vendors, and pedestrians, and Randy gambled the spies would not attempt an attack where there were witnesses. She intended to get back to the busiest part of the sailor district, Magsaysay Boulevard. There, they would stand a chance of disappearing into any number of alleys, bars or stores, and could find alternate transportation. They traveled up Third Street, and Randy opened up the throttle to the extent she was able. She wanted to make Makarov believe they were trying to get away. To Randy's relief, Makarov took the bait, and the Lada also sped up. When Rizal merged with Magsaysay, Randy took a hard right and gunned the car back toward base. Once again, she waited until Makarov was close behind. Randy made a hard right turn on Third Avenue, once again forcing the Lada to turn around. She quickly pulled the car in front of the Olongapo Police Department, and the two jumped out. Luck was on their side as a Jeepney was stopped across the street, loading and unloading passengers. The two ran for the Jeepney and jumped in the back just as it was pulling out. The gaudy colored taxi passed in the opposite direction of the Lada, just as it turned onto Third, then left on Magsaysay. They watched from the back of the Jeepney as the Lada stopped. Two people got out and cautiously approached the navy sedan, seeing it was empty. As the Jeepney headed down Magsaysay, the four spies stood on the sidewalk in front of the police station. They appeared to be discussing the next steps. It didn't appear that the spies had spotted them, as the Jeepney disappeared on the crowded Magsaysay Boulevard.

20

BAGUIO BOUND

Randy shouted up to the driver, "How far are you going?" Because of the presence of the navy in Olongapo, most people in the area spoke fluent English.

"We go all the way to Baguio this ride," the driver responded.

Randy looked at Matt. "That's pretty far from here. We could get off just outside of town, but Baguio is pretty remote and would probably be a safe and quiet place to wait for help. I can't imagine them looking as far away as Baguio for us. What do you think?"

Matt nodded and handed the driver twenty pesos, sufficient for the three-hour drive. This was the first moment in several hours that either of them had a chance to take a breath and allow themselves to calm down. As they sat in the back of the crowded Jeepney, open on the sides to the fresh air, sounds, and smells of the city, they watched the crowds of people on the street gradually diminish. The large commercial buildings began disappearing, replaced by small homes. Within fifteen minutes, they were in the rural countryside. Matt had never been to Baguio, but it was a popular spot for sailors to spend a weekend on liberty. His friends who had visited talked about the beautiful small city in the mountains of Luzon. The way his friends described it, the countryside surrounding Baguio sounded to Matt a lot like his hometown in the mountains of New Mexico, with tall pines and hill country. Baguio was very different from the Philippines of Matt's experience, mainly the ubiquitous jungles of southern Luzon. Sailors visiting Baguio bought souvenirs of handmade wooden bowls and sculptures for friends and family back home. It was a quaint place with crafts people and open-air markets. If they needed a remote and quiet location, they could not do better than Baguio.

As they drove along the countryside, Matt mused at how beautiful the Philippines were. Most of his experience had been confined to the sailor district of Olongapo, apart from spending a week in the Philippine jungle during jungle survival school. That opportunity did not include time to appreciate the scenery. He resolved that if he got out of this in one piece, he would use future liberties to spend time sight-seeing the countries his ships visited. He stopped, mid-thought as he realized that everything had changed. *If I do survive this assignment, what happens then?* Matt decided to restrain his worry over that issue for another time.

Lester and Clay leaned against the dented Lada, nervously watching Makarov shouting into a pay phone in front of the Olongapo police station. Matt and his lady friend had successfully outsmarted a man who was presumably one of the most skilled KGB agents the USSR employed, and that man was furious. Because the Russian was speaking in his native language, the two sailors-turned-spies could only speculate what Makarov was saying based upon his body language. That led them to believe that he was employing his best skills in crisis management. Makarov slammed the phone on the hook, closed his eyes, took a deep breath, and walked to his agent.

Speaking slowly, he stared the man in the face as the man gawped back, not saying a word. When Makarov finished talking to the agent, he approached the two Americans.

"I have authority to employ every asset currently available in this country to find these troublemakers," Makarov said with his most serious tone. "You need to know that I am taking these measures because your information has been valuable to us in the past, and we wish to continue the flow. I cannot believe that if the US government is involved in this matter, the two would still be on their own. There would have been reinforcements long before this, so it is worth the risk to continue pursuit." Gone were Makarov's amusing Russian accented cowboy colloquialisms. In their place were the words of a capable Soviet spymaster.

As Makarov glared at the sailors, two sedans pulled up behind the smashed-up Lada. Three men exited each vehicle. Dressed relatively casually, they held the appearance of tourists rather than KGB agents. Makarov engaged in intense discussions with these men. Makarov turned to Lester and Clay, and after a moment's hesitation, said, "You are going in pursuit with us. It is not because you have any skills I need. Your inept actions caused this, and you need to share in the responsibility of capturing them. We have agents on each major highway going north and south and more men searching the neighborhoods here in Olongapo. We have people at the gates of the naval base to be certain they do not attempt to find safety on their base. You will both participate in this search while I go to our office here to monitor the search. You will do whatever my men tell you to do without question. Do you understand?"

Both sailors nodded their heads, and without further conversation, the cars left in different directions.

21

A RESPITE IN THE PINES

The trip to Baguio was uneventful. The Jeepney occasionally stopped to allow riders off and to pick others up. Matt and Randy kept a close watch on the road behind for any signs of being followed. Other than an airplane flying overhead for a short time, the proverbial coast seemed clear enough. As the time passed, each began to relax, if just a bit. The adrenaline was gradually draining from Matt's brain. He was feeling shaky and more aware of the fear and nervousness that filled his consciousness. Even so, with each passing mile further from Olongapo, Matt felt more at ease.

As the jeepney left the jungles of southern Luzon, Matt could feel a gradual increase in altitude. The usual stifling heat and humidity steadily declined, slowly replaced by cooler air. Jungle trees and broadleaf undergrowth transformed into forests of Khasia pine and grasses. The jeepney made its final stop at a makeshift terminal on Hilltop Street, not far from Baguio's town center. The two stepped from the rear of the truck, and Matt, looking from left to right, said, "Where now?"

"I got this covered," Randy quickly replied. "We'll check into the Pines Hotel. We might as well enjoy ourselves."

As they began walking, Matt asked, "How is it that you know this area?"

"I had a case here once. A sailor killed another sailor in an Olongapo bar, and we tracked him here. I had a chance to take some time off and stayed at the Pines. It's an icon of Baguio. I think it was built around 1905. They have some great posters in the lobby where its owners touted the hotel as the 'Pinehurst of the East' and as the 'Premiere Resort Hotel of the Orient.' The original hotel was destroyed during World War II but was rebuilt in another location not far from the first. Lots of tourists stay in the hotel, so it's a fascinating place to people watch."

As they walked through the center of town, they stopped to purchase a change of clothes and some essential toiletries. It was only at that point that Matt realized he was still wearing the same clothes he had been wearing since that morning, which had been through pool water, ocean spray, rancid river water, and an enormous volume of sweat.

After they had the necessary changes of clothes, the two walked the mile or so to Luneta Hill, and Matt smiled when he saw how beautiful the Pines Hotel was. It looked like something out of the Catskills, not that Matt had ever been. He had read about the annual summer trips people from New York City made there and had seen photos of the beautiful resorts. The hotel had an air of quiet elegance. It was surrounded by tall pines. Broad steps led up to an exceptionally large front porch, leading to the hotel's elegant lobby. Once inside the hotel, the faces changed dramatically from those on the street. Guests were obviously from around the globe, with Europeans, Arabs, Africans, Asians, Americans, and many other nationalities among them. The hotel staff was consistently Filipino, each in uniform, dressed as he imagined staff in the Catskills were attired.

The hotel, not coincidentally, had a contract with the US Navy to serve its visiting dignitaries and senior officers. As such, Randy secured two rooms by providing her NIS badge and ID and completing a US government requisition document. Matt assumed the restaurant and room service would be just as accommodating.

The desk clerk assigned them adjoining rooms. As they made their way up the stairs, Randy suggested they get showers and perhaps take naps before finding food, to which Matt readily agreed. "I'll make a call to Subic to let them know where we are, and, with any luck, our folks will arrive quickly. Until then, I suggest we have a well-deserved meal and a good night's sleep."

Matt entered his room, and shutting the door behind him, took an intense breath. It was the first time he felt safe that day, a day that at times could very well have been his last. He peeled off his soiled and ripe-smelling clothes, turned on the shower, and stepped in, feeling the warmth of the water on his sore body. He could have stayed in the shower all night. He toweled off, put on his new clothes, and sank into an overstuffed armchair beside the bed.

The knocking on the door jarred Matt awake from a sleep to which he did not even realize he had yielded. From behind the door, he heard Randy's voice. "Wake up, Petty Officer Bertram!" It's time to find some good food!" When Matt opened the door, Randy stood in the doorway wearing a skirt and buttoned blouse, fresh make-up, and in Matt's eyes, was the loveliest woman on earth. He had never wanted to kiss anyone as much as Randy at that moment.

The hotel was located on Luneta Hill, just south of the old Baguio Square. No more than two blocks away was Sessions Road, known to be the best place to eat in Baguio. They found a small restaurant located in a converted home with an outdoor patio. Both enjoyed excellent traditional Filipino food. They washed it down with the national beer of the Philippines, San Miguel, and they could hear live music coming from a bar two doors down. The early evening air was exhilaratingly cool and washed over them like a soft blanket. After they finished their food, they ordered more beers. "Matt, you were amazing today. I am so proud of your bravery. You kept your wits about you as though you were a seasoned veteran, and if it weren't for you outsmarting those assholes, we know what could have happened."

Matt, blushing, said, "Thanks Randy, but it's you who was the brave and smart one. Your quick thinking saved our lives. I can't tell you how much I respect your skills as a Special Agent. You are also the most beautiful woman I have ever known." As soon as those words left Matt's mouth, he was mortified. He did not mean to say that last statement. The weariness and a couple of beers had impaired his ability to self-edit. He looked at Randy, chagrined, and said, "I, um, I didn't mean to say that last part out loud." However, as he looked at Randy, he saw that she seemed genuinely flattered and did not appear to be outraged in the least.

"Thank you, Matt, that's very kind," Randy managed to say. She stood quickly, saying, "We probably should get going. Even though it's early, it has been an exceedingly long day."

The two strolled the few blocks back to the Pines Hotel, and as they began walking up the steps to the porch, Randy stopped, looking at Matt. "Matt, sometimes the adrenaline causes you to feel things that in retrospect were more imagined than real. I am attracted to you, also. But you're involved far over your head in this mess, and it would not be even a little appropriate to take it any further. *For now.* Let's get this behind us and see where things go, OK?"

For now? There is a chance she might consider something more than a professional relationship? Those words were virtually all Matt heard of the conversation. "Fair enough, Randy, I completely understand." After a few seconds of awkward gazes, they continued their walk into the hotel, up the stairs, and to their rooms. Matt walked Randy to the door. She inserted the key, turned the lock, and opened the door. From the dark, a heavily accented voice emanated. "I have a gun. Both of you come in, or I will kill you." Each looked down the hallway to see if escape was possible, only to see two men, one on either side of them, holding pistols. A quick glance at one another, and Randy and Matt walked into the room to see Senior Chief Lester, Clay Young, and Major Pyotr Makarov, all with pistols aimed at them.

22

A STRUGGLE TO GET TO BASE

Randy and Matt had dropped Leon off two long blocks from the bridge on Magsaysay Boulevard. At the end of the bridge would be Leon's goal: the main gate to Subic Bay Naval Station. As he exited the car, he quickly ran to the doorway of a building and watched the car speed off. A few seconds later, the damaged Lada sped past him. It appeared to Leon that the occupants had not noticed him exit the vehicle, as the Lada increased speed as it went by him. He looked at his shoulder with Matt's makeshift bandage and realized he was losing blood much faster than he had previously guessed. He was already feeling dizzy, and the pain was penetrating. His goal now would be to get back to base, connect with the NIS office and involve them in the process of extracting Randy and Matt. Based on his physical condition, Capelli hoped he could make it to the base entrance without passing out or attracting the attention of whatever KGB operatives were probably surveilling that area. He anticipated that if he could get to the gate without looking suspiciously impaired, he would be able to slip past the Soviets unnoticed. For the moment, just making it to the gate was his biggest challenge.

Capelli decided to turn directly onto Magsaysay at the corner, mainly because the streets were pretty crowded. He would more easily blend in with the fusion of sailors and locals. Capelli stopped at a sari-sari store, a Filipino version of a US convenience store. He purchased a T-shirt, a long-sleeved shirt, and a cold beer and asked the proprietor if there was a private place to put them on. He placed a $50 bill on the counter. The old man behind the counter gazed at Leon's blood-soaked arm, then at the money, and directed him to a curtained doorway. Leon moved behind the curtain, sitting on a bench for a moment's respite. He removed his shirt and guzzled the beer. He then wrapped the t-shirt around his wound, tying a makeshift tourniquet, and put the long sleeve shirt on. He hoped the additional covering would be sufficient to hide the wound and the blood for the ten minutes or so it would take to get him to the bridge. Leon finished the beer in seconds, grateful for the tiny rush of pain relief, thanked the owner, and stepped back out on the busy street toward his goal.

The beer and clean dressing had helped. Leon was doing his best to try to walk normally -- not too fast, which would fuel blood loss, but not too slow, as he was aware that at the pace he was losing blood, he had a finite amount of time before shock would set in.

The sound of his own beating heart in his ears was a cue that he needed to increase his speed. He was sweating now, another sign that he was close to shock. He tried to focus with laser clarity on his goal, which, much to his relief, was now in sight, perhaps a football field away. As he approached the bridge, he bolstered his effort to blend in with the sailors coming back from liberty, struggling to smile. He carefully observed people standing or sitting on the bridge in an attempt to identify any nefarious sentinels. Leon's years as an investigator paid off this time. He immediately identified two men, who were watching the passersby with interest, feigning casual people-watching. The two were, to Leon's trained eye, obviously something much more perverse.

His hopes mounted as Capelli successfully walked past the two men, watching them scrutinize him but making no move toward him. Just as Capelli passed the men, a wave of nausea swept over him.

Helplessly, he observed his brain dim, and he began hearing a loud buzzing in his ears, drowning out all of the many sounds on the busy bridge. His world was gradually losing color, and all around him, the spectrum turned to brown. He knew he was well on the way to passing out. Seizing the last bit of energy he had, Leon grabbed his wallet with his NIS badge in it and attempted to run toward one of the three marine sentries. The run appeared more like a drunken stagger, which was a common sight for the marines. Even so, all three marines drew their weapons. As he approached the closest marine sentry, he held his badge as high as possible and said, "I've been shot. Please help me," and fell into the arms of the young marine, unconscious.

Leon heard sounds before he could see or move. The sounds, at first, were not discernable but gradually became recognizable as people speaking. The blackness gradually gave way to brightness as he became conscious that someone was lifting his eyelid and shining a light in it. He tried for a moment to speak, but the sounds he made were more like gargles than words. "Special Agent Capelli – Leon, can you hear me?" came a voice.

"You better not be God," Leon replied, "or I'll be pretty pissed."

The men in the room gave relieved chuckles, and another of the men spoke. "Capelli, I'm Director Jordan Connery, C.O. of the NISO here in Subic Bay. The Doc here says you were close to checking out from blood loss. A little surgery on that shoulder and about three truckloads of blood, though, and you're going to be right as rain."

"How long have I been out?" Capelli replied.

"About four hours."

"Thank God. There's still time. We need to talk, Director, right now."

"We do. We found an undeveloped canister of Soviet film in a bag in your pocket. While you were out, we had the film developed. We found photographs of an unbelievable array of Top-Secret Documents, crypto cards, and more. Does this have to do with the investigation onboard the *Oklahoma City*?"

Capelli, struggling to stay conscious and coherent, said, "It's conclusive evidence, Director. Our undercover radioman took them from a gym bag belonging to Senior Chief Morris Lester. But there is much more I need to tell you. The KGB is pursuing special Agent Glasscock and our undercover man. We need to find them before the KGB does."

"We are already on it," Connery replied. "Randy called into our office and let them know where they are. She didn't give any other information other than that, but we've dispatched three of our agents and one *element*. Sorry, that's a term you probably don't know: Four members of SEAL Team One. They're riding along, just in case our agents need assistance. Now, if you have the energy, fill us in on the details."

As Leon briefed the Director and the other Special Agents in the room, there was a gradual realization that this was perhaps the most extensive spy ring in the Navy's history. As the Director and his staff left Leon to recover, Connery said to his assistant, "We need to get a call to HQ. They are going to shit their pants."

As the door to Leon's room shut, the nurse administered something that made him feel like he was floating on a cloud, and, although it had been a long time since he had done so, he said a quiet prayer that his friends would be OK.

23

UNWELCOME VISITORS

T he silent, stony stare on Makarov's face was as disconcerting as the Stechkin suppressed machine pistol he held in his hand. Every passing second felt like an hour to Randy and Matt, who each sat eight feet from Makarov, directly facing him. Lester and Clay were armed also. Lester had a look on his face that spoke nothing but anger. Clay, on the other hand, appeared almost as uncomfortable as the two NIS agents.

Makarov stood and went to the window, shutting the curtain. He raised a finger in the air and finally spoke: "This meeting, I promise, will be very short," he said, almost casually. "But before we begin, it would seem prudent to be certain you are not armed. He turned to Clay and said, "Hey pardner, would you give these two the once over to make sure there aren't any six-shooters?"

Clay looked at Makarov, then at Randy and Matt, and hesitantly walked toward them. He opened Randy's handbag and withdrew her service revolver. He handed it to Makarov, who examined it and placed it on the nightstand. Clay moved to Matt and began patting him down. When he reached Matt's side where his weapon was holstered, he hesitated for just a second, then stood and said, "He's not armed." Matt sat in shocked silence as he knew full well that Clay had felt the weapon under his shirt.

"Interesting," exclaimed Makarov. "The lady friend is armed, but the desperado is not. What do we make of that? You may be wondering why we have gone to such lengths to find you. I find it important to understand who you work for, if anyone, or just *patriotic* Americans protecting your silly capitalistic ideals. Once we are done with that, like your Mr. Eastwood says, 'The way I figure, there's really not too much future with a sawed-off runt like you.' Either way, you're going to be buzzard bait." Clay mused at how Makarov could have the demeanor of a stone-cold KGB one moment and then put on the goofy façade of a Hollywood cowboy the next.

Makarov had never concerned himself much with political philosophy. He had picked a side early on and had created a good life for himself. He was loyal to the KGB, and little else was a concern of his. Makarov had been born in 1920, just three years after the Bolshevik Revolution. It was a turbulent time as Russia cast off an entire monarchy to become the USSR. In 1921, as Makarov turned one year old, Russia was in the midst of a bloody civil war and famine. He watched as Joseph Stalin brought the country under significant control as he forced industrialization on a nation that had been largely agrarian up until that time. Makarov had been conscripted into the Russian army in 1937 and served admirably. He rose through numerous promotions to become a senior intelligence officer during World War II. Following the war, he joined the People's Commissariat for State Security or the NKGB. In 1954, Soviet premier Nikita Khrushchev established the *Komitet Gosudarstvennoy Bezopasnosti*, or the Committee for State Security, more commonly known as the KGB. Now, at 56 years old, Makarov's family *was* the KGB. What the KGB believed was all that mattered to Makarov. It was his entire life. And these two tiny piss ants were a threat to the KGB. Therefore, that threat needed to be eliminated and quickly. He hoped they were vigilantes because if they were not, there would be hell to pay from his superiors, and his place in his KGB family would be at risk.

"So this is my question for you. Who do you work for? Yourselves, or someone else?"

Randy could see that it was most likely in their best interest to inform Makarov that the NIS was her employer and that Lester and Young would go down hard. She started to answer just as a knock came at the door. Clay opened it, and one of the other agents came in. In Russian, he told Makarov that one of the agents watching the gate at Subic Bay was on the phone with important information that could not wait. Angrily, Makarov stood up. "Blue, come with me. Clay, my compadre, I'm promoting you to be my right-hand man. Keep an eye on these goat heads. That means if they so much as sneeze, you be quick out of the chute. My comrade will be outside the door." With that, the two rushed out, slamming the door behind them.

It was just the three of them in those few minutes. Matt, a look of baffled curiosity on his face, said, "Clay, what the fuck? Why didn't you take my gun?"

"I didn't know what to do, Bert," Clay blurted out. "I'm in *way* over my head. I was just making some money to take care of my kid, and everything I did for and with the senior chief seemed pretty harmless and a big "fuck you" to the navy at first. By the time I realized that I was a... well, a traitor, I was just in too deep. This situation is not what I planned, and I don't want to be a part of it anymore. I like you, Bert. I'm sorry. I'm so sorry this happened. I couldn't shoot a rabbit, much less a person." Tears growing in his eyes, Clay shook his head. "Help me get out. Please. I just don't know what I can do."

"It's pretty bad timing that you decide this now, Petty Officer Young," Randy interjected. "But it's all we have. You need to know that we are both Special Agents in the Naval Investigative Service. Your actions today will have a lot to do with the consequences you receive. But that's for discussion later. We have to get out, now, before Makarov gets back."

"Bert? Are you a fucking undercover agent? I was screwed from the start, wasn't I?"

Matt stood up and touched Clay on the shoulder. "You're doing the right thing now, man. That's what counts." Clay did not look convinced, but Matt could see a bit of relief come over his friend's face.

Makarov entered Matt's room next door and picked up the phone. The agent in Subic explained to Makarov the events that had unfolded at the main gate that afternoon and the wounded NIS agent collapsing in the marine's arms. In Makarov's mind, the timing was a bit too proximate to be unrelated to the events with Bertram, which meant that it was likely that the US Government *was* involved in this. Knowing this changed everything.

His immediate reaction was to pull the plug, get the hell out, and give up this intelligence resource that had provided so much rich material. Unfortunately, the information he had just received was not entirely conclusive. One downside of being in the KGB was that mistakes were not only career-enders. They were very often life-enders. Makarov decided not to take that chance. The next decision was to consult with Moscow and necessitated a call to his superiors for guidance. He hung up the phone, took a deep breath, and dialed the number that would connect him with the director of the First Chief Directorate of the KGB.

As Makarov began dialing, Clay walked to the door of Randy's room, opened it, and said to the agent outside, "Hey, dude, something's happened, and I need your help." The agent drew his weapon and walked past Clay into the room to see Matt standing, weapon drawn, aiming at the agent's chest. Without a moment's hesitation, the agent squeezed his trigger as calmly as if he were waving. Before the trigger could release, however, a shot exploded from behind the agent. The bullet from Clay's weapon hit the agent in the back of his head, entered his brain, and exited with a fountain of blood from his eye. The agent was dead before he hit the ground. Clay was shaking uncontrollably, alternately looking at the dead man on the floor and Matt. He dropped his weapon on the floor as though it was radioactive. Randy shouted to Matt and Clay that it was time to run. Randy picked up the dead agent's pistol and three magazines, handed Clay the gun he had dropped, and the three ran out of the room toward the stairs. Randy led the way, followed by Matt, with a wobbly Clay

Young in tow. They were ten feet down the hallway when Makarov and the second agent rushed out the door, guns drawn.

Clay turned back and fired twice in their general direction, hitting a light on the ceiling above his head with his first shot and a fire extinguisher with his second. Both bullets ricocheted in the general direction of their pursuers. That was enough to buy a second or two while Makarov and his comrades ducked. The pause gave them another few steps toward the stairs. If they turned the corner to the stairs, they would have some protection from return fire. As the three approached the stairs, the shots from Makarov's weapon injected a unique frightening sound. Makarov was using his Stechkin machine pistol with a suppressor, better-known as an APS. The automatic pistol had a twenty-round double-stacked magazine and was capable of firing 750 rounds per minute.

As Makarov squeezed the trigger, the weapon released a rapid-fire spray of 9-millimeter bullets, allowing for a wide jet that could cut a person in half. One unfortunate downside of the pistol was that it was delicate and easily jammed. The Americans became the beneficiaries of this design defect. Makarov had fired ten rounds of the twenty available when the case of the tenth round jammed in the extractor. It would take a few seconds to unjam the case, and it was just enough time for the three to make the turn down the stairs.

As they began running through the lobby, Matt stole a quick look behind. Clay had stopped and was bent over, holding his gut. He straightened up, trying to run, and when he did, Matt saw the reason he was no longer running with them. Clay had been hit by several of the bullets fired by Makarov. As Clay fell, face-forward, Matt turned to help. Randy grabbed Matt and said, "No, we have to go!" and the two left their friend and unexpected savior to his fate.

Makarov stood at the top of the stair, assessing his next move. The lobby would be public, and there would be an excess of witnesses. Chasing the two through the entrance would be a wrong choice. He ran back into Matt's hotel room and looked out the window toward the hotel's front. He watched his enemies cross the street and go inside a church. *Perfect*, he thought. *A place of sanctuary with a shortage of witnesses.* They gathered their weapons. Makarov stood for a moment and stared at an untenable sight. One of his best agents, a highly trained and dependable man, was dead, on the floor. The American sailors, including Clay Young, whom he had believed he could trust, were gone. "How in the hell could this have happened?" he thought. It was not conceivable that amateurs had managed to escape. He thrust his fist on the end table, cracking it in two. Underneath the chair in which Randy had been sitting was her handbag. In his fit of rage, Makarov failed to notice the purse, which contained her NIS badge and ID.

Makarov, his remaining two agents, and Lester exited the hotel room, and left through the back stairs. Makarov had not completed the call to his superiors for guidance. Rationalizing to himself, he decided that he could make a valid argument that the situation was far too exigent to make the call at this point. The Russian language can be very colorful. One of Makarov's most-used slurs was *podonok*. The word is translated into English in various ways: Jerk, schmuck, riffraff, and crud, but the closest English equivalent is *fucker*. That is how Makarov liked to use the term. At this point, he did not care whether the podonoks were vigilantes or CIA, and he did not care what the Directorate would order. He was happy that his call to the Director did not connect. The KGB Major was livid at having been thwarted twice by those two, and he quite simply wanted them dead. Reason left the brain of the disciplined spy, replaced by the basest of human emotions: Hatred and the desire to murder. He would not allow these podonoks to humiliate him again.

24

CAT AND MOUSE

The four Soviet spies crossed the street, weapons hidden. Makarov stopped them before going in, spoke to one of the agents in Russian, who nodded and silently left the group, heading somewhere Makarov chose not to reveal to Lester. The Senior Chief's head was spinning as he quickly reviewed the bizarre day he had experienced, that was not over yet. It had started so well. He had been firmly in charge, as he was used to being. It was going to be *his* day to be the cunning and clever controller of Bertram's fate. He had happily embarked upon the day, believing it would impress Makarov and elevate Lester's status in his eyes. He was going to use his passion, poker, to bring Matt to his knees and prove that he, a senior chief and master spy, was the superior strategist and maestro of deception and authority. Now he found himself in quite a predicament. Lester was not a trained fighter, assassin, tracker, or even slightly proficient with weapons. He lacked all the skills that Makarov had, and the skills he did have were not helpful in this situation. Lester was just a greedy man with no loyalty and a senior enlisted position in the US Navy which allowed him to gather extremely sensitive intelligence and pass it on for a paycheck. Had he had a bit more insight, he would have realized that he was merely a massively immoral, well-paid clerk. That lack of insight left him worrying that if Matt and the lady were working for the government, he would be arrested and tried as a spy. In terms of the volume of information he passed on, he was most likely the most prolific spy in US history; a benchmark that until today was a source of immense and warped pride. Suppose Bertram was not some sort of agent, which Lester desperately hoped. In that case, they could kill him and his lady friend, go back to Subic, and he could return to his comfortable, perverse life. As much as Makarov had lost his sense of perspective as a calculating spy, Lester formulated at that exact moment a highly rationalized belief that Matt must be just a misguided do-gooder in over his head. He needed to die, and then life would be good.

As the agent Makarov had sent on an errand silently walked away from them, the group of three remaining spies watched at least a dozen police cars arrive in front of the Pines Hotel. The police rushed into the hotel, weapons drawn. From across the street, the three spies watched the police disappear into the hotel, then slowly walked up the steps to the church.

Iglesia de la Sagrada Concepción, a substantial stone church and monastery, was built in the early 1800s by Father José Del Rosario, an ardent advocate for the reform of Spanish rule in the Philippines. Father Del Rosario's role in Spanish politics led to a first-hand experience of Spanish justice, as he was jailed, tried, and summarily disemboweled and beheaded. Makarov would have smiled had he known the history of the spot he intended to murder the podonoks.

While smaller and less ornate than its European counterparts, Iglesia de la Sagrada Concepción was nevertheless a beautiful work of architecture. As Father Del Rosario was overseeing the building of the church in the early 1800s, his vision was to create his own version of St. Peter's Basilica in Rome, which included multiple layers of basement spaces, including catacombs and tombs for deceased priests, monks, and church leaders. The church had a large narthex at the entrance. The narthex was adorned with several statues by local sculptors and artists. Attached to the church was a small monastery that now served as a large storage area since the monastery was permanently closed during the Japanese occupation in World War II.

As Randy and Matt entered the church, their first thought was to find an exit. There was a likelihood that the spies had seen them enter the church, and even if they didn't, they weren't going to take any chances. "I don't know much about Catholic churches," said Matt, "but do they have a back door?"

"Churches like these have lots of doors," replied Randy. "The trick is to find one that gets us out fast." The two entered the church's sanctuary, their flight precluding appreciation for the hundred-foot ceiling above their heads, the dozens of paintings and frescoes, and the classical beauty of the massive room.

"I don't see any doors," bemoaned Matt. He found it odd that at this moment, he was concerned for the parishioners worshipping in this church if a fire ever broke out.

"There have to be doors," said Randy. They were in the middle of the nave, heading toward the altar at the far end of the church. There was a Bema, a raised platform the clergy used during mass. In the center was a large altar. Behind the altar was a large semi-circular bay. As they ran toward the altar, hidden in the bay they saw stairs. The stairs were a welcome exit from the sanctuary. Having no other choice, they raced downward. Just as they disappeared behind the altar, the spies entered the sanctuary. They momentarily stopped, assessing the site. It would be a perfect place for the two Americans to ambush them.

Makarov told the two other men to spread wide through the nave and aisles. "Look between the pews. It is a good place to hide out," he said in English. The three advanced carefully, but it became evident to Makarov that Bertram and his lady-friend had found a way out of the sanctuary. They picked up their pace, eventually finding the stairs hidden behind the altar. They advanced carefully down the stairs, the two agents in the lead, followed by Makarov with Lester trailing.

Matt and Randy reached the bottom of the staircase. Matt wondered if he could find a torch to light when suddenly overhead fluorescent lights came on. Randy was standing next to a switch, smiling. "Torches would have been pretty melodramatic," Randy said.

Although it was dim, as several fluorescent bulbs had burned out, there was enough light to see their surroundings and find their way. The lights revealed a truly medieval scene. There was a complex of mausoleums, each with an engraving memorializing what were presumably priests who had served at the church. In the middle of the complex was an aedicula commemorating and doubtless containing the remains of the headless Father Del Rosario.

The passage continued down a dark hallway, which appeared to be the only direction they could go. There were several doors along the hallway. Randy and Matt methodically tried each door they passed. Some were locked, and some led to other rooms, none of which appeared to be good opportunities to find an exit. The final door opened into another stairway, heading further down. They looked at each other, and with a shrug of the shoulders, Matt started down the stairs. As they reached the bottom of the stairs, their adversaries appeared at the top of the stairs. Randy turned and fired her weapon twice, hitting the remaining Soviet agent in the chest, causing Makarov and Lester to drop and find cover before returning fire. The spies returned fire, but their prey had disappeared through another door by the time they had done so.

Once again, now two stories below the church, the two found themselves passing more graves and tombs. These tombs became more modest with each passing step until, finally, they were running past catacombs containing visible skeletons, sometimes stacked ten or fifteen high. Matt found himself hoping he would not be the next addition to the population of bones in this completely disturbing chamber.

They turned the corner, hearing the echoing footsteps of the predators behind them on the concrete floor, increasing their speed despite minimal lighting and narrow, sometimes treacherous passageways. They turned yet another corner, finding a hallway much like the first, with doors on each side. The first door they approached was a small closet. The second door was locked. The third had a sign over it that said "monasteryo." Randy tried the door, and with a creak it opened. They entered a large room with stairs, this time leading up. As they shut the door behind them, Matt locked it, and they ran for the stairs.

They raced up the new set of stairs and found yet more doors. The first door was locked. The second door, with a push of Matt's shoulder, opened into a much larger room. This room had six or seven rows of storage shelves filled with boxes, religious paraphernalia, and maintenance and painting supplies. As Randy shut the door behind her, she was thrilled to discover the door could be locked and bolted. Randy quickly turned the ancient bolt. This room had ambient light coming from small basement windows, but they could see little else.

Below them, they could hear their pursuers trying doors and shooting locks off of the doors. "We have to hide. They'll find this room in no time," Randy said.

Looking around, Matt said, "Look up at the top storage shelf. It looks like there are boxes up there. What if we climbed and surrounded ourselves with the boxes? They might look in the room and see that we aren't in here and move on."

"I don't like that idea much," said Randy, "but I can't think of anything else." They climbed up to the top shelf using each of the lower shelves. The top shelf was about eight feet above the ground, higher than the line of sight. They found enough boxes to create a fence of cardboard around themselves. It was very tight, but Randy and Matt squeezed together to fit.

Below them, they could hear their pursuers moving from room to room. Random shouts and door locks being shot fostered fear in Randy and Matt. They listened to voices and footsteps clapping on the stone floor, gradually progressing in their direction. Randy started intentionally slowing her breath down and encouraged Matt to do the same. He realized this was the first opportunity to rest and catch their breath since entering the church. It felt good to have a few moments to relax just a bit. Matt realized his muscles ached from tension, and he suddenly felt more tired than he had felt in quite some time. His mind went back to his jungle survival training, climbing into a tree at night as high as he could climb and resting, out of reach of the jungle animals intent on making him their dinner. Matt's head pushed against Randy's with his nose against her hair. *Wow, her hair smells terrific and sexy,* he thought to himself, and just as quickly, he thought, *why in the hell is that what I'm feeling right now? This is a terrifying situation!*

"Matt, I need to tell you something," Randy whispered. She looked down, taking a deep breath. "Things are not looking good, and I would not forgive myself if I didn't tell you. I like you—a lot. I'm probably making a mistake saying this out loud, but I want you. *Badly.* And I wouldn't be doing this unless I thought we were probably going to die, and... and, um... if we get out of here, I'll probably regret doing this, but what the hell." With that, she turned her head so that their lips met and softly touched her lips to his. Matt thought to himself, *and this is not just an 'oh I'm going to die, goodbye' kiss.* No, it was a passionate, soft, sensual, and over-the-top romantic kiss. Matt, now sure that he was in the most bizarre situation of his lifetime, kissed back, raising his hand to her cheek and brushing her hair behind her ear. And for just a second, Matt could not have cared less whether he died that day or not.

A hand rattling the doorknob and attempting to push it open ended the kiss. Randy and Matt both held their breath to see if they would shoot the lock. The blast of a gun answered that question. The sounds of shoes on the floor were like small explosions as someone entered. The steps indicated it was just one man in the room. Perhaps they had split up to multiply their search efforts. The footsteps suggested the man had begun searching the aisles of shelves, thoroughly, systematically combing every potential hiding place.

The set of steps turned onto the row in which they were hiding. Because boxes surrounded them, they could not see what the hunter was doing. Still, he was moving slowly and discernibly, being methodical. Not five feet from them came the sound of a loud, reeking fart. *Lester* thought Bert. *Nobody else can lay a wind loaf like that.* He shook his head at the peculiar predicament they were in, and he imagined, just for a second, telling his grandchildren this story. He hoped he would live long enough to get out of the church, much less to have grandchildren. Finally, the steps moved back to the door, and Lester shut the door behind him, saying, "Nobody was in there." The sounds of the footsteps began fading, suggesting the sound of retreat until they could no longer hear steps or voices. Both Matt and Randy took deep breaths, at last able to let some of the tension go.

"Now what?" Matt asked.

They both scanned the room. The only door out of the room was the one the two came in through. "We could wait until they move on and double-back the way we came in," Randy said.

"Or," said Matt, looking at the basement window. We can go through the window and get out of here."

Randy looked closely at the windows for the first time. "I like that idea if we can get it open," replied Randy. "I hate the thought of leaving the way we came. They could have left people at the front to watch."

With that, Matt got down off the shelf they were on, helping Randy down, holding her, perhaps, just a little too long. Randy turned and climbed up below the window. It was looking out on the street. She looked for a latch but found that it had long ago rusted off. "I can't open the latch," she said in frustration. Matt appeared beside her, a heavy silver candle holder in his hand, and using it as a hammer, broke through the window, smashing out plenty of glass to make their escape. They scrambled through the window and pulled themselves onto the sidewalk, catching wary glances from the pedestrians on the sidewalk. "We did it, Matt!" cried Randy, who gave him a big hug and then began searching the street to try to determine where they were.

25

THE LATE, GREAT CAVALRY

Captain Manolo Panganiban was on the telephone with Director Jordan Connery, trying to brief him on the status of the incident in the Pines Hotel. He explained to Connery that there had been a shooting. One person was wounded and rushed to the hospital with a life-threatening gunshot wound. A second man with Soviet diplomatic credentials was dead in a hotel room rented to a NIS Special Agent named Randy Glasscock. "Witnesses informed us that two people, a man, and a woman, ran from the hotel and entered Sagrada Concepción Church about an hour ago," said the Captain. "We searched the church but found no trace of them. During our search, we discovered the body of another Soviet in the catacombs in the basement. We found no other sign of them. I know to call you, Director, because in searching her room, we found her handbag containing her wallet, I.D. and badge. I decided, because of the special relationship we have with the U.S., to give you a call before doing anything further, including calling the Soviet Embassy to inform them of the shooting."

"Thank you, Captain, for your consideration," said the Director. "Captain, I must tell you that this is a highly confidential operation we are in the middle of, and we very much need your help. We have dispatched a team to assist in this matter. They will be arriving by helicopter in a matter of minutes. Captain, does your station have a helipad we could use?"

"Unfortunately, no. Our small police department does not have much need for helicopters. But just across the street from our City Police Station is a football ground with plenty of room to land a helicopter," said Panganiban.

"I will contact our team and have them land there. If you could lend assistance with our team, the United States would be incredibly grateful."

"It would be my honor, Director," said the captain. "My small department is at your disposal. But might I ask, what would you suggest about contacting the Soviets?"

"If you could just hold off until our team gets oriented, it would be greatly appreciated."

After concluding the call, Director Connery had the helicopter contacted and asked them to call his office when they arrived to discuss a plan. He was grateful that his agents had still been alive when they left the hotel. He hoped Randy would be able to call his office so that he could let them know the cavalry was about to arrive.

No more than ten minutes later, a hulking Sikorsky SUH-60a flew over the Baguio police department and landed in the football stadium across the street. Four US Navy SEALS in light combat gear, carrying M-16 Carbines and .45 caliber pistols, and three NIS Special Agents disembarked. They walked across the grounds and crossed the street to enter the Baguio police department. The men were met at the door by Captain Manolo Panganiban and four of his best-trained officers. One of the NIS agents held out his hand, "I'm Roger Nesbitt, Captain, and I'm leading this little boy scout troop. We sure appreciate your help, but we've been in the air with limited radio contact, so I'd appreciate it if you would bring me up to date."

Captain Panganiban explained the situation at the Pines Hotel and the search of the church, which turned up a Soviet corpse. "We began searching the area after we discovered the body but decided we would wait to do anything further until you arrived," said Panganiban. "My department's resources are at your disposal."

"Thanks, Captain. I think we might want to borrow a couple of cars and officers and head toward the church. Our helicopter can head there also. They have a few gizmos to help, and an aerial search will allow us to cover more ground. If we can go in your station and call my Director, I'll get his guidance and direction, and then we'll hit the ground."

26

WHO IS CHASING WHOM?

Randy and Matt climbed out of the window and onto the sidewalk of a busy street. From what she could tell, they were no more than a block or two from Session Road. "I think our best bet is to get to a police station. We can call for help from there." She ran up to the first person walking by, an older woman carrying a shopping bag, and asked where the police station was. She stared at Randy, giving no response. Randy guessed she either did not speak English or was utterly stunned by the sight of the two Americans. "Himpilan ng pulis," Randy tried. This time the woman nodded and pointed down the street. "Doon," the woman said. "Kalsada Harrison!"

Randy said, "Salamat," and she grabbed Matt's arm and started running.

"You speak Tagalog?" Matt inquired with unconcealed surprise, running beside Randy.

"It's always good to learn a few important words wherever you are, Matt," and she smiled, glancing at him, looking a bit proud of herself.

"I think I know about eight profanities in Tagalog from my liberties in Subic but never thought to learn anything useful like that."

Randy smiled at Matt's attempts to lighten the moment. "Harrison is the street we walked in on this afternoon. The station can't be more than a half a mile ahead -- God, it was just this afternoon?" she remarked with disbelief. She had no idea how late it was, but it was twilight. Summertime sun meant it was probably no later than 10 p.m.

As they increased their speed toward the police station, Matt glanced back to a disappointing sight of two men running behind them. "Damn, I thought they'd be in that church for hours," he said with dismay. "We had better run faster."

"They wouldn't shoot us on the street with all of these bystanders," Randy said more as wishful thinking than with certainty.

They decided to detour down a side street to see if they could lose them. Turning into an alleyway, Randy quickly realized they might have made a strategic error. The alley appeared to be blocked by a fence. A trash dumpster was sitting against the fence, and they vaulted on top of it and over the wire. Still, the time that it took allowed Makarov and Lester to close their gap while at the same time making it safer to fire their weapons, now that they were off the main street. Both men drew their guns, Makarov stopping and taking the time to take a shooting stance, and fired five rounds through the fence. Makarov's weapon had a suppressor, making it the quietest weapon and attracting the least attention. Frustrated, Makarov saw that none of his shots met their target. Both Matt and Randy slipped into an alcove, drew their weapons, and returned fire. Makarov quickly realized that he would expose himself and Lester if they repeated the maneuver Matt and Randy just made. Their best hope was to use the power of his automatic pistol to dispatch them in the alley. Because of the rapid-fire of the gun and a magazine holding just 20 rounds, it was quickly empty. Randy, seizing the opportunity, screamed at Matt, "Run!"

The two ran to the end of the alley and down the street. As soon as Matt and Randy were in retreat, Makarov and Lester jumped onto the dumpster and over the fence. Lester, although in good physical condition for a CPO, was in far worse shape than Makarov. He caught his belt on the top of the fence, tipping head down, hanging like a spider dangling on a single strand of web, looking at Makarov, who was considering leaving him to hang there. Makarov reluctantly returned, prying Lester from the fence, tearing his belt off at the same time.

The time it took to rectify that situation caused a delay, and the gap they had closed with Randy and Matt had widened. They turned left on a street that Randy hoped paralleled Harrison, came to the next corner and turned left again. Her guess paid off as the sign by the next corner indicated it was Harrison.

The spies kept up the pace, with Lester losing a bit of ground as he was now sans belt, which meant that he had to run, holding his pants up with one hand. Makarov was not interested in Lester's pants issues at this point, but only in catching the podornoks and ending their lives posthaste. Makarov assumed they would try to get back onto the main street they were on and followed the turns the two had made. Soon they were back on Harrison, with their prey, once again, in sight.

The two ran as fast as they could, and as they did, Matt stole quick peeks behind them. Although disappointed, he was not surprised when the two men once again came into view. He noted, however, now that they were back on the main street, they had put their guns away. Matt could see the police station with great relief, but the spies were shrinking the distance between themselves and their targets. "Shit!" Matt shouted. Another glance revealed the spies reconsidered concealing their weapons and had drawn them, perhaps because they realized that if the two could make it safely to the police station, they would have lost their chance to stop them. Randy and Matt both looked back to see Makarov stop, draw his pistol, and take a shooting stance.

The three NIS Agents and four Navy SEALS were preparing to go inside the police department when someone looked down the street. "Is that Glasscock?" one of the agents asked.

Nesbitt and the others looked down the street to see the sight of

Randy and Matt sprinting toward them, with two men chasing them. One, curiously, was half-running, half-hopping as his pants were riding just below his buttocks. They watched the two pursuers stop and one draw a weapon. The agents and the SEALS ran down the stairs of the police department, weapons drawn and aimed at the two spies. When Randy saw the men with the guns drawn, her first thought was that the Soviets had positioned their men ahead of them, but a sense of delight quickly coursed through her head. "It's our guys!" she shouted to Matt. Randy and Matt reached them seconds later, and one of the agents said, "Special Agent Glasscock, I'm Special Agent Nesbitt, and I brought some help. I'm assuming those guys are the spies?"

"Yes," Randy squeaked out. "Please help."

"That's what we are here for, Randy," Nesbitt said, weapon raised, preparing for a firefight. "United States Federal Agent! Freeze! Put down your weapon!" shouted Nesbitt. At that moment, Makarov, with a look of shock on his face, turned and began running in the other direction as the SEALS started their pursuit. As the NIS agents and the SEALS chased the two men, two black sedans passed them and screeched to a stop in front of the spies. The two fleeing men vaulted into the cars, launching quickly to put distance between themselves and the threat heading in their direction. Nesbitt, pistol raised, looked around at the dozens of bystanders on the street and decided it was best not to fire at the escaping spies.

The Americans came running back. "We have a helicopter and the resources of the Baguio police department at our disposal. We'll get them," said Nesbitt, barking orders to the others. Matt, exceptionally relieved, mused at the turn of events. The predators, who moments before were close to dispatching him, were now the prey.

27

A CHANGE OF COURSE

The drivers of the black sedans turned right at the first available corner. They raced to put as much distance between themselves and the federal agents as possible. In the rear seat of the lead vehicle, Makarov sat, stony-faced, next to Lester, who cast an unequaled air of fear and apprehension.

The sun had set, which meant it would be much more difficult for the Americans to find them. Makarov ruminated to himself on several options to evade capture. He had trained for this. Escaping the grasp of the Americans was not his greatest concern. His most significant problem was that he would have to answer to his superiors about the numerous blunders that had occurred during this one, awfully long, day.

The longer Makarov sat staring out the side window of the sedan, the greater Lester's discomfort grew. Finally, Lester could stand the silence no longer. "What the hell does it mean that those federal agents were there? Are we completely fucking screwed?"

Makarov turned his head toward Lester. "I believe saying we're 'fucking screwed' is redundant," he said sarcastically and then turned his face back toward the side window. He said something to the driver in Russian, who responded with what sounded to Lester like 'da cer.' The car pulled up to a payphone, and Makarov exited, briskly walking to the phone. He spoke on the phone for a minute or two, hung up, and returned to the car. He once again gave the driver instructions in Russian, and the car pulled back onto the street.

"Blue, here is the situation. I'm assuming that you will have already considered much of this but listen carefully to what I am about to say. The next twelve hours will be critical in your life, as it is about to change dramatically. Because federal agents came to the aid of the two podonoks, there is little doubt that they were federal agents also. Your little radioman infiltrated your operation on your ship, intending to stop the information hemorrhage that was going on. What this means is that probably for some time now, the American government wants you as a spy and traitor. If they successfully capture you, you will go to prison, most likely, for the rest of your life, or if you are lucky, you will be shot. What this also means is that you are worthless as a sidesaddle on a sow to me.

"From our encounters today, I am confident my role has been compromised. I will be required to return to Moscow to answer for the blunders for which *you* are accountable. That I will be required to account for your screw-up is very upsetting to me, Blue. It is so disturbing that I would turn you out on the streets for the Americans to find and dispense their justice if it were up to me. I would hope for Americans to administer it with extreme prejudice. Please believe me when I say that this is indeed the course I would prefer. Despite your past usefulness, you are the root of what will be extreme aggravation in my life for some time to come.

"Unfortunately, my preferred course of action is not acceptable at this time. Our program to recruit new spies from the ranks of your military and government would suffer. It would be a tough sell in the future if our recruits thought it would end poorly for them. For that reason, we told you in the beginning that if you were ever compromised, you would receive a pleasant 'retirement' in USSR for your life. And it is for that reason, despite my desires, you shall receive that opportunity."

"Pyotr, what can I say – I'm... I'm sorry, but I've done my best, and I am grateful that you will keep your promises."

"I think it best that you listen and not talk, Blue. Here is the plan. We are going to drop you off at a small hotel. It isn't the best place, but it is safe. I must leave you tonight. Once I have made the arrangements, I will send instructions to you. We have used a small private runway outside of the city on occasion, mostly during Vietnam, when we monitored troop and ship movements from Subic Bay. I must see if it is still usable and must secure the runway with my men. We can't risk landing a plane at Loakan Airfield as it is certainly under surveillance. The window for a successful departure will be very brief. The jet will fly in, land, pick us up and then take off again, quickly, for USSR. You must be there at the time I tell you. Do you understand?"

"Yes. Yes, I do," Lester mumbled.

"Good," said Makarov.

Fifteen minutes later, the black sedan slowed and stopped in front of a shabby hotel, somewhere on the city's outskirts. Lester stepped out and went in the hotel's front door as the car door slammed shut and the two sedans sped out of sight. He walked up to the front desk clerk and was handed a key without the clerk saying a word. Lester started walking toward the stairs when he stopped and turned around. "You got some booze?" Lester said to the clerk, who nodded in the affirmative. "Great. Please send up some rum and a couple of cokes." Lester walked up the stairs, found his room, and walked in the door. The hotel was a far cry from the Whiterock Hotel where he had started his day, but he was grateful to feel safe.

Before he could sit down, there was a knock at the door. Lester's nerves, justifiably on edge, shot jolts of panic throughout his brain. "Your rum, sir," came a voice. Lester let his breath go, opened the door, gave his thanks, and shut it again. He walked to the bed and poured a little coke and a lot of rum into a glass, downing it in one breath. He poured another and walked to the window overlooking the street, checking to see if anyone was watching him. This ritual would repeat itself several times over the coming hours, interrupted only by his pacing from the bed to the door, opening the door, and peering out.

Lester sat down on the bed and poured himself another rum and coke. He thought about the incredibly awful day he had just experienced and how it turned from what he believed would be a masterpiece of strategic mastery into a lump of excrement. Lester was more than a bit chagrined as he reviewed how things had gone so terribly wrong. His mind gradually took him back to the day he raised his right hand and swore his oath of enlistment: *I, Morris Lester, do solemnly swear that I will support and defend the Constitution of the United States against all enemies, foreign and domestic; that I will bear true faith and allegiance to the same; and that I will obey the orders of the President of the United States and the orders of the officers appointed over me, according to regulations and the Uniform Code of Military Justice. So help me God.*

The moment of change came just as Lester completed two full hitches in the Navy. He served eight years and held the Petty Officer First Class rate when he received a transfer to the Naval Communications Station in Pearl Harbor. By this time in his career, he was supervising two dozen radiomen. He was well-respected both by his subordinates and his superiors. He was squared away and did his job by the book. During his second hitch, he had married Maddie, falling in love with her the instant their eyes met. But it soon became evident that she expected to live a lifestyle that exceeded the means a sailor could accommodate. Maddie loved expensive jewelry, expensive trips, nice cars, nicer handbags, and regular trips to big-ticket spas with names like *Tranquil Times, Luscious Lather*, and her favorite, *Beauty Bomb Spa*.

Lester did the best he could to keep up with Maddie's predilections, but it was clear that he would have to supplement his income to do so. Lester had stints as a bouncer, taxi driver, and bartender, none of which provided sufficient income to meet Maddie's desires. Lester had been playing poker for years and considered himself a pretty good player. Most of his games, however, were with his fellow sailors. The meager pots he took home, combined with the part-time jobs, couldn't begin to cover Maddie's monthly bill at Luscious Lather, much less all the other gear she so enthusiastically embraced.

Because of Lester's skills at poker, he began to receive invitations to private games off base. These began to yield more money. It was not enough to cover everything, but it went a long way toward keeping him from bankruptcy. During one of these games, he played with a couple of guys with "foreign accents." After several nights playing with them, they invited him to have drinks afterward, which turned into regular get-togethers. After four or five times together, the two foreigners brought a friend. The three offered to pay Lester for a bit of what he considered trivial information in exchange for a handsome wad of cash. Being in the financial fix he was in, Lester took him up on the deal, followed by another and another, each yielding more money. Without giving what he was doing so much as a moment of reconsideration, Lester was all-in and loving it. Lester had a fistful of reasons to rationalize his actions. It was several years before he looked himself in the mirror and said to the face staring back at him, "Shit, Moe, you're a fucking spy." By then, he was too deep to walk away, even if he had wanted to.

Lester poured himself another rum and coke, stood up from the bed, wobbling just a bit, and walked to the window for the umpteenth time. He looked at his watch: 2:45 a.m. As he stared out at the street, he saw a black sedan pull up. A man got out of the car and entered the hotel. If it were the feds, they would have had a dozen cars, so he assured himself that it was a courier. As expected, a note slid under his door. He opened the folded note and read:

Benguet Farm
223 Aspiris-Palispis Highway
6:00 am
45-minute taxi ride
Don't be late

He folded the note back and put it in his pocket. He thought about Maddie, and it seemed just a bit strange that this was the first time he considered that he would never see her again. She was going to have a hell of a time finding somebody to pay for her Louis Vuitton shit and her cucumber facials at the Beauty Bomb Spa. Nobody would call him "Senior Chief," and he would be at the mercy of whatever regime was in control of the USSR. He thought about the maxim his father would say to him when he was growing up every time he left the house, "Make wise decisions, son. The decisions you make today control the choices you have in the future." Well, his decisions had left him with two choices: First, he could turn himself in or be caught and tried as a spy, in which case he would, more likely than not, spend the rest of his life in prison, or, second, he could move to Russia and build a new life there on the Soviet's dime. He could learn to drink vodka. Easy decision. Da. Legkiy, or something like that.

28

A FRUSTRATING SEARCH

After the Soviets drove away in the two cars, Special Agent Nesbitt scrambled the crew of the Sikorsky UH-60A and sent them in the air to attempt to locate the spies. The four SEALS stayed on the ground, each teaming up with a police officer to search the streets. When three Volkswagen Beetles with police lights drove up, the Americans had trouble not showing their surprise at the choice of vehicle for the Baguio police department. Matt stifled a grin as he imagined a high-speed chase in a bug. In addition to the three VW's, a fourth unmarked bug arrived.

It was already dark, and with the darkness, Nesbitt was aware that it was unlikely the chopper would find much. Night vision technology in 1976 was rudimentary and generally operated on intensifying the ambient light and combining it with heat sources to increase sight in the darkness. While elementary compared with future technologies, it proved helpful in the Vietnam conflict and had improved significantly by the 1970s. As the helicopter flew over a widening circle around the police station, a crew member held the night vision device like binoculars, hoping to see more than the naked eye could.

The UH-60A helicopter was a new weapon available to the navy.

It was just one of several dozen helicopters the navy was in the process of evaluating for use in the fleet. It carried a more significant number of passengers and equipment than their workhorse from the 1960s, the SH-2 Seasprite. Ultimately, the adapted version would become the mainstay in the navy for almost fifty years. Dubbed the *Seahawk*, it was a blatant attempt to navy-tize the army version of the helicopter, the *Blackhawk*. At least for trial purposes, the chopper was proving a valuable tool in the navy's assemblage. Unfortunately, the technology available to use onboard had its limits, proving true in their search for the spies.

While the SEALS and their police officer partners drove the city in a growing circular pattern similar to the one the helicopter was using, Nesbitt and Captain Panganiban had a quick conference. Communications among the police in Baguio were rudimentary. Still, they would put the equivalent of an "all-points bulletin" out as quickly as possible, with explicit instructions not to intervene but observe and report.

With the most urgent actions taken care of, Nesbitt turned his attention to Randy and Matt. "You cannot believe how happy I am to see you," he said. "I'd say that was about as close a shave as anyone could stand, but you're safe now. I'm sure you are completely exhausted. It's late; you should get showers and some rest. I'll arrange for accommodations for you."

Matt looked at Randy and smiled, and Randy reciprocated, knowing just what Matt was thinking. "Roger, if it's just the same to you, we could never rest knowing what's going on. We both want to pitch in and help. There's no way we're stepping back at this point."

Nesbitt looked at Randy, then looked at Matt. "Bertram, you agree?"

"Most definitely, sir. There's no relaxing until we've finished this."

"Very well, you two can come with Captain Panganiban and me, and we'll join the search. We've coordinated the car radios with the eyes in the sky, so we'll know if they find anything." He handed Randy her handbag and a weapon, then turned to Matt. "I can provide you with a weapon, Matt. You should be armed as well."

Matt opened his shirt to reveal the pistol Randy had given him. "I think I'm good, Special Agent Nesbitt."

With the darkness came much-desired camouflage for the spies. Baguio had few streetlights, and with their limited night vision apparatus, the helicopter crew had no advantage in the air. Nesbitt ordered the chopper to head to Loakan Airport in Baguio to refuel and stand by for further orders. It may prove to be valuable in the apprehension of the spies, but under the challenge of darkness, it was not. Another hour of searching yielded no hint of the Soviets.

At about 3 a.m., the car's radio came alive with a call from an officer in the city's western end. He reported seeing a black sedan park in front of a seedy hotel, with a white man walking in and moments later leaving. He noted that there was only one window with lights on in the second story of the hotel.

Nesbitt smiled when Captain Panganiban translated from Tagalog. "Why is it the fucking Russians insist on driving black sedans? They might as well have a sign painted on the side of the car saying, 'We are Russian Spies.' At any rate, I'd say we probably have found our quarry."

Panganiban told the officer to take no action but to keep an eye on the hotel. He ordered the officer to let him know if there were any changes in the situation or if anyone else came or went. Nesbitt then called out to the cars with the SEALS riding along. The hotel was on the corner of Bengao Road and Ben Palispis Highway. Nesbitt asked the SEALS to rendezvous about a block away to put together a mission plan. The helicopter was scrambled and would be close by if needed but not close enough to be heard. Nesbitt did not want the noise from the chopper to make the occupants of the room suspicious.

By 3:30 a.m., all the team had arrived. LT Jason Fuerte led the four SEAL team members. "Lieutenant," said Nesbitt, "This is your specialty and expertise, so you are in charge of this operation."

"Thanks, Agent Nesbitt." LT Fuerte turned to his team and said, "Our element is a little less than a block from the hotel. We have not confirmed that these are indeed our targets, and we do not know how many people occupy the room, so we need to exercise extreme caution. We do know that our targets have fully automatic weapons in their possession, so we will not have much time to confirm our targets and take them. Our rules of engagement are to defend ourselves and not fire upon them unless it is clear they intend to use force against us. As such, we will employ stealth in gaining access to the hotel and their room. Let's consider this mission a 'snatch and grab.' You're the best operators in the navy, men. Now let's go make mama proud!"

At 3:45 am, two events happened almost simultaneously. The first was the SEAL element reached the alley beside the hotel and were preparing to enter. One operator was assigned to be on the roof, one behind the hotel, and one in front. LT Fuerte would enter the lobby to seek to confirm their target was in the room they suspected and ascertain how many were there. Once he confirmed those two important facts, all four would converge on the hotel room door.

The other event that was happening was that Senior Chief Lester's tolerance for anxiety reached its limits. He was alternately pacing the room, drinking his rum and coke, and peering out the window. As he approached the window for at least the seventieth time, he saw something he had not seen in the sixty-nine previous times. He spotted a Baguio police officer. To Lester's eye, the cop appeared to be watching the same window from which Lester was peeking. Lester immediately panicked and ducked back from the window. "What should I do? I can't just stay here like a sitting duck," he mumbled to himself. Lester's fight or flight response immediately screamed into flight. He chugged the last of his drink, grabbed his pistol, and opened his hotel room door, half expecting to be met by other police. Seeing none, he took a deep breath, headed to the stairs, and started upward for the roof. He remembered that the hotel had a metal external fire exit that many older buildings have. He hoped to use it to climb down without being seen in the lobby or by the police officer.

Two stories later, he was on the roof. Lester quickly stole a look down the fire escape. Another infusion of panic set it as he saw shadows of people on the ground. The fire escape would not provide a successful flight. Quickly, he scanned his surroundings. Other buildings were close enough to the hotel that he thought he could jump from the hotel to another building. *After all*, he thought to himself, *I'm in terrific shape. I work out all the time.*

Left with few options, Lester started running for the building with the smallest gap in between. As he gained speed, he regretted drinking as much as he had. Lester needed good reflexes and judgment right now. On the other hand, he decided, the alcohol provided him with some much-needed courage. He reached the end of the hotel building, leaping with all his might. He easily made it past the gap but landed hard and rolled into a vent, cutting his arm and causing a sharp pain to his ankle. He grabbed his ankle and stifled a groan as he crawled around the vent, peering back to the building he had just exited. As he did, a man wearing military combat gear came over the fire escape rail at the hotel, took a quick look around, and proceeded in the door to the hotel.

Once the man was inside the hotel, Lester stood, feeling the pain more intensely. He tried walking on it and decided he was probably still mobile. He limped to the fire escape on the building and gingerly took the steps down to the ground, a shot of pain hitting him each time the ankle bore weight. Once on the ground, Lester made another scan. Nobody in sight. He began to feel encouraged that he had made a clean escape from the hotel and not a moment too soon. The Ben Palispis Highway was just a few hundred feet away. He hoped he could flag down a taxi and get on the road to his rendezvous with Makarov. Just a few minutes standing on the corner yielded his target: a taxi coming his way. He whistled and waved, and the driver pulled over. He showed the driver the note he had with the destination written on it. The driver shook his head, "No, no, too far, not go. Get another taxi!" the driver shouted.

Unfortunately for the taxi driver, Lester was frantic and armed. He pulled out his weapon, pointing it at the driver. The driver, amazingly, still refused. Finally, in desperation, Lester grabbed the driver, pulling him out of the taxi. The driver fell onto the ground, and impulsively, Lester fired the gun, point-blank, into the driver's chest. Lester jumped into the car and sped away, having no clue how to get to the address Makarov had provided. The entire incident happened in front of a sari-sari store. The owner, who had been opening his store for the day, watched the whole melee. As Lester left the scene, the owner came running out to help the taxi driver. He shouted to his wife to call the police and an ambulance. The driver was losing blood quickly. The owner applied pressure to the driver's chest, hoping the ambulance would arrive soon.

LT Fuerte, entering the hotel's lobby in full combat gear and carrying an automatic weapon, gained quick cooperation from the desk attendant. The clerk confirmed that it was a white American who was staying there and that he was alone. The clerk neglected to tell the SEAL how the room was acquired. The man with the gun didn't appear to care.

LT Fuerte gave the word that their target was indeed in the room, that he was alone, and to converge. When the team reached the room's floor, they found the door open and the room empty. Fuerte alerted Nesbitt. Just as he did, Nesbitt and the others heard the sound of a gunshot. "We are heading to where we heard the gunshot. I'm guessing that's not a coincidence. Get back to your vehicles, and I'll let you know if we find anything."

Captain Panganiban sped the patrol car down the street, made a right turn, drove another half-block, pulled over to the curb to see the store clerk trying to save the taxi driver. Matt and Randy took over the first aid. At the same time, Captain Panganiban and Nesbitt questioned the store owner, who explained what he had seen and pointed in the direction the car traveled. They tried asking the taxi driver a few questions, but he was in shock and unable to provide any information. There was no doubt that Lester had somehow escaped from the hotel without being seen and was driving the stolen taxi. Panganiban assured the store clerk that an ambulance and other police officers would arrive shortly. The four jumped back into the squad car and took off in the direction Lester was heading.

Once he was in the car, Nesbitt ordered the chopper to move

ahead and look for the taxi. Dawn quickly approached, which allowed the helicopter crew to gain visual contact with the cars on the ground. Nesbitt's instructions were short and clear: "Keep enough altitude that he won't see you, and keep us informed of where he is and each turn he makes."

Nesbitt turned to Randy and Matt. "I think we need to be strategic about this. Once we have a visual of Lester, we should be able to follow him as he progresses. He may just be trying to escape to anywhere, but I have a hunch that he's going to try to meet up with Makarov. I think we should at least try to get them both. It would be a big win to get Makarov, simply for the political value. He'll end up back in Moscow anyway, eventually. Still, it would be a huge embarrassment for the USSR and would seal our case against Lester. If it appears he's just trying to escape, we'll go ahead and take him, but I think we should try to get as many fish in our net as we can."

Matt thought Nesbitt's idea had merit, but they had yet to spot Lester's car. The limited light of dawn remained a challenge for the chopper crew, and Matt hoped that Lester had not diverted from the main highway in the short time since he stole the taxi. As Panganiban did his best to maneuver the police car through the increasing traffic with no lights or sirens, all four kept an eagle's eye out for the taxi. "Agent Nesbitt, it is going to be difficult to catch up without lights and sirens," lamented Panganiban.

"Alright, it's better to catch only Lester than to lose them all," groused Nesbitt. Panganiban turned on the lights, and cars began to move over to allow him to pass.

"There!" shouted Randy. "The taxi!"

Panganiban immediately shut off the lights and edged up behind Lester, hoping he hadn't seen them. Unfortunately for them, he had. The taxi swung to make a right turn onto a side street, its tires screeching and buffeting. The car slid around the corner, sideswiping a jeepney going the other direction, then speeding up as it cleared the intersection. Matt was amazed at Captain Panganiban's driving skills and the stability the little VW had as he negotiated the turn successfully, quickly catching up to Lester. Lester attempted another turn, feinting to the left, then at the last moment straightening out. Panganiban took the bait and committed himself to a left turn, allowing Lester to put enough distance between the cars to slide into traffic. By the time Panganiban was back on the street, Lester had vanished. Nesbitt called the chopper, but unfortunately, they had missed the pursuit due to the limited light. Nesbitt gave the chopper details of where they were when they lost him. He hoped that with each minute, the light would improve enough for their eyes in the sky to see sufficiently to be of help.

Lester saw that his maneuvers were successful, and he smacked the steering wheel with an open hand, laughed out loud, and flipped his middle finger in the air. "You should know not to fuck with me, you bastards!" screamed Lester. "You're not dealing with some dumb-fuck common criminal! I am the most successful spy ever!" Never short of ego, Lester felt like James Bond at that moment. *OK, maybe Goldfinger and not so much James Bond*, Lester thought to himself, but a mastermind just the same.

Lester the Mastermind now focused on the crucial business he needed to attend to, the first of which was to figure out where the hell he was and how he would get to the rendezvous point. Once he was confident he had lost the police car, Lester pulled into a gas station. Lester jumped out of the car and took the note with the address out of his pocket. There was an attendant at the station who appeared surprised to see an American driving a Philippine taxi. Lester showed him the message and asked the attendant if he could point him in the right direction. The attendant explained to Lester that he needed to get back onto the highway from which he had just diverted. That highway would turn into Aspiris-Palispis Highway. He asked the attendant how long a drive it was, and the attendant guessed about 45 minutes. Lester looked at his watch: 5:30 a.m. He had thirty minutes to make a 45-minute drive. He would have to stop being Goldfinger and start being A.J. Foyt.

29

LESTER THE GREAT

N esbitt speculated that the best place to start their search was the road Lester was driving on before they spotted him. As they turned to find their way back to Ben Palispis Highway, Nesbitt directed the chopper to fly to that spot. Once they had arrived, they should get enough altitude to scan as great a distance as possible while at the same time not being spotted by Lester. He asked Captain Panganiban to call the other squad cars with the SEALS accompanying the officers and route them back to their location. One of the four other police cars was an unmarked car, which could come in handy at some point.

The light available for surveillance was improving by the moment, and the chopper crew kept a steady eye for the taxi. Unlike the United States, the taxis in Baguio tended to be painted white and were more often than not vans. Ridesharing was common, not just in the ubiquitous jeepneys but also in taxis. The white color of taxis was not quite as distinct as the familiar yellow color in America. Still, it narrowed down the vehicles somewhat. As the crew searched, they began to realize a disturbing fact. Baguio was a tourist town, and where there are tourists, there are a lot of taxis. As they looked down on the highway below, the pilot radioed Nesbitt. "Sir, we're going to have a tough time finding the target. I'd guess every tenth vehicle on the road is a goddam cab."

Listening intently to the conversation, Randy said to Nesbitt, "Tell him to look for one with damage on the side. He side-swiped that car when we were chasing him."

"Good point," agreed Nesbitt. "Lieutenant, look for vehicles that have damage on their sides and also look for anyone driving erratically. You know, too fast, weaving in and out of traffic."

The pilot acknowledged Nesbitt's request, somewhat relieved that they had narrowed down their search. The chopper crew continued hunting for Lester's taxi. Nesbitt called out to the unmarked police car. "I want you to come forward and take the lead," he told them. "If the chopper finds a taxi that fits the description, we are going to need you to get a visual confirmation, and it can't be from a marked police car."

The officer and the SEAL in the unmarked car affirmed the order. Soon, a grey Volkswagen Super Beetle came alongside. The SEAL in the passenger seat, who looked a bit like a giant in a go-cart, waved, and they passed the captain's car. Nesbitt was still trying to get used to the fact that Baguio police mainly used VW bugs for patrol cars. Matt said quietly to Randy, "If the police all drive bugs, aren't they easy to spot, even if they are unmarked?" Randy shrugged her shoulders and hoped there were enough civilians in Baguio who also drove bugs.

The chopper crew continued combing the traffic on the road, looking from taxi to taxi, hoping to find one with a damaged side. It was just a few minutes later that the sole enlisted crew member, AW1 Klinequist, an Aviation Systems Warfare Operator, shouted to the pilot, "There! Just behind that big truck!" The pilot looked below and ahead and saw a damaged taxi. The taxi was attempting to pass the truck in a frighteningly reckless way, popping into the left lane and then diving back behind the truck as an oncoming vehicle approached. The pilot radioed Nesbitt that they had a likely suspect about a quarter-mile ahead of them, and Nesbitt radioed the unmarked car to take a look.

The officer in the bug put the accelerator to the floor, which increased the patrol car's speed an unremarkable ten miles an hour. Gradually, however, thanks to the fact that the taxi could not successfully pass the truck at this point, they caught up. The highway changed names to the Aspiris-Palispis Highway, and they quickly approached the Baguio-Benguit border. The road widened to four lanes at this point as the route began climbing in altitude quickly. The taxi moved around the truck, as did the unmarked police car. As the elements of the city gradually began to disappear, tall pine trees covered the sides of the road. The traffic was noticeably diminished, along with commercial buildings and houses.

Lester looked at his watch: 5:45 A.M. He had just fifteen minutes to get to his destination, and being behind that truck held him back. He looked in the mirror and saw a VW Beetle following close behind him. He had seen the police cars in Baguio and found it amusing that they used bugs, but this one did not appear to have lights and was not the white color of the rest of the police cars he had seen. Nevertheless, it made him nervous. He alternately glanced out the windshield and into the rear-view mirror, keeping a close eye on the car. Remarkably, it sped up and moved to the left lane as though to pass but kept its nose just behind the passenger space of the taxi. He glanced at it and was stunned to see what looked like an American in the passenger seat. *I don't know if they are after me or not, but I can't take any chances*, Lester thought to himself. Without hesitation, he rapidly swerved to the left, hitting the bug on the front fender. The bug spun in a counterclockwise direction and then jumped the curb on the left, flying into a gravel pit beside the road. "Fuck you, assholes!" screamed Lester as he shouted victory. He quickly scanned his rearview mirror. There did not appear to be any other possible pursuers. Led by his rapidly recovering ego, Lester decided that if it had been feds in that car, he had dispatched them successfully. He put his gas pedal to the floor, hoping to make up lost time.

Captain Panganiban slowed his car as he drove by the unmarked car in the gravel pit. Both driver and the SEAL were standing and waved that they were OK, so they returned to their safe speed. Nesbitt radioed the other cars to pick up the SEAL and continue following them. He called the chopper on the radio, telling them they had confirmed the suspect vehicle and to continue following at a safe distance and altitude. Nesbitt told them to stay in touch and provide their observations as they happened. He informed them that the cars would be a quarter-mile back, hoping that Lester would think he was in the clear, which he indeed did, incorrectly.

30

AN ATTEMPTED ESCAPE

The Yakovlev Yak-40 executive jet was flying at about 7,000 feet in altitude, just 500 feet above Mount Kabuyao. The sleek Russian-made aircraft was on approach for a small runway on an open farming area just off the Ben Palispis Highway. The pilot was skilled at short and dirt runway landings and take-offs, having dropped KGB agents, military, and others on hundreds of covert missions. It was a tricky landing. Once over Mount Kabuyao, he would have to lose half of his altitude in a few miles and slow the jet enough not to overrun the runway. With great precision and skill, he slowed the three engines on the plane, pushed the lever for full flaps, and brought the jet to a smooth landing on the 1800 foot landing strip with 300 feet of runway to spare. He gunned the engines and taxied to the two waiting black sedans. He left the jet's engines running as instructed, and his co-pilot lowered the rear integrated airstairs. The time was 5:50 a.m.

Makarov turned to the agent beside him and said in Russian, "We wait ten minutes. No more. If Blue is not here, we go without him." The agent nodded and carried their luggage to the waiting jet.

Lester was frantically looking for signs for Benguet Farm and any street address signs he could find. He knew he was close, as a half-mile back, he had seen an address sign for 1000. He continued to take glimpses into his rearview mirror, fearing he would miss the turn-off. Finally, an old sign, rusty and probably not painted in ten years appeared on the right, indicating the road to the Benguet Farm. He quickly turned right, glancing at his watch. It was 5:55 a.m. He was going to make it in time. He took a deep and relieved breath and smiled, knowing that he was going to be safe.

The pilot of the chopper radioed the news that Lester had turned on the road. Nesbitt instructed him to gain some altitude and look at the surroundings, which the pilot did, just as the police car made its turn onto the road. In a few seconds, the pilot radioed back, a sense of urgency in his voice, "Agent Nesbitt, there's a runway with a jet, and two black sedans are parked next to it. You're about a third of a mile from it."

Nesbitt acknowledged and implored Captain Pantagiban to use haste. They were gaining on Lester. "We've got to get there before Lester can get on that plane," Nesbitt entreated. Panganiban nodded and sped up, gaining on the now confident Lester, who was no longer looking in the mirror but looking for the runway. He smiled as the sight of the jet came into view.

"Glavnyy!" cried the agent next to Makarov. "Smotryu!" He was not pointing at Lester but the four cars following him. At that moment, the helicopter also came into view.

Makarov shook his head, calmly walked to the jet with the agent, climbed aboard, and shut the rear air door. The agent shouted at the pilots to leave quickly. The pilot had anticipated that order had already pushed his throttle levers all on, and the three powerful AI-25 engines roared to life.

Lester was honking his horn as an unbelievable scene unfolded in front of him. Makarov was leaving him! "What the fuck!" he screamed, at the same time looking behind to see multiple vehicles in pursuit. "Oh no, no, no!" he screamed, banging his open hand on the steering wheel. Not only was he being left behind, but he was also on the verge of capture. With pitiful moaning, Lester began repeating "Oh fuck, oh fuck, oh fuck," repeatedly.

The jet was quickly up to flight speed and arced upward in the air just as the helicopter arrived. The chopper's pilot saw it was too late to stop the jet as he watched the aircraft put distance between them. Since catching the plane was futile, he turned the helicopter toward Lester. The latter was speeding down the runway in an unrealistic and pathological attempt to catch up to the jet. The chopper pilot brought the helicopter down in front of Lester, who slammed on the brakes. He grabbed his gun, momentarily hoping he could shoot his way out of the net. Lester watched impotently as the cars stopped in a circle around his taxi. He dropped his gun to the floor of the vehicle as he witnessed what looked like some kind of commandoes taking shooting stances in his direction.

Lester sat in his seat for a moment, considering putting the gun to his head, which his narcissistic nature would not allow. He slowly shook his head back and forth, opened the door, and stepped out of the taxi with his hands raised. Within seconds Lester was in handcuffs. As Nesbitt leaned Lester against the back of the car, he said, "Senior Chief Morris Lester, you are under arrest. Under Article 31 of the Uniform Code of Military Justice, you have the following rights: You have the right to remain silent; Any statements you do make may be used as evidence against you in trial by court-martial. You have the right to consult with legal counsel prior to any questioning. This legal counsel may be a civilian lawyer retained by you at your own expenses, a military lawyer appointed to act as counsel without cost to you, or both. You have the right to have such retained civilian lawyer and/or appointed military lawyer present during any interview. You have the right to terminate this interview at any time. And I recommend you just keep your pie hole shut until we get you locked up."

As the Soviet jet reached its cruising altitude of 20,000 feet, gradually heading northeast to avoid Japanese and Chinese airspace, Makarov sat in the luxurious light tan leather seat, staring out the window. He quietly said to himself in English, "Hell, that was just a bunch of sixes and sevens. Damn scamp, Blue."

The jet's flight attendant walked up and asked in Russian, "May I get you something, sir?"

Makarov, looking her in the eyes, smiled and said, "Whiskey, ma'am. And leave the bottle."

31

THE RIDE HOME

There was just enough room on the UH-60a for the four SEALS, the three NIS agents, Randy, Matt, and Lester. Nesbitt, who was the last to climb aboard, shook hands with Captain Panganiban and thanked him and his force for their considerable help. As the chopper started its ascent over the town of Baguio, Matt suddenly felt exhausted, realizing that he had been awake for the last 26 hours. With the last bit of adrenaline draining from his body, all Matt wanted to do was sleep. He looked over at Lester, handcuffed and shackled, head slumped down. Matt remembered the proud man who was his senior chief, in great physical shape, unlike pretty much every other CPO in the navy. He recalled that cocky, confident leader whom he had respected. Matt thought about how well-liked and esteemed Lester had been, and the bleak future he now faced. Had it not been for the ordeal Lester had put Matt through the last 26 hours, Matt might have even drummed up some sympathy for him. But Matt had no kind-hearted thoughts toward the man who had betrayed his country and his duty. No, he wanted Lester to pay for his crimes.

The UH-60a touched down in an empty parking lot close to the brig at Naval Base Subic Bay. Eight armed marines met the chopper and took Lester into custody. SA Nesbit looked at the two and said, "I know you two are exhausted, and we'll get you billets and showers as soon as we can, but we need to check-in at the NISO to be sure they won't need you for a while."

They walked to the NISO, which was a short walk from the brig. Both Matt and Randy walked as though their feet weighed fifty pounds. They had a quick briefing and headed, with escorts, to the Bachelor Officers' Quarters, referred to by a typical three-letter acronym, 'BOQ' for showers and, finally, some sleep. Matt did not bother to mention to anyone that he was not an officer and therefore not allowed to bunk there. He assumed the NIS had arranged to make an exception in this case.

Matt stepped into the shower, his own *personal* shower, in his own *private* room, something he had not experienced since he was home on leave. He was used to showering with the company of five or ten other of his shipmates and sleeping on a tiny bunk in a compartment filled with at least fifty sailors. He stood, back to the nozzle, allowing the hot water to wash over him. He could not recall anything feeling so good, as the water, soap, and solitude granted him some renewed vigor. When he came out of the head, he saw that someone had placed a uniform, skivvies, gym shorts, and a t-shirt on his bed. *Summer whites must be the uniform of the day*, he thought to himself, laughing when he saw the Petty Officer Second Class Radioman rate patch on the arm. "They fucked that one up," he said out loud, thinking it was just another thing that could get him in trouble. He put on the gym shorts and T-shirt, pulled back the covers of the bed, and was asleep immediately, giving himself no time to review the events of the last day. Sleep was much more critical.

Matt had pulled up the covers at 11:00 a.m. the previous morning and had slept through the night, waking feeling like a different man. He showered again, put on his summer whites, and, feeling very self-conscious, walked downstairs to the mess, and ordered breakfast. He was wondering at what point a challenge would come when a man wearing the hard shoulder boards of a navy commander walked in, scanned the room, then walked straight toward him. As the officer approached, Matt stood, saluted him, and said, "Good morning, sir," bracing himself for a confrontation. The officer returned the salute and then stuck out his right hand, "Petty Officer Bertram, I'm Commander Hopkins. Welcome back from your mission. May I sit with you a moment?"

"Of course, sir," Matt said, confused by the senior officer's demeanor.

"I work on the staff of the Seventh Fleet and am the liaison officer here in Subic. The admiral is aboard the *Okie* right now, or he would be here with us. First, I want you to know that we're all damn proud of you. Second, I'll be escorting you to your meetings today. We have a busy day ahead of us. The investigators and the prosecutors in the Judge Advocate General's office want to interview you, as well as the Director of the Naval Investigative Service Office here in Subic."

"Thank you, sir," said Matt, a bit overwhelmed by both the attention to be given to his information and the rank of his escort. "Sir, you may not know the answer to this question," Matt said, "But Clay Young. Did he, um, *die*?"

"No, he survived and is making a good recovery. He's in one of the brig cells at the hospital here. He's been more than helpful in putting some of the pieces together and has agreed to testify against Senior Chief Lester."

"Sir, I'd like to ask a favor," Matt said, looking directly into the commander's eyes. "I'd sure like to see him today if that's possible."

"I'll put in a word for you with the JAG office. I'm not sure if they'll allow it, but no harm in asking. Oh, and by the way, that second class rate badge on your shoulder is the admiral's way of giving his thanks. He's promoted you to E-5."

Well, cool, thought Matt, but, having a moment of fun in his mind, reflected, *after all I've been through, khakis and an ensign bar would have been cooler.* Keeping the thoughts to himself, Matt gave his thanks and could not help feeling a little proud of himself.

The rest of Matt's day and the following day were filled with what the JAG officers and NIS agents called "interviews." Somehow these *interviews* felt more like interrogations. They took place in the small interrogation rooms the NIS used to interview suspects and witnesses, the bathroom breaks were few, and the food came in bags. Matt surmised that they needed to know every second of Matt's time from the day he set foot on the *Oklahoma City* until Lester was apprehended. The interviews were grueling.

At the end of the second day, Commander Hopkins let Matt know that they had completed *this* round of interviews. "I have a little surprise for you," Commander Hopkins said. "They'll let you have fifteen minutes with Petty Officer Young."

The two walked to the naval hospital, and the two marine guards opened the cell/hospital room and allowed Matt into the room. Clay's face lit up when he saw Matt. "Look what the cat dragged in!" He lowered his head, then raised his eyes to meet Matt's. "Look, man, I'm so sorry. I'm really sorry."

"Clay, you ended up doing the right thing. In my book, that's big points. I hear you've been cooperating with the JAG in their work. That's got to be good for you."

"Yeah, but I'm definitely going to be court-martialed, dishonorably discharged, and will have to serve some time in Leavenworth. Probably looking at ten years. Believe me, it could be worse. Lester's probably going to get life. But my photographic memory is really coming in handy in giving the JAG everything they want."

"Well, man," said Matt, "I'll be pulling for you." The two hugged, and Matt left the room. None of the hostility he felt for Lester did he feel for Clay. *He screwed up, no doubt, but you've got to give him credit for trying to make it better,* he thought as he left.

32

UNCOMFORABLE ATTENTION

As Commander Hopkins and Matt walked back to the BOQ, Hopkins said, almost casually, "You have two more meetings tomorrow, Matt. And no interviews, I promise. A few people want to meet you, and then a wrap-up meeting with some NIS mucky-mucks. Dress blues are waiting for you in your room. Shine your shoes, and I'll meet you at 0800."

Matt turned to go into the BOQ, then hesitated and turned around. "Sir," Matt said, "I haven't seen Special Agent Glasscock since we arrived back at Subic. Is something wrong?"

Hopkins smiled and said, "I know you're anxious to see Special Agent Glasscock again. We have been intentionally keeping you apart. The JAG wants to be sure that everything is done by the book in prosecuting Lester. They have kept you apart during the interview process so that the defense cannot claim collusion on your stories. Don't worry. You'll see her tomorrow."

As promised, when Matt reached his room, there was a full-dress blues uniform, with appropriate rank and name tag, along with the meager ribbons he had earned, in his size. Along with it came the most-shined dress shoes he had ever seen. Wondering for a moment how they managed to know his exact size, especially his hat size, he gave up, realizing that they had access to much more information than he would have ever wanted them to know.

At 0800 in the morning, Matt was waiting for Commander Hopkins in the mess, finishing a cup of coffee. Matt could not help but note how much better the food for officers was than the enlisted crap, which was not much of a surprise to him.

They walked the distance to the NIS headquarters building. Instead of going to the central office, they walked one floor up to the conference room. Matt's jaw dropped as they walked in the door, as there were at least twenty people in the room. Everyone stood and gave a round of applause as Matt entered, completely stunned. Commander Hopkins escorted Matt to the front of the room and sat him in a seat in the front row.

Matt glanced at the man to his left and gulped to see that he was a Rear Admiral. Next to him were two civilians. There was more gold in the room than King Tut's tomb. The thought crossed his mind that he was more afraid of being in this room than everything that happened with Lester. Or perhaps not. But at least a close second.

A Vice Admiral stood and made his way to the podium. He pulled out paper with notes on it, cleared his voice, and said, "Good morning, ladies and gentlemen. I am Vice Admiral Teddy Howard, Commander of the United States Navy's Seventh Fleet. Over the past few days, it has become clear that a serious breach of intelligence has been effected by men in our own uniform and furnished to the USSR. I cannot give you too many details quite yet, as we do not want to compromise any ongoing investigations and prosecutions. I can say that it is probably the most serious loss of intelligence in the history of the United States Navy. Others will tell you more in a moment. However, our purpose today is to recognize someone who willingly put his life in harm's way to stop this criminal activity. In so doing, he may have saved the lives of many others and most certainly the precious secrets of our nation. It is today that we have an opportunity to express our gratefulness. I will turn it over to Rear Admiral Keith Redmond, Director of the United States Naval Intelligence Service. Admiral."

Matt was now shaking from his neck down, and as the Commander of the Navy's Seventh Fleet returned to his seat, he slapped Matt on the back. Currently, Matt was struggling to comprehend anything that was going on. *Surreal* would have been an understatement. All he could do it try to stay calm and not puke on the admiral.

"Good morning, all. As Admiral Howard said, I am Rear Admiral Keith Redmond, and I have the privilege to serve as Director of the Naval Intelligence Service. The NIS has a proud tradition of service to our country dating back to 1882. We have protected the United States Navy's interests both domestically and abroad, both overtly and covertly. For the press who are present today, we have a full sheet for you. After our presentation, my deputy Director and I will hold a press conference, with full details of our operation. We will provide you with the current status of the prosecution of the alleged spies apprehended in the last few days. Although we are still investigating the details, as Admiral Howard stated, we now believe this is the biggest betrayal of the United States Navy and the citizens of the United States of America in our country's history.

"Our purpose today, however, is to honor a sailor whose heroism showed no bounds, and without whom we might still be losing precious information to those who attempt to undermine our American way of life. I want to ask three people who are present to come to the podium. First is William J. Atwater, the Secretary of the Navy, and second is Senator Pete Wilkovich, Chair of the United States Senate Committee on Armed Services."

Matt realized that his jaw had literally dropped, and he struggled to maintain composure. When the Admiral called him forward, he was not sure he was capable of standing but managed to do so and came to the dais, standing behind Admiral Redmond.

The Secretary of the Navy came to the podium. "The navy awards conduct above and beyond the call of duty in several ways. We can give promotions, and we can award medals. Medals may seem like trivial awards for tremendous acts. The truth is that medals are and have always been important throughout the militaries of every nation. Medals are a great inspiration to young men and women and reassure them that their works have tremendous value. In truth, for the acts we are awarding medals for today, they do fail to express the paramount importance of the tasks which were undertaken. And lest I say, undertaken without any expectation of recognition. Nevertheless, our navy's proud tradition is to reward valor, honor, and duty, which we will do today.

"Petty Officer Second Class Matthew Bertram volunteered to become an undercover agent for the Naval Investigative Service. He brought what will probably be remembered as the most destructive spy ring that the United States Navy has ever experienced to its end with little direct support. In recognition of his actions, and on behalf of the President of the United States, our Commander-in-Chief, I am awarding him two medals today. The first is the Navy Distinguished Service Medal. This medal is bestowed upon members of the Navy or Marine Corps who distinguish themselves by exceptionally meritorious service to the United States government in a duty of great responsibility clearly above that normally expected. This medal is usually awarded to Captains of Ships or the highest enlisted members. In this rare case, it is justified to award it to someone of lower rank. The second medal to be awarded today is the Navy and Marine Corps Medal. This medal is the senior non-combat award for heroism. To be awarded this medal, the recipient must have experienced a 'life-threatening' risk. For heroic performance to rise to this level, it must be clearly established that the act involved a very specific life-threatening risk to the awardee. As our press release indicates, Petty Officer Bertram is more than deserving of this award."

The rest of the meeting was a fog for Matt. The reading of the citations, pinned medals, shaking hands, more speeches, none of which Matt could recall later. Overwhelmed was an understatement to describe his feelings. At some point in the proceedings, he recalled his "debriefing" following his combat experience in Cambodia. With shock, he had been informed he would receive no recognition or medals for what, to this day, would be treated as though it never happened. In retrospect, he almost preferred that. His perception of the last few months was that he was simply trying to accomplish his job, not get killed, and was over his head from the first moment he met Special Agent Davis McNutt in that drab office in Pearl Harbor.

As the dignitaries left the room, followed by Matt and his cohorts, Randy and Capelli walked up to him, beaming with pride and self-consciously giving him hugs. "I'm not sure I deserve all of this," Matt said with embarrassment.

"I think that's what qualifies you for this, my friend," said Capelli.

"Matt, I hate to rush you, but we've got one more short meeting downstairs in the NIS office," Randy said. "Then maybe we can all go get a beer and come back to reality." Matt readily agreed as they took the stairs down one level.

As they walked into the office, Matt was surprised yet again to see the Director of the NIS in the room, several JAG officers, and the Director of the Subic Bay NISO, with whom he had spent the last two days.

"I know this is all far from over for you, son," said Admiral Redmond. "There will be depositions, inquisitions, interviews, and, ultimately, a trial. Your participation will be required for all of these, for perhaps several months. I know you've been admonished not to talk to the press, but the fact is that if we send you back to the fleet, every sailor in any command will know all about you. It would be practically impossible just to blend back into your role as a radioman."

Matt had not given a return to the fleet one moment's thought, but as the admiral was saying that, he realized the truth of the matter.

"So, we are kind of struggling with what to do with you, son. We could put you someplace out of the way, perhaps with a flag command as an assistant, but, in truth, that would not be much of a reward. We could offer you a discharge, but, frankly, from a publicity standpoint, it would look more like punishment than a reward.

We've spent a good deal of time trying to find an appropriate opportunity for you, Petty Officer Bertram. I think we've come up with just the ticket. What we would like to do is to offer you a promotion of sorts. Well, let's call it a 'change of scenery.' We believe you have shown all the grit and professionalism that we want to see in one of our special agents here at the NIS. I don't know if you're aware, but we are only recruiting civilians these days to the service. Over the past few months, you have endured the most grueling job interview anyone has ever encountered, I'm sure. We have run this up and down the chain of command and gotten the green light. What I'm saying is, in short, I am offering you an honorable discharge from the United States Navy *and* a job as a Special Agent with the United States Naval Investigative Service.

"Now, I know you're probably in shock, not from the offer, but your experiences the last few months, and I want to give you some time to make a clear-headed decision. So why don't we give you thirty days of leave? You can head home, hang out with your family and friends, and we can talk on the phone in a few weeks."

Matt smiled, looking at Randy, then at Leon. "Admiral, my friends over there know something about me that you don't know. I make decisions far too quickly without giving them anything close to a reasonable amount of thought. I have often thought that this is a shortcoming that I need to work on, and I definitely am planning on working on it--sometime in the future. But for this decision, I think I'll stay impulsive. I'd like to take the thirty days, if you don't mind, Admiral. And I'll be honored to report for duty as a Special Agent in the NIS thirty-one days from now."

EPILOGUE

Senior Chief Morris "Moe" Lester was charged in military court under UCMJ article 106a, entitled "Espionage." A conviction allows a military court to execute the defendant for treason or sentence him to life in prison without parole. Because the information stolen by Lester was so damaging to the United States, the military prosecutor wanted to pursue the death penalty. Lester managed to plea to life without parole by cooperating with the NIS with in-depth information on the materials he provided to the Soviet Union and the KGB personnel he worked with over the course of twelve years. He also implicated two other radiomen as accessories to his crimes. In exchange for his actions with Matt Bertram and Randy Glasscock and his full cooperation in the matter, Clay Young received a sentence of ten years in prison.

In the early 1970s, the navy and all the other military branches had shut down their prison systems. The military prison at Fort Leavenworth, Kansas, became a consolidated prison for all service members. Both Lester and Clay Young were incarcerated there. Lester's rank was lowered to E-1, Seaman recruit, and he was dishonorably discharged from the US Navy.

Lester wrote a book in 1977 entitled "Poker Spy," which was

number five on the New York Times Bestseller List for fifteen weeks. He received compensation of $2.5 million in royalties from his book. He sold the movie rights to both the book and his life to MGM for $3 million. Lester's wife, Maddie, filed for divorce three weeks after the book and movie contracts were signed. She was awarded 75% of the royalties and movie rights money, bought a condo in the Cayman Islands, and moved in with her masseuse Javier from Tranquil Times Spa. While in prison, Lester wrote nine books on poker strategy. He was interviewed by Morley Safer on 60 Minutes, the hosts of Good Morning America and America's Most Wanted, and from his prison cell in Leavenworth, became a celebrity.

In 1977, many states and the federal government enacted what were known as "Son of Sam" laws that prohibited felons from profiting from book royalties or movie rights. The Supreme Court struck those laws down as a violation of the felons' First Amendment Rights.

Like most other high-profile crimes, the dedicated law enforcement officers who stopped the most massive spy case in history, for the most part, remained unknown to the public. Yet, among their peers, they became legends.

ABOUT THE AUTHOR

Mark David Albertson is what some of his friends call a *Renaissance Man*, which, in Mark's mind, is an excellent term for someone who couldn't decide what to do in life. Joining the US Navy after high school, he served at the end of the Vietnam era during the Cold War and was honorably discharged (mostly). Mark enlisted in the Texas Air National Guard during college, serving as a Staff Sergeant in the Security Police. He attended college at the University of Texas at San Antonio, and then Law School at St. Mary's University. Mark was a prosecuting attorney and in private law practice for over 30 years in Washington State before returning to his beloved Texas. Along the way, he worked as an armed private investigator, a hypnotherapist, a public speaker, and an attorney. As an attorney, Mark wrote numerous articles for Law Journals and Law Books. He spoke internationally on legal issues and taught college and graduate courses as an adjunct professor. In his family life, Mark managed to help with the raising of three fine children. Mark lives with his sweetie, Karen, in the Hill Country of Texas on their ranch, Los Perros Locos, and all of the children at home now have fur or feathers.

See Mark's website, www.journeytalker.com, for updates and information on Mark's latest projects.

AUTHOR'S NOTES

After writing my second book focusing on US Navy Radiomen, I decided that it might be helpful to those who did not serve in the navy or who were not radiomen to explain a bit about the rating.

In the navy, enlisted personnel have rates and ratings, which are often confused. A rate is the equivalent of rank or military pay grade. The navy has rates from E-1 to E-9 or seaman recruit (E-1) to master chief petty officer (E-9).

The rating is the enlisted sailor's job specialty, and there are many. Each rating has a symbol that is worn on the arm patch that also indicates the sailor's rate. They can either go to "A" school to learn their rating, or can "strike" for it, which means they are allowed into an apprenticeship onboard their ship. Once they gain their rating, they wear a symbol of that rating along with a patch indicating their rate. The US Navy Radioman rating was established in 1921, and its' symbol has always been sparks, which look something like this:

The Navy Radioman "trade" dates back to about 1914-1918, with the advent of the Marconi wireless transmitter/receiver. Radiomen of the US Navy operated and maintained the navy's voice and tone-modulated radio equipment. In addition, Radiomen were responsible for handling incoming and outgoing classified message traffic and antenna maintenance at both ship and shore stations. The radioman's work also included the destruction of classified messages.

Radiomen were traditionally nicknamed "Sparky" or "Sparks," stemming from their early use of spark-gap transmitters.

Pretty much from the beginning, Radio Central or the "radio shack" was generally known on the ship as the place to go for "rumor control" because the Radiomen knew what had or would happen before anyone else on the ship. Stateside sports scores were of particular interest. Occasionally people would accuse radiomen of only releasing baseball or football scores for certain "return favors," such as clean, pressed uniforms from the ship's laundry. My experience was that it just made RM's a little more popular on the ship during those times.

Perhaps the most famous radioman was the actor, Paul Newman. He was nominated for best actor six times. Still, few people know that Paul Newman enlisted in the U.S. Navy and became a radioman. He enlisted on 22 January 1943, after he graduated from Shaker Heights High School in Cleveland, OH.

One radioman was awarded the medal of honor: Thomas James Reeves. Born on December 9, 1895, he died during the Pearl Harbor attack on December 7, 1941. Chief Reeves served from 1917 until 1919 in the reserves and was on active duty from 1920 until 1941. At the time of his death, he was a Radioman Chief Petty Officer (RMC).

RMC Reeves was serving on the battleship California (BB-44) when the Japanese attacked Pearl Harbor, 7 December 1941. During that attack, the mechanized ammunition hoists in the battleship were destroyed by a Japanese bomb. Chief Reeves "... On his own initiative, in a burning passageway, assisted in the maintenance of an ammunition supply by hand to the antiaircraft guns until he was overcome by smoke and fire which resulted in his death." For his distinguished conduct, RMC Reeves was posthumously awarded the Medal of Honor. In 1943, the destroyer escort USS *Reeves* (DE-156) was named in his honor.

The RM's job changed as the technology changed. In a 1932 publication, the navy described the job as follows:

The first essential of becoming a radioman in the navy is the development of accuracy and speed in transmitting and receiving the telegraph alphabet. In order to attain speed of receiving, you will have to learn the art of printing letters and numbers rapidly and how to operate a typewriter by the touch system, as both of these methods of copying messages must be used on board ship.

In the 1950s, radio teletype equipment became the primary method of communications in the navy, and morse code, while still used, gradually declined. By the 1970s, a typical radio shack would have one or two RM's who knew how to read and transmit code, but it was only used as a backup method of communication. By 1978, satellite communications began to replace HF broadcast communications. With the advent of internet communications in the late 1980s, the need for radiomen diminished. In November of 1999, RM's merged with the Data Processing Technician (DP) rating to form the Information Systems Technician (IT) rating, and radiomen were relegated to history.

In preparing for this book I did quite a bit of research on the history and structure of the Naval Investigative Service, now known as the Naval Criminal Investigative Service. Please keep in mind that this is a work of fiction, and as such, there are places where the actual history of the NIS is a bit different than that portrayed in the book. I worked to keep it as accurate as possible, but, on occasion, I needed to change dates and locations in order to make it work for the plot.

If you have an interest in learning more about the NCIS, the US Navy or Radiomen, take a look at my website, www. journeytalker.com as I have links to a number of great resources.

(Former) RM2 Mark David Albertson (September, 2021)

www.ingramcontent.com/pod-product-compliance
Lightning Source LLC
Chambersburg PA
CBHW070617130626
46556CB00001B/392